# HIS 'N' HERS

*Also by Mike Gayle*

My Legendary Girlfriend

Mr Commitment

Turning Thirty

Dinner for Two

# HIS 'N' HERS

MIKE GAYLE

flame

FLAME
Hodder & Stoughton

Grateful acknowledgement is made for permission to reprint excerpts from the following copyrighted works:

The lyrics to *The Smile On Your Face* © Arthur Tapp 1989

Extract from Meg Ryan interview with Margot Dougherty published in *LA Magazine* (January 1999), reprinted by kind permission of the publisher



First published in Great Britain in 2004
by Hodder and Stoughton
A division of Hodder Headline


A Flame Book

2 4 6 8 10 9 7 5 3 1



A CIP catalogue record for this title is available from the British Library

ISBN 0 340 82537 5

Typeset in Linotype Benguiat by
Rowland Phototypesetting Ltd, Bury St Edmunds, Suffolk
Printed and bound in Great Britain by
Clays Ltd, St Ives plc

Hodder Headline's policy is to use papers that are natural, renewable and recyclable products and made from wood grown in sustainable forests. The logging and manufacturing processes are expected to conform to the environmental regulations of the country of origin.

Hodder and Stoughton
A division of Hodder Headline PLC
338 Euston Road
London NW1 3BH

For Claire (again)
and my monkey (for the first time)

# Acknowledgements

I owe a huge debt to everyone who helped out on this book. Special thanks, however, must go to the following who went above and beyond the call of duty: my editor Phil Pride (for being the most patient boss an author could wish for), everyone at Hodder (for all their hard work when I made their work harder), Mark, the designer (for my cracking cover – Heal's sofas, no less!), my trio of agents (it's a long story), Jane Bradish-Ellames (for being a good cop and bad cop rolled into one), Hannah Griffiths (for hours of conversations about the meaning of life) and Euan (for seamlessly stepping into the breach), Chris McCabe (for not yawning every time I came up with a new idea), Nadine Baggott (for some of the spot-on observations), Blaire Palmer (for pointing me in the right direction on several occasions), Jackie Behan (for early feedback), John and Charlotte (for the earplugs), Carol Flint (for research activities), Arthur Tapp (for introducing me to eBay, the Liberty Thieves and writing 'The Smile On Your Face'), Rodney Beckford (for his work as a sounding-board), Phil Gayle (for a key suggestion), Liz Hitchcock (for *nearly* offering me her life story), Richard Corbridge (for music-guru services), the Thursday night pub people (for being excellent drinking companions), the Monday night footballers (for my only exercise), Danny Wallace (for being Danny Wallace), Liz and James (for rescuing an early draft from my garden) and last but not least everyone @ The Board (for making the hours at my iMac go that little bit faster).

'There's so much mythology about getting together, and there's none about staying together. And staying together is what's so hard.'

Meg Ryan in an interview with *Los Angeles* magazine, 1999

# PART ONE

## Now

## Thursday, 16 January 2003

### 6.45 p.m.

With a remote control in one hand and a Budweiser in the other, I'm slouched on the sofa in front of my widescreen TV and *The Matrix* on DVD. I'm not really watching it, though, in the sense of following the story from beginning to end. What I'm doing is pointing my remote control at the DVD player and making it skip to the best bits, which constitute any moment during a film where there's loud music preferably leading up to an explosion, gun battle or slo-mo fight scene. I know exactly where the best bits of all my favourite films are – from the bank robbery scene in *Heat* to the biggest explosion in *Mission Impossible* (the final one in the tunnel on the train) and the gun battle at the end of *Leon* (which is probably my favourite gun battle ever). I'm enjoying my search through my favourite DVDs even more than usual because I've just spent a considerable amount of money on a home-cinema surround-sound system, which is now turned up so loud that it's making the mirror vibrate above the fireplace.

A huge grin is fixed to my face as I skip to my favourite scene in *The Matrix* where Keanu Reeves's character sets off the metal detector with the arsenal of weapons slung around his chest. The noise is tremendous. The bass from the thumping soundtrack is punching me in the chest. It's fantastic. I feel like I'm in a boxing ring with Ali, and when the guns start firing I'm in ecstasy. I never imagined that TV could be this good. I never imagined that there was a way of making my favourite thing in the world even better. Thanks to my surround-sound, it's not just the explosions that are clearer: there are new, more subtle noises I've missed on a plain old TV. Having the sound separated out into front left, centre, front right and a sub-woofer to handle the explosions is one thing – but with my left and right rear speakers it almost feels like I'm there in the film with Mr Reeves. I can hear bullets whizzing past my head on the left, the *ching-ching* of empty cartridges falling to the ground on my right, and the low rumble of falling masonry surrounds me.

As the scene continues, though, I realise something's wrong – or, rather, not one hundred per cent right. I look at the manual that came with the surround-sound system. After a few moments browsing through it I come to the conclusion that I need just a little more volume from my rear speakers. With the remote, I carefully adjust the levels, and close my eyes tightly, concentrating on the rear speakers.

*That's it,* I tell myself. *That's perfect.*

As the ludicrously loud *Matrix* scene comes to a close and moves on to boring talky bits, which home-cinema surround-sound does little to enhance – other than make it seem like all the actors are shouting at each other – I press pause. Keanu is frozen in time and space. I think about swapping over to *The Phantom Menace*'s pod-race scene, which is the only bit I've watched since I bought the DVD on the day it came out. Just as I'm getting the new disc out of its case the phone rings.

'Hello,' I say.

'Hi, it's me,' says Helen.

'Hey, you. Are you on the train?'

'Yeah, it's a bit of a nightmare. It's running an hour late because of signal failures.'

'Trains these days are useless,' I say sympathetically.

'The only good news is that I'll be able to get some work done.'

'I suppose so.' I reach across to the coffee-table for my beer and take a swig.

'What have you been up to?' asks Helen.

'Nothing much,' I reply, surveying the box the surround-sound system came in and the bits of plastic and polystyrene around it.

'Well,' she concludes, 'I'd better go. I just wanted to make sure you were all right.'

'I'm fine,' I reply. 'You're coming round to mine tonight, aren't you?'

'Of course,' she replies. 'See you later, then.'

'Yeah, babe,' I reply. 'See you later.'

I hang up and, with Keanu still frozen in suspended animation, look around the living room and think about the way my life has turned out. On paper, for a thirty-two-year-old divorced but financially secure accountant, life probably doesn't get much better than this – 'this' being everything in my living room: my new home-cinema surround-sound system (of course), my widescreen TV, DVD player, VCR, digital cable box, hi-fi, CDs, records, books and prerecorded videos. Stuff. Stuff that makes me happy. Or, at least, it used to make me happy.

Buying the surround-sound system today after work was an experiment. A testing of a hypothesis that has been worrying me for a while. Have I reached a point where 'stuff' no longer makes me happy? The surround-sound system has certainly made me cheerful. But this is nothing in comparison to the happiness I feel knowing that Helen is coming round tonight. This is bizarre, because Helen isn't matt black or shiny silver. She's not made by Hitachi, Sony or Panasonic. She doesn't even have an on/off button. She's just a woman who fulfils in me the basic need not to be alone.

And I realise now it's time to grow up again.

It's time to stop being so self-centred.

It's time to ask Helen to move in with me.

## 7.03 p.m.

I've just got home from work. The flat is in darkness. I kick my shoes off in the hallway and go through the post I've brought in with me from the communal entrance. There's a bank statement that's supposedly addressed to me but it says Mrs Alison Owen. I take out a pen from my bag and scribble 'MS ALISON SMITH' in large block capitals and throw it on to the small table in the hallway where house keys and junk post tend to reside before they get tidied away. The rest of the post (a gas bill and two credit-card statements) is addressed to Mr Marcus Levy, my fiancé. Walking further into the hallway I call his name but there's no reply, so I call my cat, Disco, but she doesn't appear either. With no signs of life forthcoming I head into the living room and check the messages on the answerphone.

'Hi, babe, it's me. You're probably on the tube right now. I'm just calling to say I'm running late. It's been a really bad day here. I'll be home soon, though, and I'll bring something for dinner . . . Oh, and my mum called me again about the wedding. She wants to know if she can invite Aunt Jean, because apparently they're on speaking terms now. And before you say it, I did tell her the wedding's only a month away and she's pushing her luck, but you know what my mum's like. Anyway, I told her we'd let her know.'

At the mention of Marcus's mum I press the erase button on the machine. It emits a satisfying beep as though I have just evaporated Mrs Levy with a ray gun. Putting down my bags on the sofa I wander into the kitchen, open a new can of Whiskas and call Disco for her dinner.

'Disco! Dinner time!'

Nothing.

'Disco! Dinner time!'

Still nothing.

'Disco! Dinner time!'

Still nothing.

Disco's not the sort of cat who needs to be called three times. Normally she'd be hanging around my feet mewing like a demented ball of fur before I even get the can-opener out of the drawer. I check the garden and she's nowhere to be seen. I move my search back into the flat and eventually I find her lying in one of her favourite haunts – the space between the bed and the radiator in the spare bedroom.

'Hello, sweetheart,' I say, in what Marcus calls my 'Mummy' voice. 'It's dinner time.'

She doesn't move.

'Come on now, baby,' I say rubbing my hands together to attract her attention. 'Grub's up.'

She still hasn't moved and I realise suddenly that she isn't well. I pick her up and sit on the edge of the bed. She lies limp in my hands, and as I stroke her fur I can feel that her breathing is shallow.

'What's wrong, baby?' She doesn't even look up at me. I lay her on the bed. Although she's never been like this before I think perhaps it's just one of those things – that she's eaten something dodgy in someone's garden. Just to be on the safe side I call the vet to see if they have an emergency surgery. Thankfully they do, so I place her in an old Walkers' crisps box I find in the airing cupboard, surround her with two of Marcus's old jumpers to keep her warm and walk to the vet's.

There, I wait for two and a half hours on the hard plastic seats before our turn comes up. It's my vet's practice to call the animal's name so when the nurse says, 'Disco Smith,' everyone in the waiting room laughs.

The vet, Mr Davies, is a large man with a thick brown beard. He gave Disco her jabs last summer but I'm sure he doesn't recall me. He takes her out of the box, puts her on the table in front of him and asks me lots of questions while he checks her all over. At the end of the examination he doesn't say much but tells me that he wants to keep her in overnight for observation. Before I leave I fish in my jacket pocket and pull out a plastic ball that you put cat treats in.

'Do you mind if I leave this?' I ask Mr Davies. 'Only it's her favourite toy and when she's better in the morning she'll be really pleased to see it.'

'Of course not,' he replies.

I place the toy in the box where she can see it and then pick Disco up and kiss the top of her head. 'See you in the morning, baby,' I tell her, and then I look up at the vet. 'I'll call first thing to see how she is, if that's okay?'

'That will be no problem at all,' he replies, with a smile.

I thank the vet, look into the box once more, whisper: ''Bye, then, Sweetpea,' in Disco's ear. She turns her head slightly and sniffs the air, and this makes me smile because I'm sure she can recognise my scent.

## 11.23 p.m.

I'm lying in bed watching *Newsnight* on the portable TV. The female presenter is grilling the shadow home secretary intensely about a new policy statement and looks to be winning the argument. I'm just wondering what the next question is going to be when my concentration is broken by Helen.

'Jim?' she says, with a question in her voice.

'Yeah?' I reply.

'What's wrong?'

'Nothing.'

'It doesn't look like nothing to me,' she says. 'You've been in a funny mood all evening.'

'Have I? I thought I was just watching TV.'

'I'm not talking about that. I'm talking about earlier tonight. It's like your mind is somewhere else.'

'I'm sorry,' I say, switching off the TV.

'Are you okay?' she asks, reaching out for my hand and intertwining her fingers with mine. 'You were coughing a lot during the night the last time I stayed over.'

'Was I?'

'And you do feel a bit warm.' She laughs. 'I don't want you to take this the wrong way but I sort of hope you are ill.'

'Why would you want that?'

'You've never been ill in all the time we've been together. That's a whole twelve months. I was ill within the first week of us going out, remember? I had that massive cold and I was sneezing and spluttering and coughing all the time and you came round to my flat with your home-made vegetable soup and it tasted so wonderful and—'

'I've a bit of a confession there. The soup – well, it wasn't home-made. It was from Tesco.'

Helen punches my arm in mock outrage. 'I always thought it was too good to be true. I smelt a rat when I asked you to make it for me again and you said I could only have it if I had flu.'

'I didn't think you'd believe me in a million years. Do I look like the kind of man who can make soup?'

'Not really,' she replies. 'I just hoped you were.'

I take a deep breath. 'I'm not ill. It's just that I've been thinking . . . about you and me.'

'That doesn't sound good.'

'No, it is,' I reply quickly. 'Well, at least, I'm hoping you'll think it is . . . I was wondering . . . well, we've been together quite a while now, and you're always round here anyway—'

'You make me sound like I've got nowhere better to go,' says Helen, laughing.

'I don't mean it like that. What I mean is . . . I was wondering if you fancied moving in here . . . with me? What do you think? Feel free to say no if you don't like the idea.'

She smiles at me sort of sadly and doesn't reply.

'So?' I ask.

'I love the idea,' she replies. 'Are you sure, though?'

'Yes.'

She frowns. 'It's just that . . .'

'What?'

'Nothing . . . Are you sure?'

'Of course I'm sure. That's why I'm asking you.'

'Okay, then,' she says. 'I think it's a great idea. Really fantastic. I think this is going to be really good for us.' She pauses and bites her lip as if she's thinking. 'We should do something to celebrate. I could nip home and see if I can find a bottle of something fizzy. Though knowing my fridge expect Pepsi Max rather than champagne.'

'I'm already ahead of you on that one.' I get out of bed and walk over to my suit jacket hanging on the door of the wardrobe. 'It's not quite champagne but you might enjoy it.' I take an envelope and hand it to Helen.

'What's this?' she asks.

'You know that week we're taking off work in February?' She nods. 'Well, I've booked us a trip to Chicago. I remember you saying you went to university there for a year and that you always wanted to go back and catch up with your friends. So I thought: Why not?'

Helen leaps from the bed, runs over to me and throws her arms around me. 'That's so sweet, Jim,' she says, kissing me. 'Do you know, you're possibly the best boyfriend in the entire world?'

'Yeah,' I reply cheekily. 'I've prebooked the seats too. So we're sitting together there and back. You can be my buffer.'

'Buffer?'

'It's an eight-hour flight,' I explain. 'I'll need you to stop mad people making conversation with me on the flight. They always choose me, you know. I'm not exaggerating. If there's anyone on the flight with nothing better to do than to tell someone their life story, they're automatically allocated the seat next to me. On my last business trip to Amsterdam I had to endure the potted life history of an old Dutch lady. By the time we landed at Schiphol airport I knew all the reasons for her trip: to visit her ex-husband's brother-in-law – part holiday, part bridge-building with the difficult side of the family; how old she was – seventy-one, even though in her own opinion she didn't look a day over sixty; and that her third son was a difficult pregnancy, which she put down to the fact that her husband at the time didn't know the child wasn't his. That's why I need a buffer.'

'Okay,' says Helen, rolling her eyes. 'I'll be your buffer . . . Anyway, let's get back to the important stuff, like when are we flying?'

'It should all be there,' I reply, taking the envelope from

her hands and checking the tickets. 'We leave Monday the tenth at ten twenty-five a.m. and we arrive back at Heathrow at seven fifteen a.m. UK time on the Friday—'

'Friday the fourteenth?' says Helen. 'Valentine's Day.'

'Yeah . . . it is,' I reply. 'I hadn't even realised.'

'Well, you're obviously a genius. I think that's perfect timing. We'll come back from our nice week away and I'll move in here the same day. That way, when we celebrate the anniversary of us moving in together in years to come, you'll have absolutely no excuse for not remembering.'

## Friday, 17 January 2003

### 7.07 a.m.

It's morning and I'm lying in bed alone listening to the radio. Marcus left for work ten minutes ago and I'm just trying to summon the will-power to get out of bed and start the day. I've just been promoted to senior publicity manager at work so I've got loads to do to keep on top of things . . . and of course I've got to phone the vet. As I look at the alarm clock on Marcus's side of the bed I wonder how Disco is doing. I decide to make the call at eight o'clock because I have no idea what time the surgery opens. I close my eyes, intending to doze for just a while longer, when the phone on the bedside table rings. I pick it up hurriedly, expecting it to be Marcus because he quite often calls me on his way to work to usher me out of bed in case I'm late for work.

'I'm up, okay?' I say, laughing. 'I've been up for the last half-hour.'

When I don't hear Marcus's laughter I realise I've made a huge mistake.

'Can I speak to Alison Smith, please?' asks a young woman.

'I'm really sorry,' I reply. 'I thought you were someone else. Yes, this is Alison Smith speaking.'

'Hi, I'm calling from the Hendon Road veterinary practice,' she continues. 'You left your cat, Disco, with us last night.'

'Yes, that's right. How is she? I bet she's starving. She loves her food.'

'I'm afraid we've got some bad news for you. She passed away last night. Mr Davies believes she might have been suffering from cancer and that it was quite advanced.'

There's a long pause, which I assume the veterinary nurse has left for me to say something but I can't speak. All I can think is, I didn't even know cats could get cancer.

'Hello?'

I remain silent.

'Er . . . hello, Miss Smith?'

I remain silent trying to find the courage to speak but then I drop the phone clumsily and scrabble on the floor for it. It's as if I've lost control of my body because I can't pick it up for ages.

'Hello?' I say eventually. 'Hello? Are you still there?'

'Yes,' says the nurse. 'I'm really sorry about your loss, Miss Smith.'

'Thank you,' I reply. 'What happens now? I've never . . .' My voice trails off.

'Would you like us to take care of things?'

'I don't know.'

'Perhaps you'd like to come down to the surgery later today and we can talk you through the options.'

'Yes,' I reply. 'I'll do that.'

Having said goodbye I put down the phone, walk to my dressing-table and drag the chair there to the wardrobe on the other side of the bedroom. I stand on the chair, take down a battered old brown suitcase from the top of the wardrobe and place it on the bed. I open it and rummage among the dozens of old letters, envelopes of photographs, tickets stubs and other memorabilia from my life until I find what I'm looking for and take it out. In my hand is a red and white Marlboro

Lights packet. I open it and take out the solitary cigarette and lighter contained within. I get back into bed and light the cigarette, but before I can even put it to my lips I'm overcome by a huge wave of emotion and start sobbing as if my heart has just broken in two.

## 7.15 a.m.

'Surprise!' says Helen, entering the bedroom.

I look up from the article in *The Economist* I've been reading for the last fifteen minutes to see her standing in the doorway wearing the white shirt I wore to work yesterday and nothing else. She's carrying a tray laden with two boiled eggs, three slices of toast, a white carnation in a straight vodka shot glass and what, from this position, appears to be a copy of the *Financial Times*.

'Is this all for me?' I ask incredulously.

'Of course,' she replies. 'Breakfast in bed for one.'

'If I hadn't already asked you to move in with me I'd do it again right now.'

Helen laughs. 'When I move in here I'm afraid it won't be breakfast in bed every day.'

'Really?' I say playfully. 'Well I might have to reconsider my offer.'

'You can't,' she says, setting the tray in front of me. 'It's too late. Mentally speaking, I'm already redecorating the living room, buying new sofas and basically doing my best to take the bachelor out of this pad. I'm even thinking about getting us some his 'n' hers bathrobes so that I don't have to wander round like this . . .' she gestures to my shirt, which, I have to say, has never looked as good on me as it does on her '. . . all the time. What do you think?'

'His 'n' hers bathrobes? They're not very me.'

She leans over and kisses me. 'We'll see about that.'

## 7.22 a.m.

'I can't believe she's gone,' I say tearfully, to Marcus, on the phone.

'I know, sweetheart,' he replies. 'You must be really cut up about it.'

'Part of me feels guilty for being so upset,' I tell him. 'Part of me feels I shouldn't be crying over the death of a cat because there are so many other things in the world to feel sad about. But right now most of me doesn't care about all that. She was my cat. I've had her since she was a kitten – nearly ten years.'

'What are you going to do now? Are you going to go to the vet's like you said and—'

'Decide what to do with her body?'

'Yes.'

'I think so. There's no point in my going to work today. I'd be useless. I'll call in and make some excuse.'

'I think you're right not to go to work. I'd come with you to the vet's but—'

'I know you can't. I'll be okay.'

'You can't go on your own, though. Can't you get a friend to go with you? What about Jane?'

'She's in Helsinki with her new boyfriend. Honestly, I'll be fine on my own.' There's a long pause. 'Do you think I should call Jim and tell him what's happened? I've been thinking about it for a while but I can't decide what to do for the best. I mean, Disco was his cat too. But I don't want to upset you.'

'What's to be upset about?' reassures Marcus. 'All you're doing is letting him know what's happened.'

'You're right. But I haven't spoken to him since . . . well, you know. I just think it'll be weird. I've still got his mobile number somewhere – assuming that it hasn't changed – but what if he's living with someone else and they pick up his phone? Won't they think it's strange that I'm calling?'

'I'm amazed at your capacity to see every possible permutation of things that might go wrong. Listen, I'll leave it up to you. You do whatever makes you happy.'

## 7.38 a.m.

I'm just coming out of the shower when an electronic rendition of 'Ride Of The Valkyries' fills the air.

'Helen?' I call from the bathroom. 'Can you get my phone for me, babe? It might be work.'

I listen out as the phone stops ringing and wait, dripping water all over the floor, by the bathroom for Helen to relay the message.

'It's a woman,' she says, holding out the phone. 'She wants to speak to you. She says it's important.'

I take the phone from her and she wanders off in the direction of the kitchen. I walk back into the bathroom to save the hallway carpet from further damage and stand in front of the mirror to do my daily hairline examination. 'Hello?' I say, peering at my scalp.

'Jim, it's me.'

I nearly drop the phone at the sound of this woman's voice. There's a long pause.

'Hello . . . Can you hear me?'

'Sorry,' I reply, after a few moments. 'I'm still here . . . it's just that . . . Is this . . . Alison?'

'Yes.'

'How are you?'

'I'm okay, thanks. How are you?'

'Me? I'm fine . . . but—'

'Listen, I'm only ringing because, well, I thought you ought to know that Disco died last night. She had cancer, apparently.'

'I didn't even know cats could get cancer.'

'That's exactly what . . .' Her voice trails off. 'I just thought you ought to know, that's all.'

'It's a real shock. I feel bad I haven't seen her at all.' I laugh, sadly. 'This is going to sound stupid but I've got her photo Blu-tacked to the mirror on the wardrobe in my bedroom . . . She would've been ten this year, wouldn't she? How much is that in cat years?'

'I don't know. Old, I suppose.'

'Where is she now?'

'At the vet's in Crouch End. I'm going over there in a bit to . . . I don't know . . .' Alison starts to cry.

'I'm supposed to be working from home today,' I tell her, 'but I'll come with you if you like.'

'You don't have to. I'll be fine.'

'I want to. After all, Disco was my cat too.'

Alison gives me her address and we arrange to meet at her flat in Crouch End in the next hour or so and I put down the phone.

Helen comes into the bathroom singing along to a song coming from the radio in the kitchen. 'Who was that on the phone?'

'It was Alison,' I say.

'Alison? As in your ex-wife, Alison?'

I laugh. 'I always feel weird when you call her that. I feel too young to have an ex-wife.'

'That's what you get for marrying young,' says Helen. 'Anyway, starter marriages are all the rage, according to the sort of thing you read in weekend papers. All the best people have one – Hollywood actors, pop stars, the lot. And apparently having one means that subsequent relationships will be healthier because you tend to learn from your mistakes.' Helen kisses my nose. 'Anyway, what was she calling for?'

'She called to say that our cat died.'

'Disco?'

'Yeah.'

'Oh, baby,' says Helen, putting her arms around me. 'That's awful. And there's me rambling on about starter marriages like an idiot. I'm really sorry. How did it happen?'

'Cancer, apparently.'

'Oh, that's a real shame. How do you feel?'

'A bit odd, really. She had a nice personality. Whenever I was watching TV she'd come and join me. She was the perfect companion to watch TV with.' I pause and then add, 'I know this is going to sound weird but I agreed to go to the vet's with Alison.'

'Oh,' says Helen flatly.

'Are you going to be okay with that?'

Helen sighs. 'Do you have to?'

I think for a moment before speaking. 'No, I don't have to. But when we split up the only reason Alison got Disco was . . . Well, put it this way, we both wanted to keep her. I think it's only fair that I . . . I don't know . . . that I'm there.'

'I've never really imagined you as a cat person.'

'I'm not,' I reply. 'But Disco is . . . was different.'

'Why?'

'Because she was mine.'

Helen smiles. 'If you want to go to the vet's with her I'm fine with it. I haven't got anything to worry about, have I?'

'Of course not,' I say. 'I haven't seen her for years. I don't even know if we'll have much to talk about. Everything that happened back then feels like it happened in a different lifetime. It's like all that stuff you were saying about starter marriages. Alison and I made a mistake. It's as simple as that. But we were young enough to get over it and move on.'

# PART TWO

## Then: 1989–93

# 1989

## Wednesday, 27 September 1989

### 10.45 p.m.

It's my first night at university in Birmingham and I'm at the freshers' disco with hundreds of other brand new university students. From what I can gather Freshers' Night is the most important event of your university career. This is where you make friendships that will last a lifetime and snog men who look like extras from *Brideshead Revisited*. And I'm taking no chances of missing out on the action. Having been something of a Laura-Ashley-proper-dresses girl at sixth-form college and having had to wear a quasi-nurse's uniform during my year out working for Boots I decided to give myself something of a makeover. I'm wearing the most 'studenty' clothes I could find: a second-hand suede jacket I bought at a market in Cambridge, a T-shirt that says 'Meat Is Murder' (even though I love chicken), Levi 501's that are rolled up above my ankles, no socks, and brand new Doc Marten's shoes, which I bought two days ago and which are already rubbing my heels so badly that one is bleeding.

Jane, my new best friend of the last eight hours, and I have been keeping an eye on a boy standing at the other end of the bar with a group of cool-looking guys. Each and every one of them has a cigarette hanging from the corner of his mouth as though they're auditioning for the lead role in *East of Eden*. The one I like, however, looks the coolest of the bunch and I immediately fancy him. I like his wavy dark brown hair, his worn leather jacket, his slightly grimy-looking jeans and his barely hanging together Converse All-stars – everything. We've been exchanging long glances across the room all evening. It's as if we can't take our eyes off each other. And the longer we look at each other without speaking, the more I want to run across the room, throw my arms around him and kiss him until he surrenders.

'Is he looking now?' I ask, as I stare purposefully in the opposite direction.

'I don't know,' says Jane, dolefully. 'Do you want me to look?'

'Okay.'

Jane turns her head but I lose my nerve. 'No!' I scream. 'Don't look.'

'Fine, I won't.'

There's a long pause.

'Is he looking now?' I ask.

Jane sighs. 'You know, as much as I'd like to have built-in radar I can't actually give you that information without, you know, using my eyes.'

I take a deep breath. 'Okay, don't look.'

'Are you sure?'

'Yes . . . I think so.'

'Are you absolutely sure?'

'No – not at all.'

Jane grabs me by the hand and leads me in the direction of the bar. 'If we're going to spend the whole evening pretending not to look at men, can I suggest that we get a drink in first?'

## 11 p.m.

'So, do you think you're going to try and get off with him?' asks Jane, as we proudly sip our pints of cider at the bar.

'I don't know,' I reply. 'Do you think I should?'

'You like him, don't you?'

'He's gorgeous.'

'Then just do it.'

'I can't just do it. I'm not a just-do-it kind of person. I need a plan of action.'

'The plan of action I always find works involves cider and black-currant and a lot of babbling like an idiot.'

Between us, Jane and I come up with the following additions to her usual plan:

1) I should walk over to him.
2) I should ask him for a light.
3) And then I should ask him for a cigarette.

I'm convinced it's perfect.

It's a little bit cheeky.

It's a little bit flirty.

It's a guaranteed winner.

'There's only one problem with your plan,' says Jane.

'What's that?'

'You don't smoke, do you?'

I shrug. 'No, but now is as good a time as any to start.' I knock back the last of my drink. 'Wish me luck,' I say, as I fix my eyes on my target.

'You don't need luck,' says Jane. 'He's lucky to have you fancy him at all.'

Emboldened by my friend's words, I take a deep breath and begin the walk to the other side of the bar. Half-way to my destination, however, I'm brought to an abrupt halt. A bloke I've never seen before is standing in my path. He's wearing burgundy brogues, long Argyle-patterned socks, knee-length tailored shorts, a white shirt, a green tie and a grey waistcoat. I've never seen anything quite like him in my life.

'Hi,' says the bloke, holding out his hand, 'I'm Jim.'

I'm too bewildered to be impolite, so I shake his hand. 'Er . . . I'm Alison.'

'It's great here, isn't it?' he asks, in a broad northern accent.

'It's okay.'

There's a long pause.

'Where are you from?' he asks.

'Norwich,' I reply curtly.

'I'm from Oldham,' he adds, without prompting. 'It's near Manchester, if that's any help to you.'

'Do they all dress like that in Oldham?' I ask, taking in his ensemble again.

'No,' he says proudly. 'I'm a one-off . . . What are you studying?'

'English,' I reply, and then I look over at the guy who I'm supposed to be talking to on the other side of the room. He's still smoking a cigarette and he's still looking as gorgeous as ever.

'Cool,' says Jim. 'Does that mean you're going to be an English teacher?'

'I'm going to be a novelist,' I tell him, which is sort of true. I do want to write a novel some day.

'Cool,' says Jim. 'I'm doing business and economics. I don't want to work in business, though.'

'So why are you doing it, then?'

'Everybody needs a plan B.'

'And what's plan A?'

'I'm in a band. I'm the lead singer.'

'What are you called?'

'We haven't got a name.'

'I see. Well, are you any good?'

'There's only me in the band at the minute.'

I can't help but laugh. 'Then how is that a band?'

'I'm going to recruit some more members. You don't play any instruments, do you?'

'No. Nothing. I'm completely tone-deaf.'

'That's a shame. You'd look great with a guitar.'

I smile but I don't reply. Instead I hope that the long, awkward silence currently flourishing between us will grow large enough for me to escape, but he doesn't seem to want to go.

'You should be careful, you know,' I say, after a few moments, because I feel uncomfortable standing there saying nothing.

'I should be careful of what?'

'Having a plan B.'

'Why?'

'Because if you've got one you might use it.' I smile politely at him. 'Well, it was nice to meet you.'

'Cool,' says Jim. 'It was nice to meet you too.' He leans towards me as if he's going to kiss my cheek, which is odd. I decide it's easier just to let his strange behaviour go without comment, but at the last minute he moves his face around so that we're eye to eye and then kisses me directly on the lips.

'What are you doing?' I say, outraged.

'I thought you fancied me.'

'What could possibly have made you think that?'

'You were talking to me.'

'You think that every girl who talks to you fancies you?'

'No.'

'So why pick on me?'

'You were giving me vibes.'

'Look,' I say, unable to believe my ears, 'let's just forget this ever happened because, as embarrassing as it is for you, it's even worse for me.'

'Fine,' says Jim, and heads off in the direction of the dance-floor.

'Fine,' I retort, and spin on my heels in the direction of the gorgeous boy across the room. It's too late, though. He's gone.

'Well, that's that,' I say, on my return to Jane.

'Maybe you'll see him another time.'

'I suppose.' I sigh. 'But in the meantime it looks like I'm going to have to get my own cigarettes.'

## 11.05 p.m.

I don't let the girl from Norwich get me down. Instead I set my sights elsewhere and my romantic overtures are rejected by Liz Grey from Huddersfield (two As and a B at A level), Manjit 'My friends call me Manny' Kaur from Colchester (who's 'into' New Model Army and the Levellers), and Christina Wood from Bath (who is really pleased that she didn't get into Cambridge, and is not in the slightest bit bitter that Katie, her best friend from school, has). It's not until I try it on with Linda Braithwaite at the end of the night that I get 'lucky'. Linda is a semi-Goth from the East Midlands, who has the hair, likes the music, wears the clothes but has yet to make the transition into full-Goth mode, with the white makeup, black nails, love of rubbish horror films and quaint belief that she has joined the ranks of the undead. All in all, as we kiss in the corner of the students' union bar, I consider it a result.

## Thursday, 28 September 1989

### 8.30 a.m.

The morning after the night before, I'm walking towards campus to attend my very first university lecture. This being something of a momentous occasion for me, and desperate to give the impression that I'm a proper student, I'm wearing tartan trousers, Doc Marten's boots, a home-made CND T-shirt (made the week before utilising a cheap market-stall T-shirt, a black marker pen and very basic artistic skills), a charity-shop men's suit jacket and a flat cap. I think I look fantastic. The outfit is finished off with my Walkman, which, thanks to the tape playing in it (a Billy Bragg album), gives me the perfect soundtrack to feel that I'm in possession of the requisite amount of left-wing political idealism.

'Morning, Jim boy,' says a voice from behind me, in the middle of 'The Milkman of Human Kindness'.

I turn to see a tall, sombre-looking lad, whom I recognise as being one of the many people I'd told my A-level results to the previous evening by way of making conversation. For the life of me I can't remember his name and it obviously shows.

'The name's Nick,' he says, reading my nonplussed features. 'Nick Constantinedes.'

'Nick, of course I remember,' I lie. 'How are you, mate?'

'Good,' he replies, and then looks puzzled. 'Are you going to a fancy-dress party?'

I laugh because it's the only reaction I can think of to maintain my cool. I can see that he doesn't mean anything by it. Ordinary people not 'getting' it, I reason, is all part of being a fashion visionary. 'This is the way I dress,' I explain.

'Oh,' he replies, and then, realising his mistake, adds sheepishly, 'I like your boots. Where did you get them from?'

'Afflecks Palace in Manchester.'

He nods. 'Cool.'

'Cheers.'

'Did you enjoy last night?' he asks. 'I saw you talking to a very pretty girl.'

'Did she look like a Goth?'

'No. She was wearing a Smiths T-shirt.'

'Ah, that one.' I shrug. 'She wasn't my type. Too normal-looking.'

He nods as if he understands what I'm talking about, and as we walk along we talk about the next official get-together on the Freshers' Week party-planner. Outside the Barber Institute we come to a halt.

'The engineering department's this way,' he says, pointing up the hill.

'The School of Economics is this way,' I say, pointing towards the clock tower.

He gives me a cheerful wave. 'See you around, then.'

'Yeah,' I reply. 'See you around.'

He walks about ten feet away and then I shout, 'I don't suppose you play an instrument, do you?'

'The bass guitar,' he replies. 'I was in a band back in Sussex but we weren't very good.'

'Excellent,' I reply. 'Fancy being in a band again?'

He thinks for a moment. 'Yeah, why not?'

## Wednesday, 18 October 1989

### 2 p.m.

I'm standing inside Revolution, a second-hand record shop in the city centre watching the boy I really liked from the freshers' disco flick through a plastic box of records on the floor. I'm only here because Jane wants to buy tickets to see some band I've never heard of, but I seem to have struck lucky.

'Is he looking?' I ask Jane.

'We're not going to go through all that again,' she says firmly. 'Just go and talk to him.'

'You're right,' I say to Jane. 'I will go and talk to him.' I pause, then add, 'And if you see any dodgy-looking boys in weird clothes keep them away from me.'

I walk over to the boy, who is wearing the same leather jacket and jeans as when I'd first seen him. He still looks gorgeous. I pretend to search for a record but secretly watch over his shoulder as he systematically rummages through every single box of old records in the shop. When he picks up a twelve-inch single of the Boney M hit 'Brown Girl In The Ring' and puts it on a small pile of records next to him I finally see a conversation-opener.

'You can't buy that,' I say, pointing to the record on the floor. 'It's terrible.'

From his stooped position he looks up at me. 'You're the girl from Freshers' Night,' he says, and straightens up.

I can't believe he's remembered me. 'My name's Alison Smith,' I tell him. 'I'm studying English.'

'I'm Damon,' he replies. 'Damon Guest. And I'm doing life sciences.'

'What's that?'

'I have no idea. I ended up here through Clearing.' He pauses. 'So tell me, Alison Smith, why shouldn't I buy this record?'

'Because it's terrible. Boney M – they're rubbish.'

'But it's only twenty-five p.'

'That's twenty-five p too much,' I say, and take the single off his pile and put it back in the rack.

## Friday, 20 October 1989

### 5.47 p.m.

'So how did your date with devilishly handsome Damon go?' asks Jane, as we sit on the edge of her bed, half watching the late-afternoon repeat of *Neighbours* on her portable TV.

'Great,' I say. 'We went for a drink in the Varsity.'

'On the Bristol Road?'

'That's the one. He drank Coke all night because he said he doesn't like the way alcohol tastes.'

Jane laughs. 'What a girl.'

'I know, but you know what?'

'What?'

'I don't know why but that seemed to make me like him even more.'

Jane groans. 'Okay, so what did you talk about?'

'Music, mainly. He's passionate – and I do mean passionate – about music. He plays guitar really well apparently. He was in a band back in his home town but they've split up now.'

Jane laughs. 'You should hook him up with that weird boy who tried to snog you at the beginning of term.'

'Don't remind me,' I say, shuddering. 'I can't imagine his band was any good.' I smile, thinking of Damon. 'I love that he loves music. There's something about a man with a passion for a particular activity that is incredibly sexy. Obviously trainspotting, stamp-collecting and suchlike are exceptions to the rule, but with music you'd be hard pressed to get much cooler. I managed to bluff my way through the conversation because I've heard of some of the bands he mentioned on Radio One. Later we talked about what we want to do with our lives. He told me he wants to work in the music industry and I told him about my plan to be a novelist.'

'You sound like a right pair of pretentious idiots,' says Jane, laughing.

'I know, but it gets worse. I spent most of the night imagining us living together. Me writing novels in the spare room of our house and him in the living room surrounded by hundreds of records.'

'So all you did was talk, then?'

'No. He walked me back to mine and we kissed.'

'How was it?'

'Fantastic.'

# 1991

## Friday, 11 January 1991

### 10.45 p.m.

An hour ago – with Ed, a second-year biologist, on drums, Ruth, a first-year maths student on guitar, Nick on bass and me on vocals – all my dreams came true. Captain Magnet, the band I dreamed of forming, played their first gig on the small stage in the upstairs room at the Jug of Ale in Moseley to a crowd of ten people. It was fantastic. Better than I could ever have imagined.

It's all over now. Ed and Ruth have gone home and Nick and I are sitting in the downstairs bar. We've been talking about the gig solidly since we stepped off stage and now that the topic is wearing thin I decide to offer up another conversational gambit on a subject close to my heart. 'It's all very well being the lead singer in a band,' I say, more loudly than advisable in an overcrowded pub, 'but I need a woman. And I need a woman now.'

'Things can't be that bad,' says Nick.

'They're awful,' I say. 'I thought university was supposed to be a hotbed of depravity. I want my share. Do you know how many girls I've been involved with since I started university?'

'No, but you're going to tell me, aren't you?'

'One,' I reply. 'Linda Braithwaite.'

'The dodgy semi-Goth from Freshers' Night who you managed to get off with a further two times?'

'I know,' I say, shaking my head sadly. 'I have no shame.' I take another sip of my pint.

'Your love-life's a mess, mate.'

'I know it is, which is why . . .' My sentence trails off as the most beautiful girl in the entire world walks into the pub. She is stunning. Absolutely beautiful, in a million different ways. A goddess. She's with a tall, moody-looking guy – who, it occurs to me, should look a lot happier given the company he's keeping. The girl and the guy walk over to our table and stop.

'Nick!' says the girl. 'How are you?'

'I'm fine,' he says coolly. 'How are you?'

'Great,' she says. 'Really good.'

Nick and this beautiful girl talk for about three minutes about nothing in particular – work, living arrangements, friends in common, life in general – and then she looks at the moody guy standing next to her, and says, 'Oh, I'd better be off,' and disappears to the other side of the pub.

'Who was that?' I ask, as soon as they're out of earshot.

'Who was what?' replies Nick, just to wind me up.

'That girl. That absolutely amazing girl.'

Nick laughs. 'Oh, her? That was Anne Clarke. She lived in halls of residence with me in the first year . . . She's a bit of a babe.'

'That's the understatement of the year. She's gorgeous. Why have you never introduced me to her?'

'She's bad news, mate,' he says cryptically. 'You'll only go and fall in love with her and she's guaranteed to break your heart.'

## Thursday, 14 February 1991

### 23.05 p.m.

I'm at a Valentine's Day party in Selly Park. As a rule I don't go to student house parties if I can help it. During my time at university I've discovered the first law of student house parties: for every female who attends there will be at least ten sexually frustrated rugby-playing engineering students, who will label non-rugby-playing engineering students as a threat to their attempts to get off with a member of the opposite sex.

I discovered this law in the first week of my first year and, not believing that such Neanderthal behaviour could exist at such levels of higher education, continued to learn this lesson at Sam Golden's nineteenth-birthday house party, Elaine Doon's house party to celebrate the end of exams, and Michael Greene's Christmas house party. I hadn't been to a house party since Michael Greene's when several rugby-playing engineering students had taken umbrage at the flowery shirt I wore and the fact that I'd had my tongue down the throat of Linda Braithwaite, who turned out to be the twin sister of rugby-playing engineering student Gary Braithwaite. I'm at this party with Nick for two reasons: first, he has promised me on pain of death that no engineering students have been invited; second, he mentioned that there's a good chance Anne Clarke will be here. And she is.

She's dancing exuberantly in the living room – glass of wine in one hand, cigarette in the other – to the Happy Mondays. When the song ends she walks over to a group of guys in the corner of the room. Within seconds she's laughing and giggling with them. They're all clearly infatuated with her. It's odd watching them because it's almost as if she has them mesmerised. Their eyes follow wherever she goes. It's snake-charming at its most obvious. I determine that although I'm desperate to talk to her there's absolutely no way I'm going to walk up to her and begin a conversation. I'm going to play it cool. Not cool in an I-like-you-do-you-like-me? way but cool in an I-have-no-interest-in-you-and-am-impervious-to-your-charms way. I choose my moment carefully. She leaves the group of guys and walks into the kitchen where she heads to the sink and fills her glass with water.

'Can you pass me a glass from the draining-board?' I say, behind her.

'No problem,' she replies. And then she turns and adds, 'Nice shirt.'

I'm wearing a peach-coloured cheesecloth short-sleeved shirt with a huge seventies-style collar – if a sudden strong wind enters the kitchen, I may take flight. 'Cheers,' I reply, and smile – but not too much. The opening for a hello-who-are-you? conversation is right in front of me but I ignore it, smile again and walk away.

Two hours later I find myself in conversation with a group of people from the history and geography honours course, who are friends of Nick's. Anne suddenly appears at the edge of the group. I notice her immediately but don't make eye-contact. After a while the conversation gravitates to a forthcoming field trip so I turn to my left to speak to Anne and I'm pleasantly surprised to see her smiling at me.

'I'm Jim,' I tell her. 'I think I've seen you around.'

'I'm Anne. We met in the kitchen.'

We fall into conversation, covering such general topics as who we know at the party, what courses we're studying and where we live. Soon, however, under Anne's direction, the conversation becomes less general and more personal. Unprompted she begins telling me about her life: the odd snippet about her ex-boyfriend, bits about her parents' divorce, and about how she's never really got on very well with her sister. For the most part I listen and occasionally respond with the few nuggets of wisdom I've collected during my life on earth. They seem to have the desired effect of either cheering her up or making her laugh.

## Saturday, 27 April 1991

### 12.23 a.m.

Anne and I have been out at the Varsity. Since the party back in February we've been spending a lot of time together. Most evenings she's at my house or I'm at hers. Everyone, including Nick, and Anne's ex-boyfriend, believes that we're an 'item' or, at the very least, on the verge of being together. Flattered as I am I tell anyone who will listen that there's nothing going on and we're just good friends. The reaction is always the same: they laugh as if they think I'm lying. I can't blame them because as time has passed I find it more and more difficult to believe it too.

Anne has taken it upon herself to flirt with me outrageously.

We walk around hand in hand.

But nothing ever happens.

I'll stay over at her house and sleep in her bed while she wears nothing but a bleached-out Stone Roses T-shirt and a smile.

But nothing ever happens.

She kisses me on the lips for no reason and on one occasion even puts her tongue into my ear.

But nothing ever happens.

Tonight, however, as we have both had too much to drink, I decide that something is going to happen. So, when we're sitting on the sofa at her house, half watching *Central Weekend Live*, half falling asleep, I lean in towards her and kiss her lips.

It's better than I ever imagined. But just as I'm about to start enjoying it she pulls away from me. 'Jim,' she says, startled. 'You know I like you, don't you?'

Not that old one. 'Yes.'

'The thing is, I don't like you like that.'

Yes, that old one. 'Like what?'

'Like this,' she says, gesturing towards me with her hands, indicating that the space between us is 'that'. 'It's really sweet,' she continues, 'and if things were different I'd love us to be together but I've got a lot of things on my mind and now's not a good time to begin a relationship.'

'No problem,' I say, shrugging my shoulders as if the idea of getting off with Anne has only just occurred to me. 'Of course that's okay. It's fine. I understand.'

I don't understand, of course. I don't understand at all. Whatever game she's playing I don't know the rules.

## Saturday, 4 May 1991

### 2.02 a.m.

I'm listening to 'Strangeways Here We Come', on my record-player, and considering writing a song about Anne. Despite my best attempts to make things between us as free of awkwardness as possible, I haven't seen her at all during the week following our kiss. Suddenly she's busy every night and I decide that we both probably need some time apart. My train of thought is broken by the sound of the arm of the record-player returning to its resting-place, signalling the end of side two. I look at my watch and decide to go to sleep, but after a few moments of the do-I-need-the-loo? debate, I give in and go. Yawning, I walk out on to the landing straight into Anne.

'Jim,' she says.

I don't say anything because she's wearing nothing, apart from the brand new Inspiral Carpets T-shirt that Nick bought at their gig the previous week. A gig I'd taken him to.

We both stand there awkwardly until I say, 'I was just going to the loo.'

'I was going too, but I'll wait until you've finished.'

'See you in the morning, then,' I reply forlornly, as I enter the bathroom and close the door behind me.

### 10.02 a.m.

When I come downstairs in the morning, Anne is nowhere to be seen and Nick is sitting on the sofa in the living room, looking as if he has been waiting for me.

'Morning,' he says, as I sit down.

'Morning,' I reply. 'Is she still here?'

'No, she went this morning.'

There's a long pause.

'So, are you seeing her, then?' I ask eventually.

He shakes his head. 'If it's any consolation,' he adds, 'I think she does really like you.'

I can't believe what I'm hearing. 'If she likes me so much what's she doing coming out of your bedroom in the middle of the night?'

'Believe me,' he sighs, 'it was as much a surprise to me as it was to you. I was absolutely mad about her when we lived in halls. I thought she really liked me too. She used to flirt with me constantly but nothing ever happened. Anyway, one night I'm out with her, and I thought, This is getting ridiculous so I tried to kiss her and she gave me this whole line about wanting to be friends. So, I said, "Fine, let's be friends," and then she avoids me like the plague and then the next thing I know she's getting off with a mate from my course.'

'But why would she do that?'

Nick shrugs. 'That's women for you. Who knows what's going on in their minds?'

### 11.55 p.m.

As I lie in bed later that night with the lyrics to 'Teaser Pleaser' half worked out, I try to work out how I'm feeling. The funny thing is I don't blame Nick at all. And I don't blame Anne either. I blame me and my rubbish approach to the fairer sex. This, I decide, is going to be a watershed for all my relationships from this point forwards. From now on I'm going to be different. No more falling in love with the unattainable.

## Friday, 4 October 1991

### 7.28 p.m.

It's the beginning of the first term of our last year at university and Nick, Ed and I are at home waiting for a guy who's supposed to be coming round to audition for the band. Until the summer Captain Magnet were having a really good year. We played over a dozen gigs and have twice been reviewed by the local paper. Disaster struck, however, when Ruth, our guitarist, left following 'artistic differences' (she wanted us to play some songs she'd written and I said no because they weren't very good). In desperate need of a replacement, we asked around our friends and the only person who's even vaguely interested is coming round now. We're just about to go over what we're looking for in a guitarist when there's a knock at the door.

'That'll be the door,' says Nick, grinning.

'Fine,' I reply. 'I'll get it.'

I open the door and standing in front of me is a tall guy in a leather jacket.

'Hi,' he says. 'I'm Damon. I'm here to audition for Captain Magnet.'

'I'm Jim,' I tell him. 'I'm the lead singer. Come in.'

Damon follows me into the living room, plugs his guitar into Nick's amp and plays two and a half songs for me, Nick and Ed. He does a cover of a Stone Roses song, a cover of a Dinosaur Jr song, and half of a song he'd written himself called 'The Girl From Inner Space', which he unashamedly tells us is about his girlfriend. Given that he's a better all-round musician than all of us put together, it's a foregone conclusion that he should join the band.

'You're brilliant,' I tell him. 'You're in.'

# 1992

## Wednesday, 12 February 1992

### 1.33 p.m.

Nick, Damon and I are sitting in the bar at the students' union with three empty pint glasses and the latest issue of the *NME* in front of us. Damon has fitted into the band perfectly. Most nights since he's joined us, band practices in Nick's and my living room have turned into nights out in the Varsity. These have ended up as mammoth beery conversations about life, politics, girls and music. Damon is now much more than a band mate. He's a friend.

'Do you want another drink?' I ask everyone at the table.

'I can't,' says Damon. 'I've got an organic-chemistry lecture in ten minutes.'

I turn to Nick and do a drinking-a-pint motion with my hand. He looks at his watch. 'I've got a three-hour mechanical-engineering lecture in ten minutes. I'll definitely have another pint.'

I stand up and walk to the bar. A girl I vaguely recognise is just coming in through the main entrance. I think I know her but I can't place her. She's puffing frantically on a cigarette and looking around the room as if she's searching for someone, but when her name doesn't spring to mind I lose interest and concentrate on ordering the drinks at the bar. By the time I'm returning to where we're sitting, the girl is back on my mind again, mainly because she's kissing Damon.

## 1.44 p.m.

I must have been daydreaming because I don't notice the Boy Who Dresses Differently until he's sitting next to Damon. The Boy Who Dresses Differently is the name that Jane and I have referred to him by since he tried it on with me at the freshers' disco. He's often a topic of conversation among my circle of friends because he's one of a select group of people everyone recognises around campus, whether you're interested in them or not, because they always stand out from the crowd. These university 'characters' include the Girl With No Eyebrows, the Boy Who Wears Makeup to Lectures, the Girl Who Is Always In Tears and finally, the Boy Who Dresses Differently.

In recent times I'd noticed that the Boy Who Dresses Differently had taken his eccentric style of dress to its zenith. On any day of the week he can be spotted wearing an Oxfam suit with trainers; kipper ties with home-made T-shirts, and seventies shirts with flared collars in patterns so loud you can almost hear them screaming from across the other side of the campus. Once, during exam week, Jane spotted him wearing a peach cheesecloth shirt that was so monumentally hideous I ended up having at least five different conversations that day with friends along the lines of 'Did you see the state of the Boy Who Dresses Differently today? What was he thinking?'

And now he's sitting opposite me.

'Jim,' says Damon, addressing the Boy Who Dresses Differently, 'this is my girlfriend, Alison.'

'Hi,' he replies. 'You're the Girl From Inner Space.'

I nod and smile uncomfortably as I recall the song Damon wrote about me. There's an awkward pause. I'm hoping beyond hope that he hasn't recognised me.

'Do you two know each other?' asks Damon.

I shake my head and put out my cigarette as an excuse not to make eye-contact. 'No. Not at all.'

Damon doesn't look convinced, but he doesn't seem that bothered either. 'You just seem like you recognised each other, that's all.'

'Now you say that, she does look familiar,' says Jim.

'I've never met you before in my life,' I reply quickly.

'My mistake,' says Jim. 'The girl I'm thinking of is someone I met on Freshers' Night. She really fancied me. But I wasn't all that interested.'

Damon laughs. 'She must've been mad.'

'Yeah,' says Jim. 'I think she was a bit.'

## 6.05 p.m.

'I can't believe you were sitting at the same table as the university freak boy,' says Jane excitedly, when I reach home and tell her the news.

'It was really strange. Of course I knew Damon had joined a band – they're called Captain Magnet or some such rubbish – I even knew that one of the band members was called Jim, but I'd never thought for a moment that *that* Jim was the Boy Who Dresses Differently.'

'And you didn't say anything to him about him trying to snog you on Freshers' Night?'

'I couldn't say anything, could I? I wasn't sure if he recognised me or not or whether he was just teasing me for the sake of it. So I just bit my lip.'

'Wow,' says Jane, who never says 'wow' about anything. 'What are you going to do?'

'Nothing. I'm going to ignore him. Just because he's Damon's friend doesn't mean I have to be best buddies with him . . . The thing is, though—'

'What?'

'I have to admit that I am just a little bit curious about him.'

'Really?'

'Yeah. Is that weird?'

'Do you think he's good-looking?'

'Up close, and in relatively normal clothing, I can see that some girls might find him attractive.'

Jane laughs. 'But not you?'

'No, he's good-looking in a too obvious way. You know how some men have deep-down handsomeness – you could crack them open and you'll even find their bones fanciable?' Jane nods. 'Well, Jim's the opposite. He's surface handsome. No depth.' I think for a moment, trying to get together the perfect sound-bite description. 'He looks like the kind of boy easy girls go for.'

Jane laughs. 'He sounds like he's just up my street.'

**10.17 p.m.**

I'm in the pub with Nick having an emergency session of the What Can We Do To Sort Out Jim's Life Committee. Item one on the agenda (of which I've just told Nick the details) is that I once tried to get off with our guitarist's girlfriend.

'Do you think she knew it was you?' asks Nick.

'It's hard to say. She seemed a bit off with me but that doesn't mean much, does it? It's not like it's the first time a girl's taken an instant dislike to me. But she was acting strange for someone who doesn't remember me.'

'As far as Damon goes, I don't know what you're worrying about,' says Nick. 'I reckon if you'd told him that you once tried drunkenly to proposition his girlfriend when you were a wet-behind-the-ears first-year he'd probably find it very funny. But let's say for the sake of argument that his girlfriend does recognise you from that night, the fact is she's chosen to pretend not to know who you are. So my advice is to keep quiet.'

'That's good advice but—'

'Don't say it.'

'What?'

'I know what you're going to say and don't say it.'

'How can you possibly know what I'm going to say?'

'Because your eyes have gone all squinty.'

'They've done no such thing.'

'Okay, then,' says Nick. 'Answer me this question. When you met her this afternoon, did you ask yourself if you fancied her?'

'Yes, but—'

'No buts. You know the Rules, don't you?'

I sigh and repeat in a monotone: 'A bloke should never evaluate another bloke's girlfriend for the purpose of rating her attractiveness if the first bloke considers the second bloke to be a mate.'

'Exactly,' says Nick.

'But—'

'What did I say about buts?'

'But surely there's a case to argue that as I've tried it on with Alison before she was Damon's girlfriend the Rules don't apply.'

Nick laughs. 'You're right. That's a massive legal loophole that I should get closed the moment I start fancying women who have rejected you . . . Okay, so what were the results of your extensive calculations and observations?'

'Alison's okay, very good-looking but not really my type.'

'Given your chequered Goth-tinged past I'm not exactly sure what your type is.'

'I suppose if I were to have a type Anne would be it. Although I've sworn off unattainable women.'

'You mean unattainable women like our guitarist's girlfriend?'

'Good point,' I say quietly.

'Well, all I can say is that it's a good job you don't fancy her, then.'

'That's just it,' I reply, looking at my empty pint glass. 'I think I do.'

## Saturday, 15 February 1992

### 11.23 p.m.

Every Saturday night, Nick, some of our mates and I go to a student night called Menagerie held in a cavernous nightclub called the Hummingbird. The most notable thing about it is its notoriously sticky carpet, which lines the edge of the dance-floor. In some of the difficult-to-get-at corners of the club, the carpets are still their original brick-red colour; elsewhere they have been gradually turned sludge brown by hundreds of thousands of litres of spilt cider and lager served in wobbly plastic cups.

I'm just contemplating how disgusting the carpet really is when Nick says sharply, 'Don't look over at the bar.'

'Why not?'

'Just don't,' says Nick.

'But why not?' I turn round and look over by the bar. 'It's Alison and Damon. They've seen me and they're coming over. I wish I hadn't looked.'

'I know. That's why I told you not to look.'

We rarely saw Damon out and about on a Saturday night because it was apparently 'girlfriend night' when he was supposed to spend quality time with Alison, doing things like going out for a meal or to the cinema. Which is why I'm surprised when I see him, Alison and a bunch of her mates (one of whom is carrying a heart-shaped helium balloon bearing the inscription 'Birthday Girl') enter the club. Alison's friends disappear *en masse* in the direction of the loo as she and Damon walk over to me and Nick. My heart begins to race like I've run a marathon. This is the first time I've seen Alison since Wednesday, and unfortunately she has become something of an obsession. My fear now is that if I have to talk to her ever again it will be obvious that I fancy her.

'All right, guys?' says Damon, when he reaches me and Nick.

'Great,' says Nick, and I chip in a hearty nod.

'All right, Alison?' greets Nick.

Alison nods sheepishly and I chip in another hearty nod, and Damon looks at me as if I'm being a bit weirder than normal. 'Fancy a drink, lads?' he asks.

'Carling, cheers,' says Nick.

'Castlemaine, cheers,' I add. My voice sounds ridiculously throaty and everyone looks at me as if they've just heard Harpo Marx speak. 'I've got a cough,' I add, by way of explanation.

'What do you want, Al?' asks Damon.

'I'll have a vodka and tonic,' she replies. 'But I'll come with you to the bar and give you a hand.'

'I'll be fine,' insists Damon. 'You stay here with the boys and I'll be back before you know it.'

Alison is left with me and Nick.

'I'm going to take a slash,' says Nick, being deliberately crude. 'I'll be back in a sec.'

Now I am left with just Alison.

We stare around the room for a few moments and watch the people on the dance-floor. The song playing is called 'There's No Love Between Us', and I can't work out if it's apt that it should be playing, or ironic, or inconsequential.

'Great song, this,' I say.

Alison nods and half smiles, but doesn't speak.

'So, how are you?' I ask.

'Okay,' she says dismissively. She looks over in the direction of the bar as if willing the queue that Damon's standing in to get shorter.

She's so offish with me that I'm convinced she's finally remembered who I am. I decide to come clean and apologise in a bid to keep the peace. 'Look—' I begin, but I'm interrupted by her friends returning from the loo.

'Alison!' screams one. 'We've been looking for you everywhere,' and with that they whisk her off to the dance-floor.

## Sunday, 16 February 1992

### 1 a.m.

I'm standing on my own in the balcony above the dance-floor having a cigarette and thinking about Jim. When Jane asked me for suggestions for clubs we should go to for her birthday I could have named dozens, but I'd suggested this in the full knowledge that Jim would be here because Damon had told me he came here every Saturday. And now that he's here I'm ignoring him because I feel like if I don't act offhand with him he'll know just how much I really like him. It will be obvious – not just to Jim but to Damon too.

'If you cover your ears,' says a voice behind me, 'and just watch everyone on the dance-floor they look really strange.'

I turn to see Jim standing there and, despite myself, I smile.

'Without the sound of music,' he continues, 'all you've got are hundreds of people throwing their hands and limbs around in a darkened room.' He puts his hands over his ears. 'Go on,' he encourages me, yelling over the music. 'Do it.'

I laugh, and while he still has his hands over his ears I whisper, 'I like you. I like you a lot. But I've got a boyfriend. And I can't really do this.'

'What?' he says, removing his hands from his ears.

'Nothing.'

'You looked like you were saying something.'

'I was asking you if you wanted a cigarette,' I say, offering the packet.

'I don't smoke,' he replies. 'It's bad for my singing voice. Anyway, those things will kill you one day if you're not careful.'

'I'll take my chances,' I reply, and we share an awkward smile. 'I do know you, don't I?' I say, after a few moments.

Jim nods. 'Freshers' Night, 1989. I engaged you in conversation about my A-level results, then tried to get off with you. On behalf of me and my ego, I apologise.'

I'm about to accept gracefully when we're interrupted again, this time by his friend Nick.

'Mate,' says Nick, 'I've been looking for you everywhere.'

'I was talking to someone,' replies Jim.

Nick's eyes follow Jim's to me. 'Oh,' he says. 'Sorry, kiddo.'

That one sentence speaks volumes. I can tell straight away that Nick knows that I know Jim, which I'd already sort of guessed. But there's new information in there as well. Something that hadn't even occurred to me.

'I'd better go,' I say to Jim quickly. 'I'll see you both soon.'

### 11.35 a.m.

'You're never going to believe this. But I've got this weird feeling Jim likes me too.'

It's mid-morning and Jane and I are sitting in the living room watching Sunday-morning TV. Damon has gone to Jim's for a band practice, leaving me free to update Jane on last night.

'What makes you say that?'

'It was his friend Nick who raised the alarm.'

'So now you know, what are you going to do about your crush on him?'

'I don't know. I've been doing a bit of digging about him.'

'You mean you've been asking Damon about him.'

'Yes,' I say guiltily. 'But I did it as subtly as possible. All I could find out was that apparently he had a big thing about some girl called Anne. Damon said he reckons most of their band's songs are about her. I was really surprised when I heard that. I never imagined he'd be the type to fall in love.'

'Me either. I can't think of him as the Boy Who Dresses Differently any more.'

'You're right,' I say. 'He's just a boy now. A boy I think I'm developing a massive crush on.'

## Tuesday, 3 March 1992

### 3.42 p.m.

I'm wandering aimlessly through campus trying to kill time between my last lecture, Post-war British Economic History, and the next, Applications of Modern Economics. Sitting down on a bench outside the library I stare into space and find myself thinking about Alison. I'm not thinking anything specifically, just about her in a general sense – her likes, dislikes, what she might think about. That kind of thing. It's becoming something of a habit for me. I think about her when I wake up. I think about her when I go to sleep. And I think about her in all the time between. It has occurred to me that it isn't the best idea in the world to be thinking about a mate's girlfriend with such intensity. Then I reason that the heart wants what the heart wants. In the end I decide that the best way to stop thinking about Alison is to distract myself by checking through the reading list my Post-war-British-Economic-History lecturer has just handed out. One of the books on the list is apparently essential to this year's course and as I know that every single copy in the library is bound to have been borrowed already by the mature students on my course, I have no choice but to head for the campus bookshop and buy a copy. The second I step in I look across the shop and there's Alison, looking right back at me.

'Nice weather we're having, isn't it?' I say, when I reach her. It was the first thing that had popped into my head.

She laughs. 'Yes, it's unseasonably warm for the time of year.'

'But, then, again, it did rain a little bit yesterday afternoon.'

'That's true. And they say it might rain towards the weekend.'

'Of course, I did hear that it might clear up after the weekend . . . but it might snow and sleet towards the middle of the week.'

It's like being dropped into the middle of a black-and-white Katharine Hepburn and Spencer Tracy film. One that's set in Birmingham featuring Tracy as a slightly grumpy economics student and Hepburn as an English student with a great smile.

We carry on like that – batting meteorological platitudes

backwards and forwards – for a full five minutes before I say really something stupid.

'Enough of the weather,' I say. 'Do you fancy going for a quick drink or something?'

Alison's face immediately drops. 'No, thanks,' she says quietly.

'Work to do?'

She shakes her head.

'Other plans?'

She shakes her head again.

'So why are you turning me down?' I ask.

'You know why,' she replies.

She's right, I do know why. And now I know that she knows that I know too.

'Can't we even be friends?' I ask eventually.

'I don't think so.'

And with that she excuses herself and leaves the shop. As I watch her walk out I realise with perfect clarity that I'm more than just attracted to her. This is something deeper. More long-lasting. And, for all the talk, I feel like we both know that, sooner or later, no matter what we do or say, it's inevitable that something's going to happen between us. It's just a matter of time.

## Wednesday, 4 March 1992

### 9.33 a.m.

'Jim asked me out for a drink,' I tell Jane, the following morning, as we're eating breakfast and watching TV.

'What did you say?'

'He said it would be just as friends but I said no and now I feel awful about it.'

'Why do you feel awful?'

'Because I wanted to say yes. I've got to make a choice between Jim and Damon.'

Jane winces. 'I knew this was coming. My money's on Jim. The truth is, sweetheart, I don't think Damon's the right guy for you.'

'Why not?'

'I've always thought he's a bit too nice.'

'Too nice?'

'Too nice. Too bland. Too beige. There's no spark between you any more. No chemistry. No grit. You guys never argue, do you?'

'No.'

'You never yell and shout.'

'No.'

'See? That's not normal. He's nice to you. And you're nice to him. It's like watching a film where you know the end as soon as you've seen the beginning.'

'You're right, but—'

'I know I'm right. He's a lovely guy. But he's not the one for you. Whatever happens between you and Jim doesn't matter here. The fact is you have to end it with Damon.'

'I can't.'

'Why?'

'Because we've been together a long time.'

'That's no reason at all.'

'I know.'

'Then what are you going to do?'

'It'll be our finals soon and then we'll be graduating and temptation will be out of my way, won't it? All I need to do is avoid Jim at all costs and see if I can make it work with Damon.'

## Thursday, 9 July 1992

### 9.03 p.m.

It's the night of the graduation ball. In my hand is a rolled-up piece of paper that proves to the world I have a degree in business and economics. I'm standing at the bar in a tweed suit, waiting for Nick to return from the loo, when a voice I recognise immediately says, 'You look very smart.'

I turn around and standing there, holding a packet of cigarettes in one hand, a glass of white wine in the other and looking more beautiful than ever, is Alison wearing a cream ballgown. She sets down her glass and the cigarettes on the bar, throws her arms around me and kisses my cheek.

'You almost look normal,' she says, laughing.

'Cancer Research shop in Kings Heath,' I rely, grinning. 'Five pounds.' I deliberately look Alison up and down. 'You look very . . . ballgowny.'

She laughs. 'Cheeky sod. I didn't want to do the whole ballgown thing but all the girls in my house said they were doing it and I didn't want to be the only one dressed normally.' She picks up the cigarettes, pulls one out with a lighter and lights up. Instinctively she offers me one, but before I can refuse she says, 'Oh, that's right. You're in the these-things-will-kill-you-one-day brigade.'

'And they will.'

'I've got plenty of time to give up.'

She inhales on her cigarette deeply, holds her breath for several moments, then politely exhales in the direction of the bar to keep the smoke away from me. 'I feel like a right idiot dressed like this,' she says.

'You shouldn't,' I reply. 'I think you look beautiful.' I

hadn't meant to say that. So I cover my tracks by changing subjects. 'It's been ages since I've seen you.'

'A few months at least.'

'How did you get on with your finals?'

'Fine. How about you?'

'Okay. I'm just glad it's all over. My parents came up for the ceremony and this afternoon my dad told me, as we ate lunch in the Varsity, "The world is yours for the taking, son." I didn't bother telling him that I didn't really want to "take" the world just yet.'

'I know what you mean,' says Alison. 'Everyone seems to be getting proper grown-up jobs and I've got a job at Kenway's, the bookshop in town.'

'Snap. No career in the financial industries for me, I'm working at a record shop in town.'

'Which one?'

'Revolution. Do you know it?'

'Yeah, I do. You'll never believe it but it's where Damon first asked me out.'

'How's that for full circle? I work in the record shop where he asked you out. And here we are at the end of our three years at university standing in the same place where I first met you.'

'It's strange, isn't it?'

I pause, then ask, 'Where is Damon?'

'At the bar,' she says, pointing.

I look over and wave at him. 'I know I shouldn't ask this but . . . how are things between you two?'

'They're okay,' she replies. 'We have our ups and downs.'

'Good,' I reply, then kiss her cheek and walk away.

## Wednesday, 22 July 1992

### 9.46 p.m.

It's a couple of weeks after the graduation ball and Nick, Damon, our drummer Ed and I are sitting in the Varsity following a band practice. For a while we've been talking about going away somewhere to celebrate our new freedom and now we're taking the vote.

'Hands up for a weekend in Amsterdam?'

Ed's is the only hand in the air.

'Okay, how many for a weekend in Dublin?'

There are no hands in the air.

'How can you not vote for your own idea?' I ask Nick.

'Because it seems a bit rubbish, now I think about it,' he replies.

'Okay, and finally, how many votes for the Reading festival?'

Nick, Damon and I raise our hands.

'So that's decided, then,' I say, to the boys sat around the table. 'Our big post-graduation blow-out is going to be the Reading festival on the August bank-holiday weekend.'

I came up with the idea of going to it because Nirvana were the headline act. We'd seen them the previous September and they'd been fantastic. I'm convinced that seeing them again will be a genuine rock-and-roll moment that will make the weekend really special.

'We could take our demo tape with us,' says Nick. 'And then when Nirvana have played we could hang around by the backstage area and try to give it to Kurt Cobain. He'll wander around with it in his pocket for a while and then one day he'll be bored and slip it into his Walkman to have a listen —'

'And that'll be it,' says Ed. 'He'll think we're the best band in the world and proclaim us the future of rock and roll.'

'We'll be courted by dozens of record companies,' adds Damon, 'and they'll want to sign us for huge amounts of money.'

'And our first album will go triple platinum,' I say.

We all know it's a fantasy.

We all know that there's little chance that Captain Magnet will ever release a record.

We all know that we're never going to become rock stars.

But for that brief moment, sitting around that table, it feels like anything is possible.

## Tuesday, 28 July 1992

### 12.55 p.m.

It's five minutes until my lunch-break and I'm standing at the till in the fiction department at work, counting every second that passes, when Damon bounds into the shop. 'Hey, you,' he says.

'Hi,' I say suspiciously. 'To what do I owe the pleasure?'

'I've got a surprise for you. But in order for it to work you'll have to keep the twenty-eighth to the thirtieth of August free.'

'The August bank-holiday weekend?' I say excitedly. 'You haven't booked that trip to Paris we're always talking about?'

'Even better,' he says. 'I've got us tickets to the Reading festival.'

The disappointment must be written all over my face because Damon immediately starts trying to convince me. 'It'll be great.'

'It'll be damp and muddy.'

'You'll have fun.'

'Fun? I'll have to sleep in a tent.'

'Everyone else is going.'

'Everyone who?'

'Well, originally it was going to be just the rest of the band. But then Nick caved in because his girlfriend wanted to go, and Ed, our drummer, felt obliged to take his girlfriend so I thought you could come along too.'

'What about Jim?' I ask casually. 'Who's he taking?'

'He's not taking anyone,' says Damon. 'In fact, I haven't seen him with a girl in ages. Ed says he thinks Jim's in love with someone who doesn't feel the same way about him.'

I don't need to hear any more. I agree to go with him there and then.

## Friday, 28 August 1992

### 8.01 a.m.

I'm watching breakfast TV when the phone rings. I let the answer-machine get it. 'Hi, Jim, it's Damon. Mate, I had a dodgy takeaway last night and I've been throwing up all night. I'm still coming but Al and I might be a little late.'

### 9 a.m.

I'm in the kitchen doing the washing-up when the phone rings. Once again I let the answer-machine get it. 'Hi, Jim. It's me again. I'm still feeling really dodgy. I think there's a strong chance I won't be going. Alison says she doesn't want to go without me but I'll get her to drop round the tickets.'

### 10.45 a.m.

I'm in the living room, trying to find my trainers, when there's a knock at my front door. I answer it and there on my door-step is Alison. She's dressed in old army trousers and there's a rucksack on her back.

'That's not your usual get-up,' I say, looking her up and down.

'Apparently I'm going to a festival of some kind,' she says.

'Without Damon?'

'He insisted I go,' she says, and hands me an envelope. Inside is his ticket and a note torn from an A4 pad.

Dear Jim,
Can you do three things for me?
1) Sell this ticket.
2) Look after Alison for me.
3) Have a good time.
Cheers,
Damon
PS Don't forget to give Mr Kurt our demo tape.

## Saturday, 29 August 1992

### 3.30 a.m.

Jim and I are sharing a tent. We've been in it for all of twenty minutes, having spent most of the early hours sitting around a camp fire that Nick had made. Our evening's entertainment has been eight two-litres bottles of beer, ten cans of strong cider and (with the exception of Jim) five packs of cigarettes. And we haven't seen a single band yet. Jim is lying in his sleeping-bag now and I can see that he's on the verge of dropping off to sleep. I, however, am in the mood to talk so I elbow him gently in the ribs. 'Are you asleep?'

'Yeah.'

'Very funny.'

'Can't sleep?'

'Something like that.'

'So you've woken me up to tell me you can't sleep?'

'No, I just wanted to chat to someone and you're the only one who's awake.'

'But I wasn't awake.'

'Well, you are now.'

'So what do you want to chat about?'

'How about what's going on?'

'Where?'

'Here. Between you and me.'

'Okay, it's like this,' he begins. 'I like you.'

'Really?'

'Yes, really. And I think you like me.'

'How do you know?'

'I'm guessing. Am I wrong?'

'No,' I say playfully. 'Your guess is right.'

'You, however, have a boyfriend who is a mate of mine – and that's pretty much where we are, isn't it?'

'Yeah. That is pretty much where we are.'

'So the question is, what are we going to do?'

'That is the question,' I echo.

'Any ideas?'

'None. You?'

'None.'

There's a long pause.

'Night, then,' says Jim, moving from his back on to his side.

'Sleep tight,' I reply, in a whisper, and then I put my arm around Jim and pull myself closer.

Nothing happens between us. It's just sort of cosy. And as I drift off to sleep I hope that we'll stay 'cosy' for the rest of the weekend.

## Sunday, 30 August 1992

### 3.30 p.m.

It's the afternoon of the last day of the festival and Teenage Fanclub are on stage. Two hours earlier we all made a special trip to the supermarket in Reading town centre and bought what could only be described as a ridiculous amount of alcohol, which we ferried back to the festival site in two taxis. While most of the group are drinking at a level that keeps them somewhere around the 'merry' mark, Alison seems to be well beyond that point to the extent that I feel I'm not doing a very good job of Damon's request to look after her.

'Don't you think you're knocking it back a bit?' I ask Alison, as she attempts to open a two-litre bottle of Woodpecker cider with her teeth.

'Don't be silly,' she slurs. 'You're starting to sound like Damon.'

'Okay,' I say. 'But just watch out for yourself, okay?'

**8.21 p.m.**

The penultimate band of the festival – Nick Cave and the Bad Seeds – are now on the main stage and Alison is looking decidedly wobbly.

'Are you okay?' I ask.

Alison nods unsteadily.

'Are you sure you're all right?'

She nods again and silently mouths the words: 'I'm fine.'

**10.04 p.m.**

Kurt Cobain, in a hospital robe, is being pushed on-stage in a wheelchair – everyone goes wild. Clearly mocking the rumours that have been going round about various hospitalisations he begins singing, then falls to the ground, flailing.

'This is worth the ticket price alone,' I say to Alison, over the roar of the crowd.

She nods but says nothing. I can tell she's going to be sick some time soon.

### 10.37 p.m.

Nirvana are playing 'Smells Like Teen Spirit'. They're just getting to the chorus when I notice that Alison has started throwing up.

It's like a fountain.

Or maybe a volcano erupting.

Either way it's violent.

Quite horrible.

And exceptionally projectile.

I look around for my friends, but everyone else has moved nearer the stage. I'm on my own.

I look at Kurt on stage.

Then I look at Alison, who is now on her hands and knees retching.

I look at the demo tape in my hand.

Then I shove it into my back pocket, pick her up and take her to the first-aid tent.

## Monday, 31 August 1992

### 11.07 a.m.

I'm in a phone box talking to Jane, telling her what a mess I've made of things.

'So, what was your big plan?' asks Jane. 'Get drunk and try to snog Jim?'

'I needed a bit of Dutch courage,' I explain. 'But I miscalculated and the sheer volume of cider I drank would've provided fearlessness for the whole of the Netherlands.'

'I bet you've got a bit of a headache.'

'The headache's not the worst of it. I feel terrible because I made Jim miss the band he really wanted to see and his one and only chance of giving the lead singer a tape.'

'What?'

'The boys apparently came up with some silly plan to give Kurt Cobain a copy of their demo tape. They were hoping it would lead to fame and fortune.'

'Well, that was never going to happen.'

'I know, but they like to daydream, don't they? I'm so mortified I can't say a word to him. Not even "sorry". The nicer he is to me the worse I feel.'

'The thing between you and him just isn't going to happen, is it?' says Jane.

'You're right,' I say sadly. 'I don't think it ever will.'

## 1.33 p.m.

We're on the train going back to Birmingham and I'm lying with my head against the window and my eyes closed, not talking (and, if I can help it, not moving). I haven't even made my usual trip to the smokers' carriage at the rear of the train because I'm feeling too nauseous to smoke. Jim tries to talk to me several times during the journey to assure me that everything's okay but this just upsets me more.

## 2.45 p.m.

We've just come into New Street station. When we're all off the train everyone decides to catch the bus home to Selly Oak but Jim insists, given my fragile state, that I might be better off in a taxi. I agree and twenty minutes later we're in the back of a Datsun Cherry on our way to my house.

We reach Heely Road and the driver pulls up a few doors down. We sort out the money and the bags. Jim gets out, too, and follows me up the pathway to the house. I rummage in my rucksack for my purse, which has got my keys inside. 'Well, thanks for an interesting weekend,' he says.

'I ruined it for you, didn't I?'

'No,' he says. 'I had a great time.'

'Thanks,' I say quietly, and then I reach out and put my arms around him as if I'm going to give him a hug – which is what I'd intended to do – but all of a sudden I don't. Instead I go for his lips and he goes for mine and we sort of kiss for a very long time. And when we stop I panic and immediately feel guilty.

'I'd better go,' I say. Avoiding his eyes, I step inside my front door and close it behind me.

## Thursday, 3 September 1992

### 5 p.m.

'Hi, Alison, it's me, Jim. Can you give me a ring when you've got a moment?'

This is probably the millionth message Jim has left for me since we kissed and I haven't returned a single one. I'm deliberately avoiding him because I don't want to talk about the kiss. Although the sole reason I'd got drunk at the festival was to do exactly that, I'm now convinced it was a spur-of-the-moment thing. A one-off. It didn't mean anything in the real world. And although I'm still not sure how I feel about Damon I just know that I don't have what it takes to split up from him either. We've been together for what feels like for ever. It's the longest relationship of my life so far. And no matter how unhappy I am with us, I still can't come to terms with the fact that we might be over.

## Saturday, 5 September 1992

### 5 p.m.

Jane and I have just come back from an afternoon in town shopping. The answerphone in the hallway is beeping. I press play and listen: 'Hi, Alison, it's Jim here. I know this is a stupid message to leave, given that all your housemates and potentially your boyfriend will hear it – I mean, you might all be standing there right now looking at the phone thinking, What is this guy on about? – but I'm just leaving you a message to let you know that I've got the Message. Even if you do like me – and I'm one hundred per cent sure that you do – not only do you already have a boyfriend, not only am I friends with the aforementioned boyfriend, but to top it all Damon's a ridiculously nice human being. I can't blame you for choosing him over me because at the end of the day I think I would probably choose him over me. That's all I've got to say, really. 'Bye.'

## Friday, 18 September 1992

### 10.05 p.m.

Nick, Ed, Damon and I are in the Jug of Ale about to have a post-gig pint. It was a really good performance tonight. We played well and Nick and I have been talking about maybe sending our demo tape to a few record labels. I'm about to go to the bar to get some drinks when Damon coughs like he's got something important to say.

'I've got some bad news for you, boys,' he announces. 'I've been offered a job in London.'

'Doing what?' asks Nick.

'Recruitment consultantancy.'

'When are you off?' I ask.

'At the end of the month.'

'What about the band?' I ask, even though I already know the answer.

'I'm really sorry, guys, I'm going to have to leave. You can carry on without me, surely?'

'Well, actually,' says Ed, 'I've been trying to find the right time to tell you but I'm going home to Portsmouth.'

'To do what?' I ask.

'I'm going to move in with my girlfriend.'

'But what about all the hard work we've done?' I say to them both. 'We can't give up just like that. I think we could really make it.'

'It's just pipe dreams,' says Ed. 'University's over now. We've got to get on with real life, mate.'

**10.45 p.m.**

Damon and I are standing outside the pub with the band's instruments, waiting to go home. Ed and Nick are still inside, using the toilets. We've been talking about the band and he's apologised a million times for leaving and I haven't got the heart to give him a hard time because I think he's genuinely upset about it.

'Do you think you'll start another band in London?'

'I don't know about start, I might join one.'

I nod thoughtfully. 'And what about Alison? Is she going to London with you?' It's been the one question I've wanted to ask him since he told us his news.

'Hopefully,' he replies. 'Things are good between us. I kind of think that Alison might be the One.'

'Well, best of luck and all that,' I say, shaking his hand. 'I'm sure the two of you will have a great time down there.'

'Cheers,' he says. 'I really think we will.'

## 11.45 p.m.

It's late and I'm sitting up in bed fully clothed reading over the lyrics to the last song I'm ever going to write. It is, like most of the songs I've written in the last few months, about Alison, although in a roundabout way it's about love too, and getting older and political complacency and the band falling apart and getting a job and everything else that's on my mind.

**The Smile On Your Face**

Why do you come to me
With that smile on your face
Saying that you've heard it all before?
So full of the joys of life
To care for thought at all
But it's you who has free rein.

Why do you torture me
With looks that could kill?
My grieving heart can't take much more.
It is ironic to think that one who has it all
Could just throw it all away.

CHORUS: We're on the rise again – and you can't stop us now.

Why do you think the future is so far away?
You're young but there are younger than you.
I never thought idealism was such a crime
Till you smashed my dreams in two.

Don't believe the patriot,
I don't believe the past,
Don't believe there's anything to be gained in
compromise,
I believe in youth,
But you won't believe yourself,
It's funny you never know what you've got until it's
gone.

Smash my dreams if you like but you can't sell my soul
(*repeat*)
Take all my possessions and it might hurt a bit
But that smile on your face will be gone.

# 1993

## Friday, 26 February 1993

### 8.15 p.m.

I'm standing in the Kings Heath branch of Blockbuster with my girlfriend Louise, a second-year medical student at Birmingham University. I met her at a student night in a nightclub near Five Ways called XLs a few weeks ago. She's nice but she's nothing like Alison. All the time we've been together – three months in total – I've had this picture in my head of Alison bumping into me and Louise looking all shiny and happy and new. Alison will be so devastated at having chosen Damon over me that she will break down crying.

For the past forty-five minutes I've been waiting for Louise to make a decision about which video we're going to watch, and anyone who cares to take the time to read my body language will have observed that I am currently annoyed, exasperated and depressed – in that order. 'Come on, Lou,' I say to her. 'You need to make a decision before the shop closes.' I point to a video at random. 'What about *Cape Fear?*'

'Too scary.'

I pick another at random. *'Terminator 2?'*

'It's a boys' film.'

*'My Girl?'*

'What's it about?'

'It's got Macauley Culkin in it and some girl I've never heard of.'

'I couldn't stand him in *Home Alone*.'

*'JFK?'*

'What's it about?'

*'JFK,'* I replied tersely.

'Who's that?'

'Who's *JFK*? Are you telling me that you managed to get into medical school but you've never heard of John Fitzgerald Kennedy? He was President of America in the sixties.'

'Was he?'

'Yes.'

'Sounds boring.'

*'Thelma and Louise?'*

'Saw it.'

'Right,' I say forcefully. 'That's it. I'm going to choose the film we're going to see. Nick was banging on about some French film he saw ages ago called *Betty Blue*. You wait here and carry on looking and I'll go and see if it's any good and if it is we'll watch that, okay?' I look around the store. 'Now where's the art-house section?'

## 8.17 p.m.

The art-house section turns out to be more of an art-house shelf, featuring the following empty video boxes: *Tampopo, 8 and a Half, Bicycle Thieves, La Dolce Vita, Jean de Florette* and *Betty Blue*. I pick up *Betty Blue* and study the cover to try to work out what it's about. After five minutes or so I'm none the wiser. I have, however, come to the conclusion that there's a strong chance the lead actress – Béatrice Dalle – might be naked in it. Given that the French are, perhaps, some of the best purveyors in the world of on-screen nudity I end up putting the box back on the shelf. Is it a good idea to watch a self-confessed 'erotically charged' video with Louise when there's a good chance I'll be calling time on our relationship before the evening's out? Still undecided, I reach out to pick up the box again and reread the back when an alien hand enters my line of vision, attempting to do the same. I look round abruptly, and I'm surprised to discover that the hand belongs to someone I know.

'It's you,' I say, still clutching a corner of the video box.

## 8.19 p.m.

'It's you,' I reply, still holding a corner of the box.

I haven't seen Jim since we kissed that day after the Reading festival, although I've imagined bumping into him a million times. Each and every time I imagined such an encounter I was always looking fabulous. Never in a million years did I imagine myself to be as I am now: wearing trainers, an old pair of tracksuit bottoms, and a faded Birmingham University Women's Hockey hooded top, without any makeup and my hair tied back with an elastic band because I couldn't find a scrunchie when I'd got up that morning. I'd only intended to be out of the house for a few minutes. I'd been sneezing all day, Damon was staying in London for the weekend, Jane had gone to see her parents and my other house-mate was going clubbing, so my plan had been to get a video and an extra large bag of popcorn, have a night in and feel sorry for myself.

'What are you doing here?' asks Jim.

'I was about to ask you the same question.'

'Me and Nick moved to Kings Heath a couple of weeks ago when the lease on the house in Selly Oak ran out.' He pauses. 'I thought you'd moved to London with Damon.'

'No . . . well, it didn't work out,' I say. 'Jane and I moved here a fortnight ago when the lease ran out in Heely Road.'

'Whereabouts are you living now?' asks Jim.

'Mitford Avenue.'

'What number?'

'Sixty-five,' I say, observing the huge grin spreading across Jim's face. 'Don't tell me you're—'

'I live at thirty-six,' says Jim. 'I think we're directly across the road from you.'

'You're not the house with the blue door and the Jim Morrison poster in the bay window, are you?'

'And are you the house with the green door and the scooter in the front garden?'

'It's Jane's boyfriend Peter's scooter. He leaves it at our house because he thinks it's less likely to be nicked there. I can't believe we're neighbours,' I say.

'And I can't believe we haven't bumped into each other before now. So how's Damon?'

'He's good, thanks.' I scratch the side of my face. 'And are you . . . seeing anyone?'

'No . . . well, no . . .' he replies, '. . . not really.'

Suddenly we both become aware that we're still holding the video box. Unsure what to say or do next, we remain motionless, as if playing a childhood game of statues.

'Are you going to rent that or are you just browsing?' I ask eventually.

'Rent,' he replies, and pulls the box from my grip.

'Actually, I think you'll find I had it first,' I retort, and snatch it back. We're laughing as we do this, but at the same time there's something serious going on. We're flirting again.

Jim grabs the video, pulls the band of his jeans away from his stomach and lodges it down the front of his trousers.

'You're such a child,' I say, staring at the bulge in his jeans. 'An absolute . . .'

'Juvenile?' offers Jim, grinning like an idiot. 'Tell me something I don't know.'

'I'll give you twice the rental if you give the box to me,' I say firmly.

'Tell you what, how about a compromise? I'll let you watch it at my house. But only if you promise to keep your hands to yourself.' He held out his hand for me to shake. 'Agreed?'

I shake his hand. I feel his skin on mine. I can already see what's going to happen and I don't want to fight it any more. 'Agreed.'

## 8.25 p.m.

I can't believe it, I think, imagining what it would be like to kiss her again. Here I am leaving Blockbuster with the girl I adore most in the whole world when less than an hour earlier I'd entered with a girl I didn't even like that much . . . Louise!

Damn.

*Louise.*

What am I going to do?

*Louise.*

What if she's spotted me?

*Louise.*

What if Alison's spotted her?

*Louise.*

What am I going to do?

There's only one thing I can do.

I remove the video box from my jeans and hand it to Alison. 'Can you pay for it?'

'You really know how to flatter a girl,' says Alison, holding the video at arm's length and wrinkling her nose. 'Why don't you pay for it yourself?'

'I've got something to do.'

Alison can tell I'm being evasive. 'Which is?'

'Checking out the happy endings in the new-releases section.' Before she can say anything I've disappeared to find Louise.

'Have you got the film?' asks Louise, when I arrive. 'I've been looking at *JFK* again and I didn't realise it had Kevin Costner in it. I quite like Kevin Costner.'

'This isn't working,' I tell her firmly.

'What isn't working?'

'You. Me. This. Us. We aren't working.'

'You don't want to go out with me any more?'

'It's not you. It's me. We're too different. I like French films with subtitles, you like . . . well, I don't think you like anything. Let's face it, it was never going to work, was it? Let's just go our separate ways and try to remember the good times, eh?'

'I can't believe this,' says Louise, almost tearfully. 'Is this because I didn't want to watch that Arnold Schwarzenegger film?'

'No, of course not. It's nothing to do with videos. It's to do with us. We're just not compatible. I feel awful. But believe me when I say this is hurting me more than it's hurting you.'

Overcome by anger Louise, with all the dexterity of a discus thrower, hurls the copy of *JFK* she's holding at my head. Lightning quick, I duck out of the way and it continues across the shop floor until it meets a small child coming the other way and skids to a halt on the floor. The child bursts into tears, Louise runs out of the shop and I breathe a huge sigh of relief.

'Did you see that?' says Alison, appearing at my side some moments later with the offending article in her hand. 'Some loony girl just hurled this at a poor defenceless child.'

'I know,' I reply. 'What *is* the world coming to?'

### 8.45 p.m.

Jim and I are walking along a busy Kings Heath high street in the rain. All the pubs and takeaways we pass are overflowing with Friday-night revellers and somehow it seems strange that our Friday-night revelling will consist of an evening in front of a subtitled French film.

'So, tell me,' he begins, as I light a cigarette, 'why didn't you move to London in the end?'

'I never agreed to go,' I reply, and then take a drag on my cigarette. 'Damon kept asking me and I kept telling him I wanted to stay in Birmingham. Not necessarily for the rest of my life but a little while longer at least. I didn't know what I wanted to do. In fact, I still don't. So I didn't see the point of going all the way down there to do what I'm doing here – which is drifting. Anyway, a few weeks before he was due to go it suddenly hit me: if I loved him, really loved him, I would've gone with him in a second. You do that sort of thing if you're in love, don't you?'

'Yeah,' he replies. 'I suppose if it's the real thing it wouldn't even be an issue.'

'See?' I say, smiling. 'You get it. You understand what I'm talking about. Real love isn't just about all the romantic stuff when everything is easy and the hardest thing you've got to do is make up pet names for each other—'

'You have pet names for each other?' says Jim. 'What are they?'

'He calls me Grumpus, because I can be a bit of a grumpy girlfriend sometimes. At first I was secretly a bit offended but after three years I love it.'

'And what do you call him?'

'Housey – you know, because his surname's Guest. It's not a very good one, is it?'

Jim laughs. 'Not really.'

'Anyway,' I continue, 'we're getting off the point. What I was trying to say is that love isn't just about the cute stuff—'

'Like making up rubbish pet names?'

'Yes, like making up rubbish pet names,' I say. 'It's about the tough times when things get difficult. When it's not all hearts and flowers. When it's about two people staying together, no matter what. And the fact is Damon and I haven't got that. And if I want anything from life it's – a special kind of love. A love that can stand anything you throw at it. Surely that's the only kind worth having.'

## Saturday, 27 February 1993

### 1.05 p.m.

It's early afternoon and Nick and I are in the Jug of Ale in Moseley. We're on opposite sides of the table, two half-drunk pints of lager between us, and I'm in the process of telling him about my encounter with Alison.

'So did you get to watch *Betty Blue*?'

'We never even got it out of the box.'

'So, what happened?'

'Well, we got back to the house and I think we both knew that we weren't going to watch the video. And . . . well, I don't want to go into the details but we started kissing in the hallway and then before we knew it we were in my room and you can guess the rest. So, anyway, I woke up this morning and she was lying next to me so I said, ''Morning, stranger,'' because I thought it would be a reasonably amusing thing to say. She didn't reply. She just sort of sloped out of my bed, picked up as many of her clothes as she could from the bedroom floor and left the room.'

'Doesn't sound good at all,' says Nick. 'What did you do?'

'Well, I just lay there in bed, staring at the poster on the wall in front of me.'

'The one of Bob Marley smoking a large ''herbal'' cigarette?'

'The very same. So I asked the great reggae legend – who had observed everything that had happened in that bedroom in the last twelve hours – what he reckoned had gone wrong. He didn't reply, of course, possibly because there was no need to. It was obvious what was going on. Alison's guilt complex over Damon was kicking in big-time. I got dressed, came out and sat on the stairs just as she was shoving her right foot into her left trainer. It took a while but eventually she got them on the right way round and announced offhandedly that she was leaving. I didn't reply. I had no idea how to play this. So I just sort of decided to let her get on with it.'

'And she left?'

'Yeah.'

'Without saying another word?'

'Yeah.'

Nick laughs. 'Did she take the video with her?'

'No,' I say, barely raising a smile. 'Maybe she feels really guilty about what happened; maybe she doesn't want to call it off with Damon.'

'You're probably right. She's been with him a long time.

Right through university until now. It takes a lot of guts to end something like that, even if it's not working.'

'Good point. So, what do you think I should do?'

'Do you like her?' I nod. 'Then you've got to do something that lets her know you mean business. Something that says this wasn't just about one night. It was about her being the One. Something that shows you're going to be around for a long time to come.'

'I know exactly the thing,' I say, as I pick up my pint. 'She'll love it.'

## 2.55 p.m.

I'm lying in bed still thinking about what a mess I've made of things when someone knocks on my bedroom door.

'Ally?'

It's Jane.

'I'm asleep,' I reply, from under my duvet. 'Come back later.'

Jane comes in and sits down on the bed next to me. 'Where were you last night? I was really worried when I got back from mum and dad's.'

I pop my head up from under the covers. 'Oh, I'm sorry,' I reply. 'I should've left a note or something. I wasn't thinking.'

'Anyway, I just thought you ought to know Damon called this morning.'

'Did he ask where I was?'

'I told him you'd got food poisoning and that you'd been throwing up all night and were sleeping it off.'

'Couldn't you have just told him I was out?'

'I didn't know when you'd be back, did I?' says Jane, reasonably.

I sigh heavily for my own benefit. 'You're really good to me, you know that?'

'Yeah, I do. So where were you last night, then?'

'At . . . at . . . Jim's.'

'As in Jim Owen?'

'I bumped into him last night. Typical, really. We wanted the same video. And guess what? He lives across the road from us. You know the house with the Jim Morrison poster in the window? Number thirty-six? That's him and Nick.'

'And you still both fancy each other after all this time?'

'I don't think I ever stopped liking him.'

'So what happened?'

'He suggested we watch it at his place . . . and, well, you can guess the rest. Thing is, I was really awful to him this morning. I felt guilty about Damon and left without saying anything. He must hate me now.'

'He doesn't hate you, believe me.'

'You don't know that.'

'Well, I can hazard a good guess because he knocked on the door just now and left something downstairs for you.'

I let out a scream of excitement. 'What is it?'

'I don't know but it's in a Walkers' crisps box in the hallway and it's moving.'

Jane and I race downstairs to where my other housemate, Mary, is standing in the hallway watching my parcel.

'It's got a letter attached to it,' says Jane, unsticking it from the side of the box and handing it to me. I open the envelope and read aloud:

'Dear Ms Smith,
I was trying to think of the most inappropriate gift that I could possibly give you and this is it.
Lots of love,
Mr Owen (from across the road) xxx'

I open the box carefully – because by now whatever it is is hurling itself around noisily – and look inside. I can't believe my eyes. Peering back at me with huge green eyes is a tiny tortoiseshell kitten.

'Now *that* is cute,' says Jane. 'Did you tell him you wanted a kitten?'

'No.'

'Did you tell him you like kittens?'

'No, to the best of my memory kittens have never entered any of our conversations.'

'So why's he given you one, then?' asks Mary.

'I don't know,' I reply. 'But I'm going to find out.'

## 4.20 p.m.

The kitten is wriggling in my arms as I walk across the road. And when I knock on Jim's front door it nearly leaps out of my hands. After a few moments the door opens and Jim appears, wearing a plain white T-shirt and jeans. 'I thought you'd never come, Ms Smith,' he says.

'I've just got one question for you. Why have you given me a kitten?'

'It's not just a kitten. Her name's Alan. She's six weeks old. And she's yours.'

'If she's mine how come she's called Alan?'

'I called her that because I couldn't think of any suitable girls' names and I didn't think she'd mind because she's a cat. Anyway,' he adds, 'I didn't think you were the sort of person who'd be into giving kittens names.'

'If you didn't think I'd be into giving kittens names why would you give me one in the first place?'

Jim steps outside and sits down on the doorstep. 'Because I thought if I could change your mind about keeping the kitten then maybe I could change your mind about going out with me.'

'Okay,' I say, flustered, 'that's all well and good but you can't possibly think I can keep Alan. I mean the kitten. I don't even know if my landlord will let me have pets.'

'Fine,' he says, holding out his hands, 'give me Alan back and I'll get you a box of chocolates from the garage up the road.'

Instinctively I pull the kitten closer to me. 'You can't give me a kitten and take it back minutes later.'

'But you said—'

'Look, Mr Owen, if we're going to get along you're going to need to learn to read between the lines a bit more. I want the kitten. You're not having her back. She is mine. I just want you to know that you shouldn't go around giving girls you like kittens, okay? A kitten isn't just for Christmas, you know.'

'It's not Christmas.'

'And it's not for wooing women either.'

'Wooing?'

'Yes, wooing. Cats aren't for wooing, they're for life, and don't you forget it.'

'I know,' he says quietly.

There's a brief awkward silence as we both realise the implication of what he's just said.

'I love this kitten,' I say, regaining my composure, 'but I can't call her Alan because that's too stupid for words.'

'So what are you going to call her, then?'

'Disco.'

'Disco?'

'Or to give her her full name *Best of Disco Volume Two*. It's my all-time favourite album.'

'It's your favourite album?'

'Actually it's the only one I've got.'

### 7.30 p.m.

I'm sitting on the stairs looking at the phone. I've just had the most difficult conversation of my life with Damon. He told me that he'd been expecting something like this to happen for a long while because 'It's nearly impossible to make the long-distance thing work.' The last thing he says to me before I put down the phone is: 'I'll always love you, you know.'

## Sunday, 28 February 1993

### 5.01 p.m.

It's now late Sunday afternoon and I'm standing in the ridiculously draughty hallway of my house, staring at the phone.

'What's wrong, mate?' asks Nick, wandering in from the kitchen. 'You look a bit freaked out.'

'I am a bit freaked out. I've just been speaking to Alison and . . . well, I've sort of agreed to do something that I don't really want to do.'

'Like what?'

'It was like this,' I begin. 'Alison called to tell me that she'd told Damon it was over. Even though I was immensely pleased at this news I knew there had to be a certain amount of decorum about these things so rather than yelling, "Wooohoooo!", I made lots of appropriate sympathetic noises to let her know I wasn't completely lacking in finesse. I do feel guilty about doing this to Damon. I really do. I even contemplated calling him.'

'What? To apologise for stealing his girlfriend? I can't see that conversation happening, can you?'

'No, my point exactly. I think the guilt must have been clouding my judgement because we ended the call like this: Her: "Do you want to go out tomorrow night?" Me:

"Tomorrow as in Monday?" Her: "Yes." Me: "Monday?" Her: "Yes, Monday. Have you got something else on tomorrow?" Me: "No." Her: "I thought we could go for a drink in the Jug of Ale." Me: "That sounds great." Her: "Good. Shall we say around eight? I'll knock on your door and we can get the bus into Moseley." Me: "Great. I'll see you tomorrow." Her: "Are you all right?" Me: "What? Sorry . . . yeah. I'm fine. I'll see you tomorrow."'

'A Monday-night date,' says Nick. 'Are you mad?'

'My thoughts exactly.'

'Monday night is officially the worst night of all to go out with a new girl.'

'I know.'

'Everywhere's empty and the contrast between all that emptiness and the buzzing atmosphere of the Saturday night when you first met will be too much to bear.'

'I know.'

'Tuesdays are okay, Wednesdays are better, Thursdays are probably ideal, Fridays and Saturdays are okay at a push but they're officially the weekend and, let's face it, the expectation behind a weekend date is so high few can pull it off. Sunday dates are okay if you want your night out to be quiet and homely, but Mondays? Never.'

'I know all this,' I say to Nick. 'What am I going to do? I really wanted this to work with Alison. If I have a bad first date on a Monday I know I won't get the opportunity to have a second date on any other day of the week.'

'Why didn't you tell her?'

'She wouldn't understand.'

'You're in a right mess,' says Nick. 'Have you ever actually been on a Monday-night date?'

'Twice. The first one was in 1987 with a girl called Katie

Jones. It resulted in us sitting in an empty cinema watching *Teen Wolf*, which neither of us enjoyed as we both had a geography exam the following morning. The second time was in 1988 with Gina Marsh, who I met at a sixth-form disco and insisted on a Monday-night date because the rest of her week was so busy. We ended up going for something to eat at a curry-house, which was so empty the entire waiting staff had nothing better to do all evening than watch our disastrous date unfurl before their very eyes as if we were an afternoon soap opera with the worst kind of wooden acting ever.'

'I think you're knackered,' says Nick, laughing. 'There's no way you can get out of this one.'

## 6.45 p.m.

My housemates and I are sitting in the living room in a post-*Songs of Praise* pre-*Last of The Summer Wine* Sunday-evening slump playing with Disco. She's already become one of the family and we've taken great delight in buying catfood and various treats for her from the corner shop down the road. In return Disco entertained us all afternoon rolling around on her back on the floor, getting scared of inanimate objects for no apparent reason, using her claws to climb the curtains in the living room to dangerously high levels, and even clichéd kitten stuff like playing with a ball of wool. I'm just about to stand up and get her a treat from the bag on the kitchen table when there's a knock at the door. 'Are we expecting anyone?' I ask my housemates. 'Because if we are I'm not dressed for visitors.'

Everyone shakes their head. Quite often one of my housemates' boyfriends drops by unannounced, which is okay if I'm looking halfway decent but not if I'm not. Right now I'm not. I'm wearing virtually the same outfit that I'd worn to Blockbuster on Friday night, even down to having the same elastic band tying up my hair. The only difference between Friday night's look and tonight's is I have a smear of baked-bean tomato sauce on the front of my hooded sweatshirt.

'I suppose I'd better go and see who it is,' I say. 'But whoever it is I'm not letting them in, okay?'

I peer through the spyhole and see Jim standing on the step. As I open the front door I receive my second shock: I'm hit by the aroma of Indian takeaway emanating from a brown paper bag in his hands.

'Hi,' I say, grinning hugely, while trying to distract him from my dishevelled attire.

'Hi,' says Jim. 'I can tell from the look on your face you're wondering what I want. The thing is, I was just passing with an early Monday-night date.'

'A Monday-night date?'

'You know how everything is prepackaged these days,' he continues. 'Well, they now do dates in a box.' Jim looks at the bag in his hands. 'Well, actually this is more of a bag than a box. A bag containing a takeaway for two and a video.'

'I still don't understand.'

'Look,' he says, 'I should've explained to you on the phone. I can't do Monday-night dates.' He then begins to expound to me his long and convoluted theory on Monday-night dates. 'That's why,' he says in conclusion, 'I'm standing here on your doorstep bringing our date forward by twenty-four hours. This is a tricky time for new relationships and we don't want to jinx it, do we?'

'No,' I say, laughing. 'We don't.'

So after apologising profusely to my housemates Jim and I have our first date on the green-velour sofa in the living room. We eat Chicken Rogan Josh and pilau rice from plates on our laps, share a naan bread and play with Disco well after everyone else has gone to bed.

## 11.55 p.m.

'What do you want to do now?' I ask Jim. The house is deadly silent and we are huddled on the sofa.

'I don't mind,' says Jim.

'We could talk.'

'What do you want to talk about?'

'I'm really glad you came round tonight. I know I've been a bit useless when it's come to you and me.'

'You could say that. It's taken us . . .' he pauses, working it out '. . . a long time to get together.'

I laugh. 'Well, all I really wanted to say is that despite all my attempts to put you off –'

'– and there were many –'

'– I'm glad I didn't succeed.'

'But why did you try to put me off? Is this always the way you go about things? Did Damon have to work so hard to get you or was this a special test that you dreamed up for me?'

'Apart from Freshers' Night, which was more because I thought you were a nutter, I suppose it was a case of the more you like someone and the longer you like them the more there is at stake. And, let's face it, it's taken us quite a bit of time to get to where we are now.'

'It *was* a long time,' he says, 'but it was worth it.'

## Monday, 1 March 1993

## 7.33 a.m.

It's morning and I wake up next to Jim. I make him toast and then he leaves to go across the road to get changed and shower. He comes back ten minutes later and we get the bus into town together.

**1.22 p.m.**

Revolution Records is on completely the opposite side of the city centre to Alison's bookshop. Even so, during my lunch-break I walk all the way to Kenway's just to say hello to her for fifteen minutes. In the end I'm in such a rush to get back to the shop that I miss my lunch. I have to survive the rest of the day on three cups of coffee and a packet of Polos.

**6.20 p.m.**

Jim meets me after work and we go for a drink in the Cathedral Tavern. Jim's so hungry that when he orders drinks for us he returns to the table with two pints of lager and five packets of dry-roasted peanuts. I take him home to mine and make him five slices of toast with two tins of beans.

**Tuesday, 2 March 1993**

**7.13 a.m.**

I suggest to Alison that we should both call in sick to work. Alison decides she's going to have a cold with overtones of a fever that will suggest she might be coming down with flu. I go for food poisoning and, for the sake of my boss, I go into explicit detail about how it's coming out of both ends like a fountain. After the calls we go back to bed and sleep so late that by the time we wake up we've missed the midday episode of *Neighbours*.

**2.02 p.m.**

We have a leisurely breakfast/lunch of cornflakes, toast and jam, then take up residence on the sofa, watching the cream of afternoon television while working our way through two packets of crisps and a large bag of toffee popcorn. When Alison's housemates arrive home from work they discover us asleep in front of *Countdown* surrounded by crisps packets and popcorn bits.

## Wednesday, 3 March 1993

### 11.09 p.m.

'I don't want you to take this the wrong way,' I tell Alison, at the end of another evening together, 'but I think we should spend the night apart. I'm shattered, aren't you? Every night since we've been together we've stayed up really late. I fell asleep at the till this afternoon. It was only for a split second but the only thing that woke me up was Patrick, my boss, slipping on the new Napalm Death album and cranking the volume right up. I yelled so loudly everyone in the shop looked at me as if I was some sort of lunatic. We need sleep. So, let's just take the night off, okay?'

Alison looks disappointed. 'Do we have to?'

'Yes . . . no . . . yes . . . At least, I think so.'

At the door she gives me a long kiss goodnight. 'Shall I walk you home?' she asks.

'Will you stop at nothing to seduce me?' I ask her. 'I live across the road, I think I'll be all right, somehow.'

### 11.37 p.m.

I've been lying in bed for all of five minutes when I realise I already miss Jim too much to go to sleep. It might have been easier if he'd lived miles away but I keep thinking about him, wondering what he's doing, what expression is on his face, whether he's asleep or not. By the time it gets to a quarter to twelve I've put my shoes back on, loaded my bag with spare underwear, deodorant and a clean top for work. When I tell Jane I'm going over to Jim's because I miss him she laughs like a drain and shakes her head in pity.

## Thursday, 4 March 1993

### 12.02 a.m.

As I walk along the path to the front gate and cross the road, I'm in a world of my own until a voice breaks my concentration. 'Great minds think alike,' says Jim.

I look up and he's standing right in front of me. 'Where are you going?'

'Yours,' he explains. 'I couldn't sleep. I kind of missed you. Where were you off to, like I don't already know?'

'It's pathetic, really. Look at us. We're like a couple of lovestruck teenagers. We're twenty-two. We shouldn't be acting like this, should we?'

Jim looks at me and shrugs. Then, hand in hand, we go back to mine.

### 6.33 p.m.

After work we get the bus back to Kings Heath, but on a whim I decide to make Alison a meal from scratch, using the kind of raw materials you only find in a supermarket. We get off in Moseley and go to Kwik Save.

'I love this,' says Alison, as we walk up the first aisle in the store, which contains cereal, biscuits, fruit juice and other drinks. 'I'm so excited.'

'Well, if Kwik Save gets you going,' I say, 'tomorrow I'll take you to Poundland.'

'I'm not excited by Kwik Save – although who couldn't be excited by a store where you have to buy your own carrier bags? – I'm excited because I'm shopping with you. I normally do my shopping with the girls. Which is fine. But it has just occurred to me that I've never been supermarket shopping with someone I'm going out with.'

'You never went to the supermarket with Damon?'

'It just never happened. There's something really nice about shopping together, don't you think? It's because it's so domestic, isn't it? I love watching couples doing their shopping together, don't you?' She points to a couple in their late twenties – a man in a suit and a girl in jeans and trainers. 'People like them. They've spent the day apart and now they're here getting stuff they need: a couple of bananas, loo roll, washing powder, cereal.'

'You mean the kind of stuff we all buy every week?'

'Yes, but it's different when you buy things as part of a couple. Supermarket shopping is like the biggest symbol of togetherness. It's nice. It's comfortable . . . It's cosy.'

'Here's to togetherness,' I say cheerfully, as I drop a packet of Kellogg's Fruit 'n' Fibre into our trolley.

## Sunday, 7 March 1993

### 9.03 a.m.

'It's like this,' I explain to Jane in the kitchen, as I make the first cup of tea of the day. 'I want to kiss Jim constantly. I want to make him breakfast in bed. I want to hold hands with him and take long walks in the park on sunny Sunday afternoons. I want to buy him clothes. I want to kill dragons for him and rescue him from the clutches of anyone who wants to do him harm. I want to tell anyone who will listen: "See this wonderful, intelligent, handsome bloke by my side? This is my boyfriend, Jim."'

# PART THREE

## Then: 1994–96

# 1994

## Tuesday, 4 January 1994

### 7.30 p.m.

It's our first night back in Birmingham after the new year. I'm over at Alison's and, with Disco, we're watching *Coronation Street*, which is one of the many programmes I'd never seen until I got together with her (including other non-Australian soap operas, any programme featuring injured pets and breakfast television).

'How long have we been together?' I ask her casually.

'Ten months.'

'That's a long time.'

'I suppose it is.'

There's a long pause.

'You know what?' I tell her. 'As girlfriends go you're all right, you know.'

'All right?'

'Yeah, all right.'

'Good,' she replies. 'I think you're all right too.'

'Well, that's good,' I reply, and then we carry on watching TV.

## Wednesday, 5 January 1994

### 9.05 p.m.

'I think Jim's trying to tell me he loves me,' I say to Jane, the following night, when we're in the Jug.

'How do you know?' she asks, simultaneously offering me a cigarette.

I look at the packet. 'I'm trying to give up,' I reply. 'New Year resolution and all that.'

'Sorry,' says Jane. 'I didn't know.'

'Jim's always telling me . . .' I lower my speech and adopt the Voice of Doom '. . . THESE THINGS WILL KILL YOU.'

We both laugh, then I reach out and take a cigarette.

'I thought—'

'It's only the one,' I say, interrupting her, then giggle. 'I'll give up tomorrow.' I light up and continue my story. 'He did that whole bumbling thing blokes do and then told me that he thought I was "all right".'

Jane laughs. '"All right" is good, but when will blokes learn that it's not good *enough*? What did you say back?'

'I told him I thought he was okay too.'

'Disappointed he didn't go all the way?'

'A little bit. I've known for months now that I'm in love with him. But I'm determined I'm not going to say anything until he's ready to say it to me.'

'Trust me, he's a boy,' says Jane, 'so you might be in for a long wait. A very long wait.'

## Sunday, 1 May 1994

### 11.39 p.m.

I'm lying in bed when I'm woken by the sound of someone throwing lumps of soil at my bedroom window. I open my curtain, peer down into the moonlit street and see Jim on all fours in the front garden. He'd told me he was going out for a drink with the boys. I wasn't expecting to see him until tomorrow night when we're supposed to be going to the cinema.

I open the window. 'Jim,' I say exasperatedly. 'What are you doing?'

'Looking for stuff to throw at your window,' he slurs drunkenly.

'You're drunk,' I whisper hoarsely, in case he hasn't realised. 'What do you want?'

'I want to tell you something,' he says. 'I want to tell you that . . . that . . . that I like you. I just thought you ought to know.'

'Thanks.' I sigh. 'I'll see you in the morning.'

I pretend to go back to bed but I stay and watch from the corner of the window as he stumbles out of the garden, across the road and spends five minutes trying to find the keys to his front door. As I get into bed I ask myself whether I would've accepted a drunken declaration of love. As I fall asleep I decide that something would've been better than nothing.

## Saturday, 4 June 1994

### 2.28 p.m.

It's a sunny summer afternoon. Jim and I are walking around the lake in Cannon Hill park. The warm weather has brought everybody out and there are mums and dads with prams, little kids racing around on bikes, older kids playing football. It seems like the whole of Birmingham has come out to play.

'I'm going to ask you a question,' says Jim, 'but I don't want you to infer anything by it, okay?'

'Okay,' I reply. 'Fire away.'

'Do you think it's possible to love one person for the rest of your life?'

'Yes,' I say immediately. 'Next question?'

'That was it, really. I was hoping I'd get more out of you than a simple yes. I was looking for more of a discussion.'

'That's men all over. They like to argue about things just for the sake of it. The fact is, Jim, I do think it's possible to love one person for the whole of your life. But at the same time I realise it's pretty hard.'

'That's what I think too.'

There's a long silence.

'So, is that it, then?' I ask. 'Is question time over?'

'Not quite. I've got one more. Have you ever told anyone that you loved them?'

'Now, that's what I call a proper conversation. The first person I told was Michael Pemberton when I was fifteen and we'd been together three days.'

'Michael Pemberton? I like the sound of him.' Jim smiles.

'He was lovely. We were on a school trip to Cambridge and Michael ate his sandwiches with me rather than with his mates. I think that pushed me over the edge a little bit because in those days who you ate your sandwiches with on a school trip really meant something. I remember we sneaked off for a bit of a kissing session and in the middle of it I told him I loved him. He just looked at me blankly, then carried on kissing me.'

'You know what that was about, don't you?' says Jim.

'Of course I wanted some sort of reaction but the fact that I got none didn't upset me because I think I liked the idea of saying it so much it didn't matter that I didn't hear it back. I was over the moon that day. I really was. The next day he dumped me.'

'That's got to have hurt.'

'It did. He didn't even say why. He just said, "I don't want to see you any more."'

'Which is code for "You're coming on a bit strong there."'

'Exactly.'

'Poor fifteen-year-old you.'

'Thanks. I was upset for a while but the fact that I'd told a real live human being that I loved them more than made up for my newly single status. It was kind of losing my I-love-you virginity, not the best experience of my life but I was hoping it would get better as I got older. Plus Michael's reaction made the whole situation more tragic and that's what I wanted in my life at the time – a bit of tragedy and drama.'

'Who was next?'

'After that I think it was Andrew Jarrett, who I went out with when I was seventeen.'

'I don't like the sound of Andrew Jarrett at all.'

'Why?'

'He sounds weaselly. Was he?'

'Of course he wasn't weaselly. He was gorgeous. So gorgeous I think I was in love with him before I started going out with him. It wasn't just an obsession, I was genuinely in love with him. It's funny, I can laugh about it now but I can remember sobbing my heart out night after night because I wasn't his girlfriend. I hadn't even talked to him at the time. But I tell you – and I'm not joking – I would've done anything for him. Absolutely anything. I got off with him at a party and I told him I loved him after all of three hours' snogging him. I didn't see much of him after that because he avoided me like the plague. It took me a while but I eventually worked out that it wasn't the best idea to start declaring your love before the boy you're with declares his.'

'So when did you finally get a boy to do that?'

'The summer before university. I met Steven Sanderson on holiday in Lanzarote. He was fantastically good-looking and very trendy and we had a great time. I was so pleased with myself that I had a friend take a whole roll of film of me and Steve so that I could send pictures to all my friends from school and sixth-form college – shallow, I know, but he was gorgeous. But even gorgeousness wears off after a while – I suppose you become immune to the effect. I wasn't in love with him but I'm ashamed to say that I was desperate for him to be in love with me, if only to show that I was having some sort of effect on him. He said it about a month and a half into our relationship. He took me out to an Italian restaurant in town and we had what he thought was a romantic meal. The food was terrible, the waiters were hopeless, and Steven's attempts at looking sophisticated were cack-handed at best. Over a glass of breadsticks he took my hand and told me he loved me. Refusing to learn the lessons of the past I felt bad that I'd made him say it so I said it back to him, and that seemed to make him happy. We lost interest in each other pretty much instantaneously after that and we didn't so much split up as fade away.'

'And number four?'

'That was—'

'Let me guess . . . Damon?'

'Yeah.'

'Fair enough. I mean, he was your boyfriend, after all.' Jim pauses. 'So how did he do it? Was it an all-singing, all-dancing, full-string-ensemble declaration?'

'It was a bit sneaky, to be truthful. It took me totally by surprise. We'd only been together six weeks.'

'Six weeks?'

'Yeah, I know. We were on our way to a gig at the Hummingbird and we were walking along Bull Street when he just stopped and turned to me and said, "I've been thinking about this for a long time. And I want to tell you that I'm falling in love with you."'

'So what did you say?'

'It hadn't occurred to me to be in love with Damon at this point but I hate being rude and couldn't stand the prospect of him feeling bad all night just because I hadn't said it back. So I smiled at him and said, "I love you too," and his face just lit up and he was in a great mood all night. I felt awful about that because what I said wasn't true, although it was true in the end.'

'You really loved him, then?'

'Yeah. It was different from all the other times, though. It was grown-up love.'

'And how did it feel?'

'It's impossible to put into words. But when you feel it you know what it is straight away.' I laugh self-consciously in an effort to change the mood. 'Come on, then. I've confessed everything. So, what about you? How many times have you said, "I love you"?'

'None.'

'None at all?'

'A big fat zero.'

'I don't understand. How could you have reached the age of twenty-three and not told a girl you loved her?'

'I've never really been into the idea of saying, "I love you",' says Jim. 'I mean, before the age of twenty-three there aren't a great many occasions that a bloke needs to say those words.'

'How can you say that?' I ask incredulously.

'But it's true.'

'But you'd had girlfriends before me. And you never told them you loved them?'

'I'll concede that I quite liked a lot of them but none of them inspired in me the desire I always imagined you needed within you to say those three little words.'

'None of them?'

'None of them.'

'Did you ever even come close?'

'Not really. I had girls say they were in love with me, though.'

'And what did you do when they said that?'

'I said, "Cheers."'

I look at Jim, horrified. 'Tell me you're joking.'

'With the gift of hindsight I can see now that it wasn't the best thing to say but I'm afraid I did actually say it. I thought I was being polite.'

'So let me get this straight. They'd say, "Jim, I think I'm falling in love with you," and you'd reply, "Cheers, mate"?'

'I didn't call them "mate", that would've been daft. But, yeah, that was the short and tall of it.'

'You really must have been a charmer. The only good thing to come out of what you've said is to reassure me that I wasn't the only girl in the world to have said, "I love you," only to get the most ignorant of responses.'

'The funny thing,' says Jim, 'is that the less you say those words the more important they become to you.'

'I have no idea what you're talking about.'

'Well, look, it's like this. It's not like I don't believe in love. I do. It's just that I think I have a greater reverence for it than those people who just bandy it about in an everyday kind of way.'

'You mean like me?' I joke.

'Exactly. You see, for me the words "I love you" are like one of those big red fire-alarm buttons behind glass that say, "Smash in case of emergency" – and in any case, if it isn't an emergency, by which I mean the real thing, I'm not going to smash the glass.'

'I can see how that could make sense to you.'

'But what can I say? If I don't feel it, I'm not going to say it just to make someone feel better.'

'No,' I say, sarcastically. 'That would be too awful.'

'Anyway,' continues Jim carefully, 'this brings me to my point.'

'Which is?'

'Well, remember how I asked you not to infer anything by this conversation?'

'Yes.'

'Well, having given it a lot of thought I think you should feel free to infer what you like.'

'But you told me not to.'

'Well, now I'm telling you that you can.'

'Why? You spent ages telling me not to read anything into what you were saying.'

'Look,' he says, 'what I'm trying to tell you is that I think it's time for me to smash the glass.'

'I have no idea what you're talking about.'

Jim laughs. 'I know what you're doing, Smithy.'

'Do you?'

'You're trying to make me say it.'

'Am I?'

'Yes, you are.'

'So, why don't you say it?'

'Okay, I will—'

'Ready when you are.' I concentrate all my psychic energy on him willing him to say it.

*Say it.*

Out comes the first word.

*Say it.*

Out comes the second word.

*Say it.*

And then out comes the third word.

That's it. He said it. 'I love you.' There's no mistaking it. There's no way he can take it back.

I watch Jim as he studies my face for a reaction. I give him my best poker face.

'Did you hear what I just said?' he asks.

I nod and grin back at him like an idiot.

'So what's your response to the first time I have ever said those words to someone who isn't my mum?'

'Cheers,' I say eventually, and explode with laughter.

## Sunday, 5 June 1994

### 10.45 p.m.

Jim and I are sitting in the Jug of Ale just as last orders are being called. The contents of his pockets are on the table: three bus tickets, balled-up tissues, Chewit wrappers, an old gig ticket and some loose change. I follow by emptying out the contents of my purse: a handful of receipts, a picture of me and Jim taken in a photo booth in Woolworth's, tissues, lipstick, lip balm and some loose change.

'This is so studenty it's depressing,' I say, rummaging through the overwhelmingly copper coins on the table trying to collect enough money to get us both a drink. I pick up my cigarettes and look inside the packet. There's only one left. 'And I'm down to my last fag,' I say despairingly.

'It's all too pathetic for words,' adds Jim.

'I feel like time's moving on,' I say, lighting the cigarette. 'My friends who went straight on to teacher-training courses have graduated now; all those types who joined graduate training schemes last summer are chalking up their first year at work. Even Jane's a dogsbody at BBC Pebble Mill.'

'Nick's swapped his temp job to work for a construction firm on a new shopping centre,' says Jim, picking up two ten-pence coins from the table.

'And here we are. I'm still working at Kenway's, you're still at Revolution.' I pick up several twenty-pence pieces. 'It seems like everyone's moving on apart from me and you. And do you want to know what's worse?'

'What's worse?'

'We're not even recent graduates any more.'

'So what are we, then?'

'Old news.'

Jim laughs. 'You're being a bit melodramatic, babe. Honestly, we've got ages before we have to worry about getting left behind.'

'This summer there's a whole new bunch of graduates out in the world. A whole new bunch of people chasing the jobs we want. That's not counting the ones who graduated before us. The truth is, a year off travelling around the world or working in a bookshop or a record shop after you've graduated is easy enough to justify on a CV to an employer, these days. In fact, it's practically encouraged. If we end up taking another year off . . . well, it doesn't look good, does it?' I look at the handful of silver coins I've managed to collect together so far. It amounts to one pound forty-five. 'Have you given any thought to what you're going to do?'

'Well, if we've got enough I was thinking about getting another Carling,' replies Jim.

'You know that's not what I'm talking about. I'm talking about . . . you know . . . with your life.'

'Not really.'

'I'm thinking about going back to university to do a master's in English. I've talked to a few of my old tutors and one thinks there might be a place for me in October.'

'More studying? What's the point?'

'The point is I don't know what I want to do. And an MA will look better on my CV than "Worked in a bookshop because I like reading."'

Jim laughs. 'The first twenty-three years of my life I've never wanted or needed a career and now, all of a sudden, it's the most important thing in the world to get one. All I know is I don't want to be an accountant.'

'Who said you had to be one?'

'My dad's an accountant. His dad was an accountant. Pretty much everyone on my course became trainee chartered accountants, corporate tax planners, financial advisers or business managers.'

'What do you want to do instead?'

'I don't know. But as I'm pretty happy right now I think I'll stick with what I've got for the minute.'

I pour the money I've collected into Jim's hand and he puts it together with his own. 'Just enough for a pint and a half,' he says sadly.

'I don't fancy one any more,' I say.

'Me neither,' says Jim. 'Let's go home.'

## Monday, 13 June 1994

### 7.30 p.m.

Alison and I are waiting in the queue at the Odeon to see *Four Weddings and a Funeral*.

'I've decided what I'm going to do,' I say, as she rummages in her bag for her debit card. 'I'm going to open a record shop.'

'That sounds great,' says Alison.

'I thought if I can't make records I can at least sell them. I've already thought of the name. I was going to call it Captain Magnet's Record Shop but I thought it was too much of a mouthful. So I've gone with Jimmy Jimmy Records.'

Alison looks at me blankly.

'After the Undertones song, "Jimmy Jimmy".'

'Ah,' she exclaims, clearly nonplussed.

'What do you think?'

'Sounds like a great idea.'

## Thursday, 16 June 1994

### 6.45 p.m.

Alison and I are walking along the petfood aisle in Safeway.

'You know I said I was going to open a record shop?'

'Hmm,' she replies.

'I've gone off the idea. But I've got an even better one. I'm going to be a teacher,' I tell her.

'A teacher?'

'Think about it. It makes perfect sense. They get fantastic holidays. It's practically a job for life. And while the money's not brilliant it's better than nothing.'

'That sounds great,' says Alison, picking up a can of Felix and throwing it into the basket. 'Secondary or primary?'

'What?'

'The kids you want to teach?'

'I can't stand primary-school kids. They'd drive me up the wall.'

'So secondary, then?'

I wince at the thought of trying to control a classroom full of teenagers. 'I don't fancy that either.'

'Well, it looks like you're stuffed, then, because I think it's pretty essential for schoolteachers to teach schoolkids.'

## Wednesday, 22 June 1994

### 9.12 p.m.

'I've got it,' I say to Alison, Nick and Jane, as we sit in the bar at the Jug waiting to go upstairs to see my workmate's band Pluto perform.

'You've got what?' asks Nick.

'For the benefit of anyone who hasn't been privy to the many conversations Jim and I have had recently,' says Alison, 'my boyfriend is referring to his latest career plan.'

'I thought you were going to open a record shop,' says Jane.

'Old news,' I reply. 'I've moved on since then. I've been doing a lot of thinking about my personality and what I'd be ideally suited to and I think I've finally cracked it. I'm going to be a social worker.'

There is what can only be described as a stunned silence before Jane pipes up, 'You *are* joking?'

'I'm absolutely serious. It makes perfect sense to me. Social work is about helping the disadvantaged, it's about championing those who have no one to champion them and, most of all, it's one of those jobs that, like teaching, everyone moans about but nobody wants to do. Well, I'm going to put my money where my mouth is.'

'I'm sorry, mate,' says Nick, 'but you'd make a terrible social worker.'

'Oh, don't say that,' says Alison. 'I think he'd be great at whatever he does.'

I look at Alison and smile. It's great knowing there's someone who will always be on your side. 'I agree with Alison,' I say to Nick. 'I think I'd make a great social worker too. And that's what I'm going to do.'

## Saturday, 2 July 1994

### 11.30 a.m.

It's one of those rare Saturdays when both Jim and I have the whole day off. Jim stayed the night but got up early this morning. When I walk into the living room he's sitting on the sofa next to Jane, watching kids' TV. I can see straight away from the expression on his face that something's wrong.

'Morning,' I say, putting my arms around him.

'Hey, you,' he replies, with a sigh.

'You look a little glum, and you were tossing and turning all night. What's on your mind?'

'I couldn't sleep because last night it struck me just as if I'd been slapped in the face that I'm going to end up as an accountant. I can feel it. I'm going to end up being one and there's nothing I can do about it.'

'What are you like?' I say. 'You can do whatever you set your mind to. You don't have to do anything you don't want to.'

'That's just it. I don't know what I want to do. So I might as well do accountancy.'

'You can stay at Revolution. You like it there.'

Jim shrugs. 'No. It's time to move on. You know Darren-at-work's band Pluto?' I nod. 'They just got signed by some record label.' He sighs. 'I'm really chuffed for him. He's made it. But, like I said, I think it's just time I moved on.'

## Monday, 4 July 1994

### 1.14 p.m.

In a bid to get my career moving I call Trudy Lannagan during my lunch-break. She used to be on my business and economics course and works for the accounting firm Greene

Lowe. After some so-how-are-you? conversation, I ask her if she knows of any graduate jobs with her firm. I get a nice chat but no result. So I call Richard Price, also from my course, who now works at Foster, Williams and Hayman. Again, nice chat but no result. So then I call Chris Dempsey, who works at Future Finance Business Solutions. Again, nice chat but no result. Finally I call Paul Broughton, who now works for a corporate tax planner, Enterprise Four. Nice chat but no result. Then I run out of change for the phone-box and go back to the shop just that little bit more depressed than when I arrived.

## Thursday, 7 July 1994

### 1.23 p.m.

During today's lunch-break I call the following in my search for jobs: Sheila Austin, Edwin Fowler, Lisa Smith and Trevor Thomas. All people I didn't really like at university and who weren't all that keen on me. No result with any of them.

## Friday, 8 July 1994

### 4.30 p.m.

Having pre-booked the afternoon off work I drop into the university careers counsellor. I take one of those job aptitude tests that are supposed to tell you what you should do as a career. The results are as follows:

1. Teacher.
2. Social worker.
3. Accountant.

## Monday, 1 August 1994

### 10.07 p.m.

I'm on my way round to Alison's after a goodbye drink for Darren and I'm thinking about the future. Since July I've sent my CV to about five different accountancy firms every week. I've had four interviews so far but never got past the second round. And there's me thinking I've been rejecting accountancy when it's clear that accountancy has been rejecting me.

I reach Alison's and knock at the door. She answers straight away. 'Hey, you,' she says. 'Nick called a while ago to say that there's a phone message for you at your place. Some girl called Trudy Lannagan says you once lent her your European economics notes. She said she might have some good news for you.'

I call Trudy straight away. It isn't good news. It's great news.

'What's your news, then?' asks Alison.

'Trudy works for a firm called Green Lowe in the city centre. They're really big players in the accounting world. They've got branches all over the place. Anyway, apparently some guy has just been dismissed from their graduate training scheme and they want his space filled as soon as possible. She said if I send in my CV she'll put in a good word for me.'

'Are you going to do it?'

'Greene Lowe have got a brilliant reputation,' I say excitedly. 'People kill to get on their graduate scheme.'

'Well, that's all well and good but are you sure you want to do this?'

'What do you mean?'

'Well, don't you want to see the world first? We could go travelling. See some of the amazing places the world has to offer? I just don't want you to have any regrets about this job later in life. I want you to be happy, that's all.'

## Friday, 19 August 1994

### 19.41 p.m.

Jim and I are making dinner for ourselves round at mine. All evening he's been really agitated. He hasn't been right since he got the letter last week saying he'd got a third interview at Greene Lowe. He has been sleeping badly, grinding his teeth at night, and completely lost his appetite. Whenever I ask him what's wrong he just shrugs and says he's fine.

'It's pointless going to this interview on Monday,' says Jim, tearing leaves off a recently washed iceberg lettuce and throwing them into a bowl. 'There's no way I'm going to get this job. I'm going to call Monday morning and say I'm ill or something. I'm terrible at interviews. I think it's why I haven't got any of the jobs I've applied for so far. I don't tell them what they want to hear.'

'Well, that's easily remedied. I'll give you a mock-interview.'

'This isn't the best time for messing about.'

'Who's messing about?' I tell him. 'I'm serious.'

I rearrange the chairs at the kitchen table so that there's one on either side, then move the tomato-ketchup bottle, the salt and pepper shakers and the place mats out of the way.

'If we're going to do this,' I say firmly, 'we're going to do it properly. You go home and put on your interview suit and I'll go and get into something a bit more formal. I'll see you back here at eight o'clock on the dot.'

**8 p.m.**

I'm now standing on Alison's doorstep, knocking at her door in my one and only suit, a white shirt, a dark blue tie and a brand new pair of black brogues.

'Look,' I say, as she answers the door, 'I'm only going along with the idea because you're being so insistent. Now I'm here this all feels a little bit too much like doctors-and-nurses territory, especially with you wearing that get-up.' She's in a fitted black jacket and a long black skirt with her hair tied back. 'You look like some sort of office dominatrix.'

'I beg your pardon?' says Alison sternly. 'Did you say something, Mr Owen?'

'Ah,' I say, getting the joke. 'You're in your role.'

Alison shakes her head dismissively and tuts like a schoolteacher. 'Please follow me.' We walk through the hallway into the kitchen in silence. Then she gestures to one of the kitchen chairs. 'Please take a seat, Mr Owen.'

I sit down and stare at her across the table. Dressed formally, she looks so disgustingly gorgeous I'm in danger of forgetting that her housemates might be home any second. The last thing they need to round off the day is to catch us *in flagrante* on the kitchen table. Again.

'Okay, Mr Owen,' says Alison sternly. 'I'll be straight with you. I'm a busy woman at a very busy firm, so let's get on with it.'

And with that she begins grilling me on my knowledge of tax planning, my awareness of current and pending UK finance legislation, presents me with a problem-solving/difficult client scenario to sort out, probes me on how I might go about landing new business and finally tells me, in no uncertain terms, why 'playing badminton' should never be on anyone's CV under 'Extracurricular Activities'.

'Well, thank you for you time, Mr Owen,' says Alison, in conclusion of our mock-interview. 'You'll hear from us soon. Before you go, is there anything you'd like to ask me?'

I think for a moment. 'What are you doing in fifteen minutes?'

'Chairing a very important meeting with some clients, the outcome of which could bring hundreds of thousands of pounds in fees to the business. Why do you ask?'

'I was just looking at you in that get-up,' I confess, 'and well . . .'

Alison laughs and comes round from behind the table to kiss me. 'Just remember that if this kind of thing happens in your real interview you're a dead man.'

## Wednesday, 31 August 1994

### 7.08 p.m.

I'm at home when the phone rings and I answer it immediately.

'Hello?'

'Al, it's me,' says Jim, despondently.

'What's wrong?'

'I've just heard from Greene Lowe.'

I can tell from his voice that he hasn't got it. 'Don't worry, sweetheart,' I tell him. 'There'll be other jobs.'

'No, there won't.'

'There will. I promise.'

'No,' he says firmly. 'No, there won't be other jobs like this one. Because this one is mine. I've got it!'

## Friday, 23 December 1994

### 10.20 a.m.

It's the day before Christmas Eve and Jim and I are at New Street station with all our bags. It's been nearly three months since I started my master's degree. It's nice being a student again. It's nice to be using my brain again. I suddenly feel like I have a real sense of purpose and direction. The first term has flown by as I made new friends, learned new things and really began to think about what I wanted to do with my future. I've decided that I want to get into publishing. My dream job is to be an editor. I'm convinced I'll never get there in a million years. I didn't even tell Jim for a while because I thought he might think it was stupid. When I did tell him, he said, 'I think you'll make the best editor in the world.' And he really seemed to mean it. It inspired me to start writing off to publishing companies in London to see if I can get any work experience with them next year.

Jim's equally excited by his new job. He's taken to it as if he'd been born to do it. I'm amazed by the transformation. He brings work home all the time on top of what he has to do to pass the first stages of his accountancy exams. 'This is the best job,' he told me, a few months into it, when I came downstairs looking for him in the middle of the night. He was sitting at the kitchen table surrounded by textbooks and files. It was two o'clock in the morning.

'It can't be if you're having to work this late.'

Jim looked at the clock. 'I hadn't even noticed it was late.'

I smiled. 'Are you coming to bed?'

'Not yet,' he replied. 'I'll be up in a bit.'

He didn't come up in a bit. When I woke the next morning the pillow next to me was empty. And when I went downstairs to find him he was asleep at the table. Exactly where I'd left him.

And now here we are at New Street, waiting to go home for Christmas.

'Will I see you over Christmas?' I ask.

'I've got a lot of work,' he says. 'I was hoping to use the peace and quiet at my parents' to get some done. I'll definitely see you for New Year's Eve.' He looks at his watch. 'My train will be pulling in any second. I'd better go.'

He kisses me and we hug and then say goodbye. And as he walks away I know it's stupid but I begin to cry. We haven't even exchanged Christmas presents. His is still in my bag and I wasn't even sure if he'd remembered to get one for me.

## Saturday, 24 December 1994

### 11.20 p.m.

It's Christmas Eve and I'm at my parents'. I've just got in from the pub after seeing all my friends from home. I'm just thinking about going to bed when the phone rings, much to my mum's consternation. In her world, polite people don't ring after seven o'clock at the latest.

'Hello?'

'Hi, can I speak to Alison, please?'

'Jim, it's me. You're drunk, aren't you?'

'Very. Happy Christmas Eve, babe.'

'Where are you?'

'In a phone-box outside the pub I've been drinking in since three o'clock this afternoon. I've been telling all my old schoolmates about you. I told them you're the best girlfriend in the world and that I'm the crappest boyfriend in the world.'

'Why would you tell them that?'

'Because I forgot to give you your Christmas present. Do you forgive me?'

'Of course I do.'

'I'll come and give it to you the day after Boxing Day, if you like.'

'There's no need. I'll get it from you when I see you on New Year's Eve, okay?'

The beeps start to go.

'I haven't got any more change,' he says.

'It's okay,' I tell him. 'Happy Christmas.'

**11.25 p.m.**

Outside the phone-box the minicab driver I've asked to wait for me beeps the horn.

'Where to, mate?' he asks, when I get into the back of his car.

'I know it's Christmas Eve,' I begin, 'but how much would you charge to take me to drop a parcel in Norwich tonight?'

'Are you joking?'

'Absolutely not.'

He thinks for a minute, then quotes me a price that he probably thinks is so ridiculous I'll change my mind. Without hesitating, I reply, 'It's a deal.' Frankie the cab driver and I go to the nearest cashpoint where I take out the money and hand it to him. We then drop round to my parents' house to get the present and proceed to make the six-hour round trip to Alison's parents' front door. When I reach Alison's I think about knocking on the door but I don't. Instead I open the porch door and leave it on the welcome mat. As I carefully shut it it occurs to me that it's probably the closest I'll ever come to being Father Christmas.

## Saturday, 31 December 1994

### 11.59 p.m.

Alison and I are at a houseparty in Moseley, surrounded by all of our friends. Everyone is counting down to the new year. When we reach zero everyone shouts at the top of their voices.

'Happy new year,' I say to Alison, as I put my arms around her.

'Happy new year to you too.'

'Any new-year resolutions?'

'I think I'm going to take up smoking again,' she says. 'Someone needs to try to balance the number of people who are always giving up. Think about the cigarette manufacturers. We can't have them going out of business. What about you?'

'Only the one.'

'What is it?'

'To be nicer to you. I know I've neglected you a bit recently—'

'You haven't.'

'I have. And you know it. I just want you to know that I'll make things right.'

'Well, I'll try hard too,' she says. 'I really do think this is going to be our year.'

# 1995

## Tuesday, 17 January 1995

### 7.17 p.m.

It's a couple of weeks into the new year and Alison has just come over to my place for something to eat. She's sitting at the table in the kitchen watching me cook one of my only recipes: Jim Owen's World Famous Vegetarian Cottage Pie (which is essentially the same as Jim Owen's World Famous Normal Cottage Pie, *sans* meat).

'I've got a present for you,' says Alison, reaching into her bag.

'Whatever anniversary you're celebrating, babe, not only have I forgotten but I haven't bought you anything.'

She laughs and her eyes flit briefly to the present in her hand. Her face changes but only for a moment. It's a look that's excited and apprehensive at the same time. She hands me a small parcel and I take off the wrapping paper to reveal one of those small cereal boxes you get in variety packs. The label on the box says 'Coco Pops'. I give it a shake. It jingles. I look at Alison for clarification.

'It's a set of keys,' she says.

'A set of keys to where?'

'To mine,' she says sheepishly.

I take them out of the box and look at them. 'A key exchange? You do know what this means, don't you?'

'Apart from you not having to throw stones at my window when you've been to the pub and think you'll be able to get lucky?'

'This means you won't ever be able to get away from me even when you might want to.'

'I know,' she says. 'But I can't think of a situation when I'll want to get away from you.'

I dig in my pocket, pull out my keys and hand them to her. 'Fair's fair,' I tell her. 'Now neither of us will have anywhere to hide.'

## Tuesday, 14 February 1995

### 7.08 a.m.

It's Valentine's Day. I receive two cards in the post:

1. A picture of a single rose – inside, in Alison's handwriting, it reads, 'Dear Jim, Happy Valentine's Day. Loving you has made my life sweeter than ever. All my love Alison.'

2. A cartoon drawing of two kittens kissing – inside, in Alison's handwriting, it reads, 'Dear man with the can-opener, have a puuurr-fectly happy Valentine's Day. Thanks for all the Whiskas, feline love, Disco.'

### 7.17 a.m.

I receive two cards in the post:

1. A cartoon of two pigs wallowing in mud – the caption inside reads: 'Let's make bacon.' The inscription reads: 'To my sweetheart, Have a great day, big love, Jimmy Jimmy.'

2. A card featuring a reproduction of Modigliani's *Girl with a*

*Polka-dot Dress*. The inscription, in what I recognise immediately as Damon's handwriting, reads: 'I won't stop loving you because I can't stop loving you.'

## Friday, 24 March 1995

### 7.04 p.m.

I'm sitting in Alison's kitchen minding my own business when she comes in, looking pensive.

'Jim?'

'Yeah?' I respond, a forkful of beans on toast hovering in front of my lips.

'What are you doing two weekends from now?'

'Nothing,' I reply. 'Why?'

'I've got to see my mum and dad.'

I shovel the beans into my mouth and wonder why she considers this information worthy of disturbing my dinner. 'That's nice,' I say, chewing. 'I'll miss you, though.'

'Well, hopefully you won't.'

'You've got no worries there, babe,' I reassure her. 'I'll definitely miss you.'

'No, you're not getting me,' says Alison. 'I'm hoping you won't miss me because I want you to come with me.'

I put down my fork in an attempt to add gravitas to what I'm about to say. My action says: Look, I have put down my eating implements. I am not messing about. 'That's sweet, Al, but I don't really *do* parents.'

'I know it's asking a massive favour,' pleads Alison, 'but they've specifically asked to meet you.'

'No offence, Al, but your parents have always sounded a bit high-maintenance.'

'They are,' says Alison. 'One hundred and ten per cent.

And now they want to meet you. And I know for a fact that they won't take no for an answer because I've tried. So, what do you say?'

I think for a moment and then respond. 'No.'

'What do you mean, no?'

'I mean, no. As in ''Thank you for inviting me to your parents' for the weekend but I don't want to go.'' That kind of no.'

'But you can't just say no like that. I'm your girlfriend.'

'You're right. I'm sorry. What was I thinking? I shouldn't have just said, ''No.'' What I should've said is, ''No, sweetheart.'''

'That doesn't make it any better,' says Alison, exasperatedly.

'Well, you tell me how I can say no and have you accept it and I'll say it.'

'But why?'

'I'm just not very good at it.'

'What?'

'Meeting parents.'

'Of course you are.'

'No, I'm not. Every time I've met girlfriends' parents it's gone terribly.'

'I don't believe you.'

'I'm not joking. Samantha Gough's parents invited me for dinner. Her dad didn't say a single word and just glared at me across the table. Natalie Moore's parents invited me to their holiday cottage in south Wales for the weekend and her mum got drunk and tried it on with me. And, worst of all, I met Christine Taylor's parents one evening when I went round to pick up their daughter for a night out. They were nice enough until we were just about to go and her father shook my hand and I could feel he was holding something in the palm of his hand which ended up in mine.'

'What was it?'

'Have a guess. They usually come in threes but he'd just given me the one.'

'No!' exclaims Alison. Her laughter fills the room.

'Yes, and on top of that, he whispered, "If you can't be good, be careful." It wouldn't have been so bad but I was fourteen and it was the first time I'd ever been out with her. I'm telling you, I'm cursed.'

## Saturday, 25 March 1995

### 8.20 p.m.

Despite my protests Alison refuses to take no for an answer. Instead she badgers me until I have no choice but to give in. It occurs to me that, of all the early stages of a relationship, for me meeting a girlfriend's parents is right up there at the top of the list of 'Things that I'd Much Rather Not Do If I Had the Choice'. The fact is, however, that I don't really get the choice. As she says, I've got away with it for long enough.

I'm going to have to go.

And from the moment I agree to go Alison begins briefing me on her parents as if she's planning a military operation (which, in many ways, she is). I'm informed of what to do, what not to do, and what will be expected of me. And if that's not enough, I'm tested on a daily basis.

**Sunday, 26 March 1995**

**10.35 a.m.**
'What is the number-one topic of conversation that is absolutely off-limits?' she asks me first thing in the morning right after what we currently refer to as the Sunday Roll in the Hay.

'The general topic of politics,' I say carefully.

'Correct,' says Alison. 'And what about politics specifically?'

'The Labour Party since 1979?'

'Not bad,' she says coolly. 'Not bad at all.'

**Wednesday, 29 March 1995**

**17.45 p.m.**
It's evening and we're in the frozen-food aisle in Safeway. I'm trying to decide whether or not I want a packet of Findus Frozen French Bread Pizzas when Alison turns to me and says, 'What's the number-two topic of conversation that is absolutely off-limits?'

I have to think for a moment. 'The general topic of religion?'

'Good . . . and?'

'The state of the Church of England specifically?'

'More specific than that?'

'Er . . . er . . .' I know the answer. It's on the tip of my tongue. 'I've got it,' I say finally. 'Women priests.'

'Very good,' she says. 'Very good indeed.'

## Saturday, 1 April 1995

### 8 p.m.

Alison and her housemates, Jane and Mary, are all in the living room debating whether to make a journey to the video shop. Mary doesn't care what she sees as long as it doesn't have subtitles. Jane doesn't care what she sees as long as it has subtitles. I don't care what we see as long as it has explosions. Alison doesn't care what we see at all because she has other things on her mind.

'What's the number-three topic of conversation that is absolutely off-limits?' she whispers.

I know this one. It's easy. 'His ongoing battle with his next-door neighbour – on the left – over the size of their privet hedge.'

'Brilliant,' she says, and then she announces to the room that she doesn't care what film she sees either as long as it's got explosions.

## Wednesday, 5 April 1995

### 6.55 a.m.

I've stayed over at Alison's, I've just had a shower and I'm walking along the landing to our bedroom when I pass Alison in her dressing-gown, carrying several towels and her makeup bag, coming the other way.

'Morning, babe,' I say.

'What's the number-four topic of conversation to avoid?'

Another easy one. 'Your kid sister's recent body piercing. It's a definite no-no.'

'Brilliant,' she says, as she enters the bathroom and locks the door.

## Thursday, 6 April 1995

### 8.08 p.m.

I'm standing in the hallway with Jane and Mary waiting for Alison to come down so that we can all go to the Jug. Finally Alison comes down the stairs and before she can open her mouth I say, 'No more testing.'

'But—'

'No buts either.'

She smiles coyly. 'Just one more. I'll make sure it's not even a tricky one. I just want you to be ready.'

'Fine.'

'Okay, what is the fifth and final topic of conversation to avoid at all costs with my dad?'

'French cheeses?' I say, in a bid to wind her up.

'No,' she says, shocked.

'Gardening?' I say, continuing as I mean to go on.

She shakes her head. 'One last go.'

I think for a moment. 'Your smoking?'

'Now I know you're not taking this seriously,' she says, 'because I know that you know for a fact that it goes without saying that we'd never talk about that. If my dad so much as suspects I smoke he'll go bonkers.'

'I know, I know,' I say, laughing. 'But you do know those things will kill you, don't you?'

'You're just stalling for time, Owen,' says Alison, smiling.

'No, I'm not,' I reply. 'The answer to your question is, America's role in the Second World War. Specifically the liberation of Europe. Apparently it really winds him up. But the fact is, Al, none of these topics have ever come up in any conversation I've had in my life. You just need to chill out, babe, it'll be fine.'

## Saturday, 8 April 1995

### 12.23 p.m.

Jim and I have just arrived at the front gate of my parents' house and my mum is already on the doorstep greeting us. She's obviously been standing on lookout patrol for a while now, wanting to have the official first sighting of her daughter's new boyfriend.

'Hi, Mum,' I say, waving with my right hand while clutching Jim's hand tightly with the left. 'Tell me it's going to be all right,' I whisper to Jim, as we walk up the path.

'It'll be fine,' says Jim. 'Absolutely fine.'

My dad suddenly appears next to Mum. I study his face carefully to work out what his first impression of Jim might be. He's wearing the look he uses when he's reading the newspaper. As Jim isn't a copy of the *Daily Telegraph* I have no idea what that means. I reach into my bag, pull out a packet of extra strong mints and pop in yet another to hide any remnants of the ten cigarettes I smoked on the train journey here.

'Hello, sweetie,' says Dad, giving me a huge hug. 'How are you?'

'I'm good, Dad,' I say, squeezing Jim's hand so tightly I fear I'm in danger of crushing it.

'And I take it this is the young man we've been hearing so much about?' My dad holds out his hand for Jim to shake.

My heart stops for a second.

I'm suddenly convinced that Jim will give my dad's hand a high-five slap like an American basketball player. I have no idea why I think this will happen as I have never seen Jim give a high five in all the time I've known him.

Jim smiles widely like a TV game-show contestant and shakes Dad's hand like a normal person and I let out a sigh of relief.

'Very pleased to meet you,' says Jim. 'How are you today, Mr Smith?'

'I'm well,' says Dad. 'Thank you for asking.'

The greetings continue in the hallway. Mum smiles a lot and takes coats and bags. Dad smiles too, but less than Mum, and stands and watches her. As I open the door to go into the living room I imagine that the next few hours will go like this: Mum will tell me everything that has happened to her and everyone in the street since I've last seen her; Dad will engage Jim in conversation about cars; we'll sit down to a meal with more food than any four people could ever imagine eating; Jim and I will attempt to consume as much of it as fast as we possibly can; and then at around six I'll feign extreme tiredness, Dad will call a cab for us, we'll catch the train home and I'll be grateful to Jim for ever for being the best possible boyfriend in the world.

The second I walk into the room I realise I have been completely outmanoeuvred.

'Surprise!' says my older sister, Emma.

'Hi,' says Emma's husband, Eduardo.

'Aunty Ally!' screams their three-year-old daughter, Molly.

'All right, sis?' My seventeen-year-old kid sister, Caroline, greets me casually.

'Hello, dear,' says Nana Smith.

'Hello, dear,' echoes Nana Graham.

I'm speechless. Three generations of my family are sitting around the dining-table with the specific intention of meeting Jim. I'm struck dumb by this scene and can only look on helplessly in horror. Maybe he's right after all about being cursed. And now I'm cursed too.

I look across at him once more. He doesn't look like a man who's about to dump me even when my mother announces to the room: 'Look, everyone, this is Jim, Alison's new partner – that's the modern word, isn't it?'

I'm mortified. My mother, who has never used a word like 'partner' in her life, has suddenly started using politically correct terminology. I decide it can only get worse from here on.

But it doesn't.

My family adore Jim.

Dad talks to him about West Ham's current form, music, politics *and* religion.

Mum talks to him about his accountancy exams and his family in Oldham.

My kid sister, normally terminally sulky, is positively perky and flirts with him outrageously.

My older sister laughs to the point of choking at all of his jokes.

As does my brother-in-law.

As does Nana Smith.

As does Nana Graham, once my older sister has repeated the joke in her good ear.

Even my niece, whom I can barely get to acknowledge me without her bursting into tears, is sitting in his lap before we've finished dessert.

## 6.34 p.m.

'That wasn't too bad,' says Jim, when we're safely ensconced in the back of a taxi on our way to the station.

'I'm pretty sure my dad wants to adopt you,' I say, squeezing his hand. 'I'm sure the only thing stopping him is my mum. Mum says he always wanted a boy. I think the only reason my baby sister exists is because they thought they'd have one last go. You're the son he's always wanted. After this every other phone call will be "Jim this" and "Jim that" and "Jim the other". If it wasn't hard enough for me as the middle child to get attention from my parents it will now be almost impossible. But I don't care. You've passed the parent test, babe. You've done me proud.'

## Sunday, 6 August 1995

### 3.45 p.m.

Jim, two large suitcases and I are standing in my hallway having just arrived back from our very first foreign holiday together – a seven-day package deal to Malta. The weather was okay and we had a reasonably good time, but I think we both found it hard to relax. The past few months have been something of a blur for us both. Jim is still in love with his job and seems always to be revising for one exam or another. Meanwhile I'm still enjoying my MA and have been working intensively on my thesis. On holiday we must have looked like the oddest couple on the beach. There we were on the sunbeds, all day, every day, Jim reading books on tax planning while I chipped away at the works of Charles Dickens.

'Home, sweet home,' I say, flicking through the post.

'Anyone in?' yells Jim up the stairs. 'Everyone must be out. No welcome-back party, then.'

I carry on looking through the post: a gas bill, a letter from the student-loans company, two pieces of credit-card junk mail and a pristine white envelope postmarked London, which I open hurriedly.

'What is it?' asks Jim.

'Remember I wrote to some publishing houses for work experience earlier in the year?' I gabble excitedly. 'Well, Cooper and Lawton have got back to me.'

'Excellent,' says Jim. 'A few weeks in London sounds like a good laugh.'

'But it's better than that,' I tell him. 'In fact, it's better than I ever could have imagined – they're offering me a job interview for an editorial position. How fantastic is that?'

'Great,' he replies, wearily, then kisses my cheek, picks up my suitcase and takes it upstairs without another word.

## 8.59 p.m.

Jim and I are in the pub with my housemates. He hasn't said much all night. In fact he's been 'funny' ever since I had my good news. I've asked him several times what the problem is and each time he denies there is one.

'What's wrong with him?' asks Jane, when Jim goes to the loo.

'He's been miserable all night,' says Mary.

'You two had a fight?' asks Jane.

'No,' I sigh, 'he's sulking.'

'What is it with boys and sulking?' asks Jane.

'It's the only way they can communicate,' says Mary.

'I quite like Jim when he's sulking,' I reply. 'He reminds me of a small boy. A small boy who's afraid to say what's on his mind. I know what's on his mind, though, but there's nothing much I can do unless he wants to talk about it.'

'What is it?' asks Mary.

'I'll give you two guesses.'

'Not your job interview?'

'You can't turn it down,' says Jane firmly. 'It's too good an opportunity.'

'I know, but if I take it I feel like it's going to send my whole life in a different direction.'

'But that's good, isn't it?' says Mary.

'The thing is, I like my life now. I like being with Jim. I like what we've got. But what if I get the job in London? What if it takes us in different directions? Plus he's only just got started with his new job—'

Jim comes back from the loo and I stop abruptly.

'I don't think I'll make it to last orders, babe,' he says, yawning. 'I'm feeling really tired. I'm going to get off home.'

'To yours or mine?'

'Mine.'

'But I thought you were—' I don't finish my sentence. 'Okay, I'll see you tomorrow night.'

He nods and walks out without kissing me.

'Deep down,' I say, as I watch him leave, 'I know he's right to be worried about us because I'm worried about us too. I don't understand how relationships work. I don't know how they survive. It seems like every day something new arrives to threaten your peace of mind.'

## 11.07 p.m.

The girls and I have just got home. We sit up and have a cup of tea and talk for a while in the kitchen and then, one by one, we say goodnight and get ready to go to bed. I'm the last in the bathroom. As I'm taking off my makeup and washing my face Disco wanders in and looks at me accusingly. I must be the only person in the world who can be made to feel guilty by a cat because I suddenly decide to go over to Jim's. He's in bed when I creep into his room. I undress in the dark leaving my clothes in a pile on the floor next to the bed and climb under the duvet next to him.

'Are you awake?' I whisper.

'Yeah,' he says quietly. 'Look . . . tonight . . . the way I've been acting . . . I'm sorry, okay?'

I love the way he talks to me as if I know what he's talking about immediately because, of course, I do. We can just launch into new topics seemingly at random to people outside the relationship, or continue conversations that we began hours earlier.

'I thought you'd be pleased for me.'

'I am pleased for you. It's just that I know where all this is going and I don't like it.'

'But it's only an interview. I probably won't get it.'

'You will. I know you will.'

'But I don't have to take it.' Of course I *do* want the job. I want

**it more than anything. But it feels like it would've been wrong to say anything else. It wouldn't have been what either of us wanted to hear. This way we have a temporary solution.**

## Sunday, 20 August 1995

### 1.20 p.m.

Alison is due to go to London tomorrow for her interview. She's spent ages getting her clothes ready. I am in the pub with Nick. I needed to get out of the house for a while. Nick is good for distraction. We talk about nothing much. Nothing that matters, at least. I'm just beginning to feel okay when he says, 'Al's off to her interview tomorrow.'

'Yeah,' I reply.

'Want to talk about it?'

'No.'

He shrugs. 'Okay, I was just asking.'

'Things are strained between us,' I say, without further prompting. 'They have been since she announced she was off. I admit it's all my fault. It's just that I can't help but feel a bit . . .'

'Cheated?'

'Yeah, that's it. Cheated. I'm just getting my life sorted for the first time. I've got a great job, a great girlfriend. Everything's in place and now . . . well, now it's not going to be. She'll get the job. I know she will. And when she does that will be it. She'll be off. And we'll be over.'

## Friday, 8 September 1995

### 7.02 a.m.

Every day since the interview Alison has been waiting to hear something from Cooper and Lawton about the job. After the first week she couldn't sleep and even her twenty-fifth birthday turned into a bit of a non-event because she was so worried. After the second week it was all I could do to stop her calling them to put her out of her misery. Finally last night I said to her that, whatever time it is, when the letter arrives she should call me and we'll open it together. So, when the phone rings as I'm making breakfast, I already know she's got news.

'Hello?' I say.

'I think the letter's here,' says Alison.

'I'll be there in a second,' I say, and put down the phone.

### 7.10 a.m.

Alison's in the hallway with Jane and Mary when I let myself in.

'Morning, babe,' she says, greeting me with a kiss.

'Is that it?' I say, looking at the letter in her hand.

She nods. 'It's got their postmark on it.'

'Well, go on, then,' says Jane. 'He's here now so you can open it.'

'Yeah,' I say, trying to sound cheerful. 'Open it.'

'I can't,' she says. 'It's too weird.'

'I'm one hundred per cent sure you've got it,' declares Mary. 'Just open it.'

Alison hands the envelope to me. 'You do it for me.'

'I really think you should do it, Al.'

'I can't. Please, Jim, just do this one thing for me.'

I hand the letter back to her. 'No,' I say firmly. 'You open it. I'll be right here with you.'

She opens the envelope and scan-reads the letter. Her face says it all.

'Well?' demands Jane.

'I didn't get it,' says Alison. 'They said I was an excellent candidate but they've given the job to someone with more experience.'

I put my arms around her and she begins to cry. Jane and Mary make a diplomatic retreat. 'I'm sorry, sweetheart. I really thought you were going to get it. There'll be other jobs. Everything will work out okay in the end.'

'No,' she says. 'I don't think there will be. I knew I was no good and I was right . . . At least you'll be happy anyway. You never wanted me to get that job. I could tell.'

'If you're asking me if I'm glad you're not moving to London the answer's yes,' I tell her. 'Of course I am, because it would have made life difficult for us. But if you're asking me if I'm happy that you didn't get the job then, no, I'm not. I was sure you'd get it. And I wanted that for you. I wanted you to be happy because that's what being in love is supposed to be about. And if you'd got the job I would have tried my best to be happy for you even if it had torn me up inside. And do you know why? Because making you happy is what I'm supposed to do. It's my job. And if you're not happy I can't be happy either.'

## Thursday, 5 October 1995

### 7.13 p.m.

Jim and I are standing in a medium-sized bedsit in a huge, dilapidated house in Moseley. It's a large room with a single bed in one corner, two cooker rings on a work surface by the window, a large wardrobe next to the door and a lime-green carpet dotted with faded stains.

The reason we're standing here is because we've decided to move in together. It just seems to make sense. We're together more often than we're not, and now that I'm not moving to London there just doesn't seem any reason not to. But as we examine the four walls in front of us I can see plenty of reasons not to. The place stinks of cigarette smoke, and the bathroom is on the landing, shared with other residents. Its only saving grace is that it's cheap.

'What do you think?' asks Mr Mebus, the landlord of Flat 11c Fenchurch Avenue, as we leave the building.

'We've got some other places to see,' says Jim, cheerily, 'but we'll ring this evening if we want it.'

Once we're out of earshot the truth comes out.

'That was too vile for words,' says Jim.

'I felt soiled just standing in that room,' I reply.

Needless to say we don't ring Mr Mebus that night.

### 7.56 p.m.

Or Mrs Rawsthorne of 23a Rickman Road (dump).

### 8.23 p.m.

Or Mr Shaukat of Flat D, 453 Lake Road (even dumpier).

## Tuesday, 10 October 1995

### 6.45 p.m.

Or Mr Dixon of Flat 2, 11th floor, Abingdon House (too depressing).

### 7.33 p.m.

Or Mr and Mrs Cimoszewicz of Flat 4, Howard Street (a woodchip-wallpapered death-trap).

### 7.58 p.m.

Or Mr Potts of Flat A, Duke Street (landlord looked too much like a serial killer and mentioned several times how he had keys to all the flats).

## Friday, 20 October 1995

### 6.22 p.m.

Or Mr Dixon (again) of Flat 5, 13th floor, Warwick House (mouse droppings on the kitchen floor!).

### 6.49 p.m.

Or the Ruddard brothers of 345c Warwick Crescent (previous occupant had disappeared mysteriously leaving all his belongings).

### 7.47 p.m.

Or Mr Ho of Flat 1, Able Row (smelt strongly of Ajax and desperation).

## Monday, 13 November 1995

### 8.38 p.m.

We're in my bedroom, watching TV on the portable having had one of our most depressing flat-hunting experiences so far. Tonight we saw a one-bedroom flat on the top floor of a large house on Valentine Road in Kings Heath. It had mould growing from a crack in the kitchen ceiling and when I pointed it out to the letting agent he just laughed and said he wouldn't charge us extra for keeping pets.

'I feel like this is never going to work,' I say to Jim, who's lying on the bed half-watching *EastEnders*.

'Do you think this is some sort of sign that we shouldn't move in together?'

'I think it's just a sign that we don't really know how much anything costs in the real world.'

There's a pause as we watch Pat Butcher on the TV have a shouty, earring-jangling row with Ian Beale.

'So, what are we going to do?' I ask, still looking at the TV. 'Do we just stay as we are? Or . . . I've got it!'

'What?'

'You could just move in with me and the girls . . . or I could move in with you and the boys across the road.'

Jim pulls a face. 'I don't know about that. Some people don't like living with a couple, do they?'

'So we'll ask them right now,' I say positively. 'The worst they can say is no.'

## 10.13 p.m.

Alison's just called me to compare reactions.

'So what did they say your end?' she asks.

'Nick's fine with you moving in,' I tell her. 'But don't get too excited. He does have some reservations.'

'Which are?'

'You're not allowed to start moaning at him to keep the place tidy. Basically I think if you live here you're going to have to lower your standards . . . a lot.'

'Is that it?'

'Oh, and Nick says he'd prefer it if you didn't bring any pot-pourri into the house because, and I quote, "Dead flower petals in a bowl is the biggest scam ever."'

'Why does he think I'm going to bring pot-pourri with me?'

'I have no idea. He only has the vaguest concept of women at the best of times. Anyway, what did the girls say?'

'They were a bit reserved to begin with. I think they think it will mean that they won't be able to walk about naked any more.'

I laugh. 'Tell them I only have eyes for you and that they can feel free to walk around naked. In fact, I'll encourage it.'

'I bet you will. The other thing they mentioned is that they don't want us having rows in any public area of the house.'

'We don't row much anyway. Except for the occasional sulk – like last week when we were play-fighting and I dropped you on your head – we're very good at being nice to each other.'

'I know, but they did say it.'

'Fine. We can agree to that. What else is there?'

'That's it. The bottom line is that they think it will be nice to have a man around the place to kill spiders, take out the bin-bags on rubbish day and programme the video. Having said that, I don't think they were being entirely serious about that last bit.'

'So, that's that, then,' I say finally. 'They've both said yes . . . Which room do we go for? Yours or mine?'

'Well, I don't want you to take this the wrong way but I'd rather you moved into mine. My house is nicer. Do you mind?'

'I do, actually. The telly at yours is tiny.'

'And that's your only reason?'

'What can I say? I hate tiny TVs.'

'So what do we do?'

I reach into my pocket and take out a fifty-pence piece. 'Heads we'll live at mine, tails we'll live at yours.'

I toss the coin into the air and catch it in the palm of my hand.

'What is it?' asks Alison.

Tilting my hand I look at the coin and can clearly see the Queen's head. I've won. But suddenly I realise I don't want to win. Alison's right. Her house is a million times nicer than mine, plus Disco will like living at her house more than mine. And I want Alison to be happy.

'It's tails,' I lie. 'We're moving into yours.'

## Wednesday, 15 November 1995

### 9.02 a.m.

It's the morning of the move and we've both got the day off work. Last night I made space in my wardrobe for Jim. I emptied out two drawers in my room and I even cleared a space for his records. I was absolutely ready to go. Now it's twelve hours later and I'm standing in what's become our joint bedroom surrounded by all of Jim's worldly goods: several hundred records, two black bin-bags of clothes, several shoeboxes of tapes, a guitar, four crisps boxes of books, two carrier-bags of shoes and trainers, and a TV. I don't think either of us can believe how much stuff he has. The funny thing is, instead of sorting it all out we decide to tackle the bigger, more exciting and far more adult question.

'Which side of the bed do you want?' I ask, as Jim sits down on a bin-bag of his clothes and surveys the room.

He points to the one furthest away from the door. 'I'll have that side.'

'Just out of curiosity, why?'

'It's like this,' he explains. 'If a mad axe murderer broke into the house wanting to kill all the inhabitants who's he going to try and kill first?'

'The person nearest the doorway . . . Which is me! I can't believe that!' I say, laughing. I grab a pillow and attack him with it. Jim grabs the other and a huge pillow fight ensues. Using his brute strength he manages to wrestle mine off me and pins me down – apparently in the same manner he used with his sister when they were kids.

'If you'd just let me finish,' he says, as I struggle underneath him trying to bite his wrists, 'I would have explained my reasoning.'

'Go on, then.'

'Well, if you get attacked first by the mad axe murderer that will give me time to get out of bed and save what's left of you. We could do it the other way round, if you like, but I don't think you'd be much cop at stopping mad axe murderers.'

'You're my knight in tarnished armour,' I say sarcastically. 'Now get off me and let me kiss you properly.'

Jim releases his grip on my wrists and we're about to kiss when the phone rings.

'I'd better get that.'

'Leave it,' says Jim. 'Let the answerphone get it.'

'It might be my mum, though. She called last night and I forgot to call her back because I was so busy getting things ready for you to move in. I won't be a second, I promise, and then we'll pick up exactly where we left off.'

**9.43 a.m.**

Alison's been on the phone so long that I've turned on the TV and I'm watching one of those terrible daytime chat shows. Today's debate is entitled: 'Should We Bring Back the Death Penalty?'

I'm engrossed in it when the bedroom door opens and Alison returns. I can tell straight away that her whole mood has changed. 'What's up?' I ask. 'Is your mum all right?'

'It was the woman who interviewed me at Cooper and Lawton. Apparently they've got a vacancy for a junior in their publicity department and because I interviewed so well they want to know if I'm interested in filling the position.'

'I thought you wanted to work in editorial?'

'I can't afford to be choosy. I really want to work in publishing so I've got to take anything I can get.'

'You're definitely going to take it, then?'

There's a long silence, which I assume is my answer.

'When would the job start?' I ask her.

'After Christmas.' There's a long pause, then she adds, 'You could come too. You could apply to firms in London. I'm sure there'll be loads of opportunities for you there . . . It's nothing to do with you . . . or us . . . or anything like that. We're really good together. I just want more than I've got here.'

'But I don't want to move.' I tell her. 'I'm happy here. All my friends are here. I don't want to give up all that. And I can't do the long-distance thing. I just can't. I thought asking you to move in with me would be a way of keeping us together. But it's clear we're going in different directions. Maybe we should just split up now so that we can stay friends.'

'Well, I don't think I can stay friends with you,' Alison

replies sadly. 'I think it will hurt too much. So maybe you better just go.'

### 10.01 a.m.

Jim tells me he's going back to Nick's and as he leaves he slams the door in the process. Seconds later the letterbox creaks open and he drops his house keys through it. I pick them up and stare at them. Then Disco wanders in from the living room and starts purring loudly because she's hungry. And with her pawing at my feet I start sobbing so hard I think I'll never stop.

## Saturday, 23 December 1995

### 6.47 p.m.

The doorbell has just rung. I answer it, and standing on the step in front of me is Alison carrying Disco. A few weeks ago she'd called me to ask if I'd consider looking after the cat until she gets settled in London. She's brought over a carrier-bag full of Whiskas tins, some packets of dried food, all her toys and a little card with the vet's address on and the date of her next set of injections. Disco seems pleased to see me, which is more than I can say for Alison. She doesn't say much at all and she barely looks at me. I can't understand why she won't see things from my point of view.

My girlfriend is leaving to go and live in another city.

Long-distance relationships never work.

These are the facts and none of them is my fault.

'What time are you leaving tomorrow?' I ask, as she gets ready to leave.

'Dad came up and took most of the big items from my room last weekend,' she replies. 'I don't know. Early, probably, because the trains will be packed with everyone going home for Christmas. What about you?'

'I'll get the train home some time in the afternoon.'

She nods, and there's an awkward silence.

'Well, I suppose I'd better go, then,' she says, and stoops to stroke Disco who is scratching at the carrier-bags by our feet. 'Me and the girls are going to the Jug for a farewell drink if you fancy coming?'

'I'd love to,' I say, 'but I've got too much work to do.'

'Okay, well, have a great Christmas, won't you?'

'Yeah,' I say. 'You too.'

## Sunday, 24 December 1995

### 8.55 a.m.

It's Christmas Eve.

More importantly, it's the day that Alison's leaving Birmingham for good. Which is why I'm banging on her front door. I don't want her to go. I don't want us to split up. And I have to tell her now.

'Who is it?' says Jane, behind the closed front door.

'Quick, Jane, it's me,' I say. 'I've got to speak to Alison before she goes.'

Jane opens the door and looks at me. 'You're a bit late for that.'

'Don't tell me she's gone.'

'Of course she's gone,' says Jane, firmly. 'Why would she hang about here waiting for you to come to your senses?'

'But—'

'No buts, Jim. No buts at all. Alison loves you. And the fact is, you've let her down.'

Even with no idea of what time train she's getting I convince myself that I'm still in with a chance of seeing her before she leaves Birmingham. I race to the bus stop on the high street just as the number fifty pulls up. Jostling a number of pensioners and their shopping trolleys, I fight my way on and will the driver to put his foot down. He obviously isn't picking up on my psychic messages because he drives so slowly that, as we reach the city centre, I decide it will be faster under my own steam. I persuade him to let me off by Digbeth coach station, then run like my life depends on it – which, in a lot of ways, it does. I run from the coach station, up through to the markets, past St Martin's and into the station.

I'm assuming that Alison's going home to Norwich so I check all the timetables located on the walls. Once I've worked out the relevant information (i.e. that it's not a Saturday in March) I discover that the next train to Norwich is leaving from platform eleven in five minutes. I run through the ticket barrier and down the escalators to the platform, which is when I realise the fatal design flaw in my plan – looking for someone on a packed train is not the easiest thing in the world to do. Especially when this particular train seems to be packed full of contestants for the 1995 Alison Smith Lookalike Championship. There are fat-looking Alisons, short-looking Alisons, Alisons who look like Alison from behind and nothing like Alison from the front, Alisons who have Alison's hair but nothing else, Alisons who have Alison's body and non-Alison hair (there is, believe it or not, a Chinese Alison, who has every single Alison attribute with the exception of Alison's lack of Chineseness). So here I am searching for her, finding all these non-Alisons, and all the time the clock is ticking. Finally I reach carriage F and there she is, reading a magazine. I bang on the window and she looks round with a jolt. I wait patiently for her to appear at the carriage door, which, thankfully, she does, and she lowers the window just as the guard blows his whistle.

'I'm sorry,' I yell, over the deep growl of the train's diesel engine. 'I don't want us to split up.'

'I'm sorry too,' she yells back.

'I think we can make this work,' I say, jogging along the platform next to the train, 'and I don't care what you say, I won't take no for an answer.'

# 1996

## Friday, 9 February 1996

### 7.33 a.m.

I'm in my room in Highbury, checking that I've packed all the things I'll need for the weekend in Birmingham into my rucksack. 'Pants, four pairs,' I read aloud from my Things For A Weekend Away list. All there.

'Two bras (at least one matching pants).'

All present and correct.

'Makeup bag and emergency tampons.'

Yes.

'One full pack Marlboro Lights.'

Yes.

'Three pairs of tights (one pair at least sixty denier).'

No.

I check in my chest of drawers for my tights and then realise that they are all in the dirty-laundry basket waiting to be washed.

I grab a pen from the desk in my room and scrawl, 'BUY TIGHTS LUNCHTIME!' across the back of my hand.

## 6.45 p.m.

I've just reached Victoria by tube and now I'm facing a ten-minute walk to the coach station. I hate getting the coach. It's a four-hour trip on National Express, stopping at Oxford, Coventry, Birmingham International and Birmingham Digbeth. In a car, it takes roughly two hours to get to Birmingham – on a coach it takes absolutely for ever. I hate it more than any other form of transport known to man.

It's raining when I step outside. Suddenly my rucksack feels like it weighs a tonne, my arms feel like they're about to snap off and I remember I forgot to buy new tights at lunchtime. As I walk along Wilton Street I keep looking at my watch, thinking, Can't miss the coach! Not another one for three hours! I'm tempted to crumple on to the ground in exhaustion and give up.

## 11.09 p.m.

The coach is just pulling into Digbeth coach station in Birmingham and everyone is getting ready to disembark. I'm looking through the window for Jim but I can't see him. He always comes to pick me up. I get off the coach and wait for the driver to unload my bag. Then I spot him sitting on a bench reading a newspaper. He looks up and sees me, and his whole face lights up. We almost do that cheesy run-and-throw-your-arms-around-the-one-you-love move, but we possess just enough self-restraint not to. Instead we walk quickly towards each other, throw our arms around each other and squeeze tightly. We don't let go for a very long time.

## 11.35 p.m.

'Jim?' I say, as we climb into his single bed with its Ikea faded-green checked duvet case, 'this is ridiculous. One person trying to get a decent night's sleep in a bed the width of a razor blade is difficult enough, but two is just plain madness.'

For about a month Jim has been living in a new house-share in Moseley. The worst thing about it is that it's kitted out with basic landlord standard-issue horrible fittings and fixtures, including a single bed in every one of the three bedrooms. Jim's is particularly uncomfortable and has springs poking out in all directions and they're so rusty and ancient that if I make the slightest movement the creaks and squeaks make it sound like we're having a four-person orgy. It really gets me down.

'There's nothing wrong with the bed,' says Jim. 'It's fine.'

'Of course it's not fine,' I reply. 'Look at us. You're having to sleep on your left side with your arm underneath me and your back resting half on the bed and half on the wall and I'm having to spoon into whatever space is left over. We virtually have to synchronise our breathing in case I end up on the floor. I think you need to get a double bed.'

'You might have a point.'

'Ask the landlord to put one in.'

'I'm not sure I can do that. Have you seen Mr McNamara? Word has it that he used to be a professional wrestler.'

I laugh. 'Yeah, right.'

'It doesn't matter if it's true or not,' insists Jim. 'What does matter is that Mr McNamara is the size of a house with a short-fuse temper that could lose a man like me his home and his head.'

'And?'

Jim sighs heavily. 'I'll ask him next time he comes round.'

## Wednesday, 14 February 1996

### 7.02 a.m.

I receive one card: a black and white photo of a heart made in pebbles on a beach. Inside, it reads: 'Happy Valentine's Day. You make me complete. All my love, always, Alison.'

### 7.38 a.m.

I receive two cards:

1. A huge satin padded card with a cartoon cat on a heart-shaped cake. Inside it reads: 'I wanted to do something different this year. This is the least tasteful card I could find. It's not easy being away from you but if this card, like us being away from each other, represents rock bottom, then things can only get better. Big love, Jim.'

2. The card was forwarded to me from my parents' address. It is a plain white card with a real rose petal on the front. Inside, in Damon's handwriting, there is a D and nothing else.

## Thursday, 7 March 1996

### 7.24 p.m.

I've just been round to Mr McNamara's. The conversation went like this:

Me: 'Hi, Mr McNamara. Sorry to bother you. It's just that I've only got a single bed in my room and when my girlfriend comes to stay there's no room for the two of us. I was just wondering if you could supply me with a double bed. My girlfriend is on the verge of giving me a really hard time. I'm sure you understand what a difference a bigger bed would make.'

Him: 'I'm renting the room to you – not your girlfriend.'

I couldn't see the point of pushing the matter any further, given that this was the full extent of Mr McNamara's reasoned debate. And as I'm perfectly happy in the bed five days out of seven I decide to let sleeping landlords lie.

## Friday, 8 March 1996

### 10.22 p.m.

Jim has come to stay with me in London. He hasn't mentioned the bed so I assume everything's okay. I don't want to ask him about it because I don't want him to think I'm nagging him. My flatmate Viv nags her boyfriend constantly and never lets him get away with a single thing. I don't want to be like that. I want to be a cool girlfriend.

## Sunday, 10 March 1996

### 6.35 p.m.

'So I'll see you next weekend?' I ask, as we prepare to say goodbye at the station.

'Yeah,' says Jim. He gives me a huge kiss.

'You've got the bed thing sorted, haven't you?' I ask.

'Or course,' he says reassuringly.

'I knew you would. I wasn't checking up on you.'

'I know, it's fine. It's all sorted.'

## Friday, 15 March 1996

### 11.57 p.m.

Alison and I have just arrived at my place.

'You know what I'd really like to do?' purrs Alison, as we stand in the hallway.

'What?' I say, even though I'm pretty sure what the answer will be.

'I think we should christen the new double bed!' she exclaims, and then she begins nibbling my earlobe. Before I know it we're scrambling up the stairs and towards my room. We kiss frantically on the upstairs landing and manoeuvre ourselves into my room backwards, then flop on to the bed. This is exactly the moment at which Alison realises there isn't a new bed to christen. If I'd had a single ounce of sense I would've bought one as soon as I'd left her the previous weekend. I didn't, however, have even half an ounce of sense so instead I ignored the problem as if it might sort itself out. By the time it occurred to me to do something about it was nine thirty last night and all the bed shops I could find in the *Yellow Pages* had been closed for hours.

'Where's the new bed?' asks Alison.

'There's a little problem with that,' I explain quickly.

'But I thought—'

'I lied. I asked my landlord and he wouldn't budge.'

'Why didn't you tell me?'

'Because I knew you'd get annoyed.'

'So when were you going to tell me?'

'I was kind of hoping you wouldn't notice.'

There's a long pause. I'm convinced Alison is going to explode. But she doesn't. All she says, quite calmly and quietly, is: 'Tomorrow we're going shopping.'

## Saturday, 16 March 1996

### 2.05 p.m.

We're in Beds, Beds, Beds, a bed warehouse in nearby Stirchley. We look at dozens throughout the afternoon. We do the sitting-down thing, we do the lying-down thing and we even do the part-sitting, part-lying thing. At around four o'clock we finally make our decision: a Sleepnite pocket-sprung divan. At the till I agree to pay the extra ten pounds for same-day delivery, then scrabble for my credit card. But Alison stops me and gets out her cheque book.

'What are you doing?' I ask.

'Writing a cheque, stupid.'

'I can see that, but what's it for?'

'It's for you. You're getting the bed because of me. I get the benefit of not being permanently crippled. And, even better, I now know that when I come up here I'm going to get the best sleep ever. The least I can do is pay half.'

'You do realise what this means, though?'

'What?'

'That this bed will be our first joint purchase.'

'It's just a bed, Jim.'

'No, it's not. After this will come cutlery, vacuum-cleaners, wardrobes, TVs, fridges, washing-machines, microwaves and mortgages, everything.'

'So?'

'So, nothing. I'm just letting you know that it's a momentous occasion. For instance if we ever split up –'

'– which we won't –'

'– of course, which we won't – but if we did there could come a point where we'll be arguing about which one of us will get this bed we're buying right this very second.'

'So, what do you want me to do? Not pay for half of it?'

'I wasn't saying don't pay for it. I was making the point that it's a momentous occasion.'

'You're insane, Jim. But if it makes you feel any better, if we ever do split up –'

'– which we won't –'

'– of course, which we won't – I'll get the bed.'

'Why?'

'Because we'll agree to it right now.'

'Why would I agree to that?'

'As an incentive not to split up with me.'

I laugh. 'But I'm not going to split up with you.'

'So you won't mind relinquishing all future claims to this bed, will you?'

'You're making my head hurt.'

'You started it.'

'Come on, let's just pay and get out of here.'

'Not until you give up all future claims on this bed. I'm serious, Jim. I can't go buying beds with young men who can't promise to stick around.'

'But I am sticking around. I'm not going anywhere.'

'Then put your half of the bed where your mouth is.'

'And then we can go?'

'Yes.'

'Okay, I hereby declare in front of . . .' I peer at the name-tag of the girl on the check-out '. . . Becky Collins that should I ever split up with Alison the bed we have bought today will belong completely and wholly to her.' I turn to Alison. 'Satisfied?'

Alison kisses my cheek. 'Absolutely.'

## Sunday, 17 March 1996

### 4.03 a.m.

**It's the middle of the night and I'm lying next to Jim in our brand new bed when the phone rings and wakes me. I look at the clock, yawn, then nudge Jim.**

**'Hmm?' he says sleepily.**

**'It's the phone,' I reply.**

**'Let the answerphone get it,' he says, and with that he puts a pillow over his head and goes back to sleep.**

## 4.19 a.m.

A phone's ringing again. This time, it's Jim's new work mobile. I open my eyes and turn on the bedside light, but I have no idea where it is. I nudge Jim again. 'Hmm?' he says sleepily.

'It's your mobile this time.'

'Just ignore it, babe. It'll be the guys from work again having a laugh.'

'I wish you'd get some better friends,' I tell Jim, but he doesn't reply as he's already drifted back to sleep. So, like Jim, I put a pillow over my head and try to get back to sleep. The phone carries on ringing and I continue to lie there waiting for the answerphone to kick in. When it does I turn over in bed and snuggle up to the warmth of his body.

## 4.23 a.m.

Once again I'm yanked out of sleep by a ringing phone. It takes me a few moments to realise that this time it's my own mobile. I don't bother trying to wake Jim. I just get out of bed and search for the phone in all the usual places. I check the pockets of my jeans, which are lying on the bedroom floor, my handbag, next to the bed, and my coat pockets and I still can't find it, but my stumbling around the room finally wakes Jim. 'What's wrong now?' he mumbles from bed.

'I'm trying to find my phone.'

'Who's phoning us now?'

'I don't know,' I reply impatiently, 'because I can't find the phone.'

'It's in my jacket pocket on the back of the door,' says Jim. 'You gave it to me last night to look after.'

He's right. As I get nearer to his jacket I can hear it more clearly. I take the phone out of the pocket and answer it.

'Hello?'

'Is that Alison?'

It's Jim's sister, Kirsty. She sounds upset. 'What's wrong?'

'I'm sorry to phone you in the middle of the night. I never would normally. It's just that something terrible has happened.'

'What is it?' I ask, as my heart begins to race.

'It's Dad,' she says. 'He had a heart-attack. He's dead.'

I'm in tears as I listen and Jim, now awake, leaps out of bed to find out what's wrong. 'Who is it?' he asks.

I hand the phone to him, put my arms around him and hug him with all my strength. When he puts the phone down he cries and cries as if he's never going to stop.

## Friday, 22 March 1996

### 11.15 a.m.

It's the day of the funeral and my parents' house is packed with relatives of all descriptions from uncles and aunts to boyfriends of second cousins and even the fourth ex-husband of my grandad's former sister-in-law.

An elderly woman comes up to me, puts her arms around me and kisses me on the cheek. I have no idea who she is. 'I'm really sorry for your loss,' she says, in a Yorkshire accent.

'Thank you,' I reply.

'Your father was a lovely man.'

'Yeah,' I reply. 'He was.'

This sort of thing has been happening all day. People have been coming up and telling me that the last time they saw me was when I was a toddler, or that I've grown up to become a fine young man, or in this lady's case that I'm a credit to my father. She begins telling me about her connection to my mum's side of the family in great detail. From what I can gather she's my mum's second cousin's wife.

Apparently I met her once when I was eleven and she once bought me a train set for Christmas. I have no recollection of this. I'm just wondering how I'm going to extricate myself from the conversation without appearing rude when Alison appears at my side.

'Sorry to interrupt,' she says to the old lady, 'but Jim's mum wants to speak to him in the kitchen.'

'Oh, that's fine,' says the old lady. 'I'll catch up with you later.'

I smile at the old lady, then Alison takes my hands and leads me along the hallway in the direction of the front door.

'I thought you said Mum was in the kitchen,' I ask, confused.

Alison smiles. 'I lied. I was watching your pained expression from the other side of the room and thought you might need rescuing.'

'Very clever, Ms Smith,' I say, laughing. 'Well rescued.'

'Do you fancy coming outside while I have a fag?' asks Alison.

'Yeah,' I reply. 'Why not?' I open the front door and sit on the step and Alison squeezes in beside me. 'This used to be my favourite place to sit when I was a kid,' I tell her, as she lights her cigarette. 'I used to like watching the world go by.'

Alison inhales heavily on her cigarette and exhales with a sigh. Looking down at her calves, she picks a stray bit of fluff off her tights absentmindedly.

'How are you doing?' she asks, checking for more fluff.

'Okay,' I reply. 'I still can't believe this has happened. All morning I've been thinking how, at twenty-five, I'm too young to be without a dad. This is the kind of thing that people in their thirties and forties are supposed to deal with, not people in their twenties. People who haven't really stopped being kids yet.'

'It seems so unfair,' says Alison. 'I hate that this is happening to you.'

'I miss him, Al, I really miss him. I've been trying to remember everything he ever said to me, every moment we ever spent together. It's like I want to be able to watch it again and again like a video, but I can't because I never played those moments enough when he was alive. I never used to like looking back because the only people who look back are the ones who haven't got a future. And it's only now he's gone that I realise you have to take stock regularly. You have to rewind and review things and try to make sense of them because they might not always be there.'

**11.31 a.m.**

The undertakers have just arrived to pick up the immediate family to take us to St Mary's for the funeral service and there's a flurry of activity. The decision has been made that my mum, my sister, Alison and I will travel in the first car, with other close relatives in the second and third cars. When I tell Alison this, she seems reluctant. 'Are you sure?' she says. 'Shouldn't someone closer to your family be in the first car, like one of your aunts or something? It's just that I feel like a bit of an impostor being here. I'm not really family, am I? I'll get a lift with one of your uncles or something.'

'No,' I say firmly, as I put my arms around her. 'You're absolutely wrong about this. As far as I'm concerned you're family. I don't think I could've got through any of this without you. You've been there every step of the way. You've sorted out everything from packing my bags to sorting out train tickets. You've done all the things I couldn't do for myself. You've just seen what needed doing and got on with it. You just understood. And that's the thing, isn't it? That's when you know something's right. That's when you become family.'

Then, without saying another word, I take her hand and lead her outside to where the rest of my family are waiting for us. One by one we get into the first car, my mum first, my sister next to her, then me, then Alison.

My family.

# PART FOUR

## Then: 1997

# 1997

## Friday, 17 January 1997

### 9.34 a.m.

Jim and I are finally moving in together today. A vacancy came up in the Greene Lowe office in Blackfriars a few months before Christmas. It's on a higher grade than his old job, he gets more responsibility and more money too. The place we're moving to is a ground-floor flat in a converted house in Muswell Hill. It's got a living room and a small kitchen and bathroom. It isn't brilliant and it's overpriced, but we reasoned it would do us for a while. The best thing about it is that it's semi-furnished so we don't have to go out and buy loads of expensive stuff, only items that we need, like a pine table and four chairs. We got them from Habitat in the sale – our second joint purchase. I'm pathetically excited about having my own table and chairs because it means we can invite people round for dinner: we can entertain. It makes me feel like we're well on our way to being proper grown-ups. Finally we're shedding our semi-student status. I feel like we can now be a proper couple.

### 10.00 a.m.

Alison and I, with a fair portion of our worldly goods in the back of a van I've rented for the weekend, have just turned up at our new flat. As I get out and open the rear doors I can't help but stare at the black bin-liners, suitcases and boxes. It's weird having everything you own, everything you think makes you, packed away. And even more strange when some of the stuff belongs to the person you've decided to share your life with.

Thankfully, Nick and Jane have turned up to help us and as we bring the boxes, bags and suitcases in to the flat it strikes me that Alison hasn't got much stuff. She's never been much of a stuff person. She has the girly stuff: the must-read literary books, the candles, the Indian-textile throws, the cushions, the photos of friends and family, the crap portable black-and-white TV, the ancient top-loading video-recorder, the sackload of beauty products (including several million bottles of shampoo and conditioner despite the fact that last time I looked she only had one head in need of shampooing/conditioning), and, of course, the clothes, but that's it. Standard girly stuff. Small-volume girly stuff. Not large-volume stuff like I have. She lacks the hundreds of CDs, the CD racks, the hi-fi, the non-ancient portable TV, the non-ancient video-recorder, the two suitcases and the bin-liners of clothes, shoes and trainers, the dozens and dozens of back issues of *FHM*, *The Economist* and *Spiderman Monthly*, the life-sized cardboard cut-out of Chewbacca, the out-of-date-but-I'm-still-going-to-read-them-because-there's-an-interesting-article-in-there weekend supplements of newspapers, the video-games console, the emergency alcohol (a four-pack of Carlsberg, a bottle of Jack Daniel's, a half-drunk bottle of Absolut citrus) and more . . . much more.

**7.33 p.m.**

Our first night in the flat. Just me, Jim and Disco. A little urban family unit. We watch TV, order home-delivery Chinese and drink a six-pack of Becks from the off-licence two doors down. Best of all, when the Chinese arrives we sit down at our brand new dining-table to eat it.

'I'm so happy right now,' I say, chopsticks in hand. 'This is perfect. When we've finished eating at our jointly owned table, how do you fancy retiring to our jointly owned bed?'

Jim grins from ear to ear. 'That sounds like a splendid idea, my dear.'

## Friday, 14 February 1997

**7.31 a.m.**

I'm in the communal hallway checking the mail. Amongst the usual junk post is an envelope that has been forwarded from my parents' address. I have a pretty good idea what it is and open it with a mixture of curiosity and guilt. Inside is a cream card with a small gold heart in the centre. Inside, it reads: 'Happy Valentine's Day, still missing you, D.' I know I ought to throw it away but I don't. I take the card and the envelope and after Jim goes to work hide it in an old shoebox.

## Thursday, 13 March 1997

**6.43 a.m.**

It's been a month since Alison and I moved in together and things have been going great. We seem to be spending most of our time laughing and eating nice food. Our friends think we've disappeared off the face of the earth because we don't go out any more. It's not like we can't. It's more like we don't want to. I feel we're a bit like Tom and Barbara from *The Good Life* – completely self-sufficient from the outside world. I like the way things are between us: they seem so much more relaxed than before. Right now, however, I'm lying in bed next to Alison listening to the *Today* programme and thinking about getting up when suddenly, as if from nowhere, I smell something I've never smelt before . . . at least, I'd never smelt it from this particular source.

'Was that you?' I ask Alison, nudging her in the ribs.

'Was what me?' she replies, clearly faking sleep.

'You're such a bad liar,' I say, sniffing the air surreptitiously, 'I know it's not me and Disco isn't in the room, so who else is it going to be?' I put my arm around her and adopt an incredibly patronising manner. 'It is okay, you know. You can fart. It is allowed.'

'I've been holding it in all night,' says Alison, letting out a giggle that's nine parts laughter to one part shame. 'I'm really sorry, Jim. I'm an awful girlfriend, aren't I?'

'Why?'

'Because I've done this . . .' she pulls a disgusted face '. . . in front of you.'

'I can't believe it,' I say. 'You're right. We've been together all this time and this really is the first time I've heard you fart. How come I've never heard you before? Everyone's got to fart sometimes. Even you. Where have you been doing it?'

Alison hangs her head in shame. 'When you're around, in the bathroom mainly, out in the hallway sometimes and occasionally by the front door – anywhere that's a public space so I can blame it on someone else.'

'You're insane. Do you know that?'

Alison nods, and then she kisses me.

## Friday, 28 March 1997

### 7.09 p.m.

It's early evening, and Alison and I are watching TV with Disco stretched out between us.

'She looks like you, you know,' says Alison.

'Who does?'

'Disco.'

'You're saying I look like a cat?'

'Not exactly. I just think that if she looks like either of us it's you. You are her dad, after all.'

I look at Disco, who's lying on her back yawning widely. 'I think you're right,' I observe. 'She does look like me.'

## Friday, 4 April 1997

### 3.45 a.m.

'Are you awake?'

In the darkness of our bedroom I turn to look in Alison's direction and then at the alarm clock on the floor next to me.

'No.' I sigh.

Alison laughs. 'I can't sleep.'

'Why?'

'I've got something on my mind.'

'You're not going to let me go back to sleep without us having a talk, are you?'

'No.'

'Go on, then.'

'It's three months since we officially moved in together,' says Alison proudly. 'I just want to make sure that things are going okay.'

'Can I just ask, you know what time it is, don't you?'

'Yes.'

'And yet you still want to know the answer to this question?'

'Yes.'

'Even though we've both got work in the morning?'

'Yes.'

'Fine. I've got no complaints. You're actually . . . okay to live with.'

Alison laughs. 'Okay? You know I'm better than "okay".'

'Okay, you're not too bad, then.'

'I know you think I'm being a bit mad and that's because I am being a bit mad. But I just want to make sure everything's okay between us.' She pauses, then adds, 'Relationships are about communicating so here I am communicating.'

'Thanks for that information. Shall we go back to sleep now?'

'Yeah,' says Alison sleepily, and kisses my chin.

She drifts off to sleep immediately, but I'm awake now so I lie next to her and wonder what disease I might have that can make the snores, wheezes and snuffles of the woman lying next to me sound so magical.

## Sunday, 25 May 1997

### 3 p.m.

I'm on the phone in the middle of a conversation with Jane. Jim's watching TV in the living room and Disco is on the bed next to me, rolling on her back and occasionally scraping at the bedcovers.

'So, how's living together going?' she asks.

'I can't fault it,' I proclaim happily. 'I feel like he really wants to be with me.'

'That's brilliant. I'm so pleased for you.'

'I think in all the time we've been together we've gone through all the stages: like the madly-in-love phase and the weird not-quite-a-real-relationship phase when we were living in different cities, and there was all that pressure. But now we're actually living together I . . . Well, the thing is . . .'

'What?'

'I feel like it's too perfect.'

'Like a honeymoon period?'

'Exactly. It feels like we're on our best behaviour all the time. I'm sure we can't keep it up. Sooner or later the honeymoon has got to end.'

## Saturday, 5 July 1997

### 6.33 p.m.

We've got some friends coming over for our first dinner party in an hour or so, but right now I'm watching last weekend's *Blind Date* on video. I want contestant number three to win but I just know that the student with the shiny shirt is going to choose number two because she's managed to work into one of her answers that she's a blonde. Suddenly I notice something. I take a surreptitious sniff of the air just to confirm whether or not my worst nightmare is about to come true.

Sniff.

Sniff.

Sniff.

Sniff.

It has.

There's a distinct smell of burning Chicken Provençal. I leap out of the armchair and pass Disco heading rapidly away from the kitchen. I'm faced with a roomful of smoke. I grab the 'Welcome to Norwich' oven gloves Alison's mum bought us for Christmas and open the oven door. I'm greeted by a smoking mass of charred black slurry in a Pyrex dish.

I've killed the Chicken Provençal.

I turn around to see a half-dressed Alison standing in the doorway. I look at the Chicken Provençal again.

The chicken is dead and now I am too.

'I'm really sorry—' I begin, but Alison doesn't wait around for an explanation. She turns and leaves the room.

## 6.36 p.m.

I'm sitting on the edge of the bed thinking about what's just happened. In a way I feel semi-responsible for the catastrophe that has befallen the meal. I'd left the fate of the Chicken Provençal in Jim's hands. I knew I'd live to regret it. I knew it. But at the same time I didn't want to get our new set-up off to a bad start by treating him like an idiot incapable of following simple instructions. And, anyway, I'd needed to have a shower, do my hair and put on some makeup.

'Look, I'm really sorry,' says Jim, standing in the doorway. 'It just completely slipped my mind.'

'All you had to do was turn off the bastard cooker when it went ping,' I say angrily. 'A child of four could've done that. Or a trained monkey.'

'I'm sorry,' says Jim.

I can't bring myself to speak to him.

'I'm really sorry. Listen, I'll sort it out, babe. You carry on getting ready and I'll sort all the mess in the kitchen. When everyone arrives I'll tell them it was my fault.'

'Fine,' I snap, but I give up all hope of an evening of sophisticated banter the moment I hear Jim pick up the phone, dial and say, 'I'd like to order the Peking Garden Banquet Meal for six.'

## Sunday, 6 July 1997

### 1.15 a.m.

Jim and I are in bed. We're lying in neither of our usual positions that involve touching or spooning but, rather, we're silently fuming with each other. Everything turned out all right in the end. The food was good, our friends appeared to enjoy themselves and Jim was at his most charming and entertaining. Most people would've considered it a success. But not me. As I lie there in bed next to Jim I wish with my whole heart that I hadn't referred to the Smeg oven in the kitchen as 'the bastard cooker'. I feel as if that one word has changed everything between us. Since we moved in together I've been desperately trying to keep that side of me hidden – to imagine that somehow it had disappeared.

We are supposed to be madly in love.

We are supposed to be new and improved, like soap powder with added cleaning power.

We aren't supposed to be yelling expletives at each other.

I wish I could go back in time and uninvite our friends, then Jim could incinerate as many meals as he likes. I could be laid-back and easy. I could laugh off even the worst disaster. But now I've broken the truce and I think it's inevitable that we'll reach this point again.

'Jim?' I whisper to the body lying next to me. 'Are you talking to me?'

'Hmm?' he mutters noncommittally.

'So you're not talking to me. Well, listen . . . I'm sorry.'

'That's okay,' he replies softly. 'I'm sorry too.'

'Friends?' I say, rubbing his calf with my foot.

'Yeah,' he replies. 'We're still friends.'

## Friday, 22 August 1997

### 8.01 a.m.

Jim and I are going to Norwich for the weekend to spend my twenty-seventh birthday with my parents. They called him and told him they wanted to throw me a surprise party featuring a whole host of distant relatives whom I haven't seen in years. When he told me the bad news I was so utterly annoyed with him for having agreed to get me there that I could barely speak. I'm calmer now, but only marginally so – I can't believe Jim made me book half a day's holiday so we could get there early.

'Right then,' I say to Jim, as I zip up my overnight bag. 'We'd better get a move on if we're going to get to my parents' before lunch-time.'

'We can't go yet,' says Jim, rummaging through the drawer in my bedside table. 'I can't find your passport.'

'That's because it's in the drawer in the kitch—' I stop abruptly and give him my full attention. 'Why are you looking for my passport?'

'Because you won't be able to leave the country without it.'

'But we're going to my parents'.'

Jim shakes his head.

'But you—'

'I lied.'

'So we're going where exactly?'

'New York.'

'New York?'

'Three days in New York, leaving this afternoon, coming back Monday night.'

'But what about work?'

'I called your boss and sorted it out.'

'I thought there was something funny going on. I kept trying to talk to her about a meeting on Monday and she just kept smiling at me enigmatically and changing the subject.'

'All my doing.' Jim opens an envelope on the bed and hands me the tickets.

'We can't afford this,' I tell him.

'No, we can't,' he admits, 'but we need a break and this is it.'

'But I didn't pack with the aim of going to New York. I packed for a boring weekend with Mum and Dad.'

'I know,' says Jim. 'Not very practical, am I? Well, the cab taking us to Heathrow will be here in an hour and a half so you'd better repack. Talking of which . . . I don't suppose you've seen my cut-off jeans, have you? I can't seem to find them anywhere and it might be hot out there.'

'No,' I reply. 'I haven't seen them in ages. Maybe you lost them in the move? Anyway, they were horrible-looking things.'

'Maybe,' muses Jim. 'But I kind of liked them.'

## Saturday, 23 August 1997

### 10.23 a.m.

The floor around our bed is littered with wrapping-paper from the surprise birthday presents I've given Alison: some pearl earrings, a gilt-edged notebook and a couple of books she'd wanted (*The God of Small Things* and *Cold Mountain*). We're now lying in bed with the windows open, listening to the sound of New York.

'Even the traffic sounds different from London,' says Alison. She pauses and looks at me. 'That was a really stupid thing to say, wasn't it?'

'No,' I reply. 'It was a pretty good observation.'

Alison laughs. 'That's one of the great things about being with you. I can say stupid stuff and it doesn't feel stupid.'

## 3.03 p.m.

Jim and I are eating a late lunch in the Dean and DeLuca deli near the Rockefeller Center. We're sitting next to the window, watching people go by. Every now and again our eyes meet across the table and we smile like we're sharing a secret that no one else knows.

## 10.34 p.m.

We're shattered. An evening of hopping around Manhattan's finest bars and clubs has been shelved for a night in and an evening of US TV. Now, though, we're in our hotel room and I'm ticking off the items we want from the room-service breakfast menu.

'Orange or grapefruit juice?'

'Grapefruit.'

'Tea or coffee?'

'I'll have a coffee, thanks.'

'Cereal? They've got muesli, cornflakes, bran flakes and porridge.'

'Not for me.'

'Fruit?'

'I'm going to stick to stuff that needs a knife and fork.'

'Okay, how many eggs?'

'Two.'

'How do you want them?'

'It's got to be over easy,' says Jim.

I can't help but laugh. 'You've always wanted to order your eggs over easy. Okay, next up. Sausage links?'

'Is that like normal sausage?' I shrug. 'Put me down for some of it anyway.'

'Canadian bacon?'

'Some of that too. In fact, tick everything else that's there. I love breakfast.'

'Okay,' I say, ticking the boxes. 'One last question from the menu:

do you love me? The options are, one, a bit; two, a lot; three, to the moon and back again.'

Jim looks at me and smiles. 'It's got to be three.'

## Sunday, 24 August 1997

### 9.47 a.m.

We're at the top of the Empire State Building. Alison is looking out through the put-the-money-in-the-slot binoculars across Manhattan. I'm reading our guidebook to New York.

'According to the guidebook, the Empire State Building is a hundred and three floors high,' I tell Alison.

'Really?' she says vaguely.

'It's 1472 feet tall from the top of the TV mast to the ground.'

'Fascinating.'

'The volume of the building is thirty-seven million cubic feet.'

'Amazing.'

'And it took seven million man-hours to construct.'

'Mind-boggling.'

'You're being sarcastic now,' I tell her. 'You should be impressed by the facts at my fingertips.'

'I am. But how about this one? There's this girl, let's for the sake of argument call her Alison Smith—'

'A likely name.'

'Well, this Alison Smith girl is, was and will always be in love with you. How's that for a fact, Mr Owen?'

'It's a good one,' I say, laughing. 'But if we're being sickeningly cute let me give you a fact of my own. There's this guy, let's call him for the sake of argument Jim Owen—'

'A likely name.'

'Well, this Jim Owen guy thinks that you are officially the best thing since sliced bread. How's that for a fact?'

'Brilliant,' she replies. 'A girl can never tire of hearing those kinds of facts when they really mean something.'

**4.35 p.m.**
We're standing in Grand Central Station. I tell Jim that this has to be the most beautiful building in the entire world. We stand watching the light stream through the windows at the top and I ask him why every single one of the hundreds of people in here isn't staring up at the ceiling like we are. He says, 'Because when you've got real life to contend with on a daily basis, stuff like this always takes second place to practicality. It's the same with love. You take it for granted and after a while it becomes invisible.'

## Monday, 25 August 1997

**1.15 p.m.**
We're in Central Park, sitting on a bench opposite the entrance to the zoo. We've been here for half an hour or so, just people-watching before we go back to our hotel and start packing.

'Do you think we'll have kids one day?' I ask Jim, as a couple walk by pushing a pram.

'Um . . . one day,' he replies. 'How many do you want?'

'Two, one of each. What about you?'

Jim doesn't reply. Instead he just sort of shrugs as if he's lost in a world of his own.

## 6.45 p.m.

We're at JFK now. We should've been on the plane two hours ago but the flight back to London has been delayed because of electrical storms. I've never seen anything like it. Huge sheets of rain are coming down relentlessly against the large glass windows looking out on to the runway and every now and again there's a bright flash and a huge crack, quickly followed by a deep roll of thunder. Jim's oblivious to this. He's in one of the news kiosks hunting around for a couple of hi-fi magazines for the flight. I watch him scanning the shelves and suddenly I feel sort of strange looking at him. It's almost like one of those moments that people talk about in books . . . I feel like it's just dawned on me that there isn't anyone in the world I'd rather be with than him. And I know this is the moment everything falls into place. By the time I walk over to him to tell him my news I have a grin on my face.

'What's funny?' asks Jim.

'Nothing . . . well, not nothing, actually . . . everything. I've just realised that I want – no, I need to marry you. I'm serious. I love you. I want us to be together for the rest of our lives.'

Jim looks at me and says, 'To be truthful I've sort of been feeling the same way. I think we should do it.'

'The idea of getting married just feels right,' I tell Jim. 'We shouldn't make a big deal of it, though. I don't want a big wedding or anything showy. Let's just go for it.'

'You mean elope?'

'Jim, we're too old to elope. We should just go away somewhere, get hitched and do all the explaining once the deed is done.'

'So where do you fancy doing it?'

'There's only one place I can think of. The place where it all began.'

## Tuesday, 4 November 1997

### 12.03 p.m.

Today is the day of the wedding. And Alison and I have just arrived in Birmingham. We're not due at the register office for another two hours. So, as we planned on the way up on the train, we get a cab to Selly Oak and have lunch at the Varsity, which, to our disappointment, has undergone a refurbishment. Afterwards we take a walk down to the university and sit on a bench outside the library. To the left of us is the beautiful ivy-covered building of the arts faculty, ahead is the clock tower and University Square, where in summer my friends and I would lie on our backs and attempt to get to grips with books on quantitative economics. Being here brings back all the memories.

'It's been a long journey,' says Alison wistfully.

'What?' I joke. 'From the city centre to the campus?'

'No, from first meeting you at university to where we are now. I mean – 1989 – it seems like yesterday. I can still remember how I thought about the world, how I thought my life would be, how I first felt about you. All those memories are still fresh in my mind. It doesn't feel like so much time can have passed so quickly, does it? Look at us. Here we are, years later, you an accountant, me working in publishing, and the two of us about to get married.' Alison lights a cigarette. 'If the student me could see me now I think she'd be quite pleased.' She pauses for a drag on her cigarette. 'She'd be a bit disappointed I'd never got round to writing that great novel I was convinced I had in me but she'd be impressed that I work in publishing. Relationships-wise, I think she'd be happy that I'd found love. I think while she put on a brave face about finding the right person for her, she always thought that the right person might not be out there or, if he was, that he'd never find her. I think she'd be surprised that she'd found it with the Boy Who Dresses Differently because she would have assumed that he wasn't her type. What about you?'

'I think student me would be a bit disappointed. I think he had big plans for the rest of his life. A lot of things he wanted to achieve, dreams he wanted to pursue. I know for a fact that he certainly didn't want to end up in accountancy.'

'Oh, that's really sad,' says Alison.

'It is a bit,' I reply. 'But on the other hand I think he'd be quite chuffed with the money he's earning.'

'Would he think you'd sold out?'

'He's a student. Of course he'd think I'd sold out. I think he'd be really annoyed for a while . . . at least until I explained to him that he was never going to be a rock star. I think he'd realise I'd done the best with the skills he'd got.'

'And what about me? What would he think about you still being with Damon's girlfriend after four years?'

'He'd be surprised it's lasted this long. I think he'd be a little bit scared at the thought of being with someone for that long. But at the same time he'd be relieved because I don't think he wanted to go through life alone.'

'Yes, but what about me?'

'What would he think of you? He'd think, Yes, you're all right.'

'Only all right?'

'Yeah,' I say. 'I think he'd play it cool.'

'But what would he *really* think about me?' asks Alison,

carefully flicking the ash from her cigarette. 'You know, when he's alone at night thinking about life.'

'He'd think he'd done better than he ever deserved.'

## 1.37 p.m.

Jim and I are sitting in the waiting room inside the register office, waiting for our turn to get married. We thought it would be really funny to dress down for the wedding so we checked into our hotel and got changed. I'm wearing jeans, trainers, a cream top and a jacket. Jim's wearing jeans, trainers and a thick black polo-neck jumper. As a special surprise, when we walked into the register office he showed me his socks: the Argyle-patterned knee-length ones he wore on Freshers' Night. I laugh when I see them. I don't know where they've been hiding all these years. I thought I'd weeded out most of the embarrassing stuff he used to wear.

'I can't believe we're getting married in less than half an hour,' says Jim.

'Me either,' I concur.

'Do you think we'll feel any different once we've done it?'

'Yes,' I say reassuringly. 'I think we will. You must feel different after you get married otherwise why do people still do it? I think I feel different already.'

Jim laughs. 'We haven't even decided what you're doing about your surname. Are you still going to be Ms Smith or do you fancy being Mrs Owen?'

'I hadn't thought about that.' I clear my throat theatrically. 'Alison Elizabeth Owen – what do you think?'

'Alison Owen has a certain ring to it. Try out a double-barrelled job.'

'Hmm,' I begin, 'I'm not sure Alison Smith-Owen works, does it?'

'Not really. Maybe Alison Owen-Smith at a push, but it sounds a bit of a mouthful. Me being a man of the nineties, maybe I should change my name to Jim Smith.'

'No way,' I say firmly, 'if you have a name that bland, people will constantly think it's false. I'm going to go with Alison Owen. I'm a bit tired of Alison Smith anyway. She was a lovely girl but she did moan a lot. Alison Owen is a much nicer woman altogether.'

'Mr Jim Owen and Miss Alison Smith?' says a kindly looking middle-aged woman in a black trouser suit.

Jim and I both look up. 'Yes?'

'You're next,' she replies.

## 2 p.m.

We're now standing in the room where we're going to get married. It's painted cream, and there are long velvet curtains at either side of the huge window in front of us. It is filled with enough plastic chairs to seat at least forty or fifty people. It seems a bit empty because there are only three of us here.

'I'm sorry,' I explain to the registrar. 'We haven't brought any witnesses with us.'

The registrar smiles. 'Don't worry. You're not the first and I'm sure you won't be the last. I'll just go and get some.'

She disappears and returns, moments later, with a young man in a security-guard uniform and a well-dressed elderly woman in a hat.

'This is Daniel, our security guard,' says the registrar. 'Most people who work here have been witnesses at some point, but Daniel's new so I thought he'd like a go.'

Alison and I shake hands with him.

'I've never done this before,' he says.

'Neither have we,' I reply.

'And this lady who's volunteered,' says the registrar, 'is due to get married after you.'

'Call me Marjorie,' she says, offering her hand.

'Thanks for doing this,' says Alison. 'I hope your husband-to-be doesn't mind.'

'He thinks the whole thing's hilarious. Just out of curiosity, why haven't you got any witnesses?'

'It's just one of those things,' says Alison in reply.

'Okay, then,' says the registrar. 'Now the witnesses are present let's begin.'

I cough nervously and Alison looks at me. I just know I can't go through with this. I can feel in my bones that this is going to be a huge mistake.

'Do you mind hanging on a second?' I say to the registrar. 'I just need to talk to my girlfriend before we go any further.'

I grab Alison's hand, lead her to the back of the room and take a deep breath. 'You know I love you, don't you?'

'You're having second thoughts, aren't you?' asks Alison. 'I knew you would.'

'I'm not at all,' I tell her. 'I just want to make sure you're happy about doing it like this. You know, your mum and dad aren't here. Your friends aren't here. It's just you, me, the registrar and two people we've never met before.'

'That's fine by me,' she says. 'I've never wanted a big wedding. I'm not sure that before I met you I even wanted to get married. But what I do know is this, I love you and getting married to you is the best thing I could possibly do.'

'Is there a problem?' asks the registrar, who has now walked down to our end of the room.

'No,' I reply. 'We were just sorting out a few details.' I look at Alison and smile. 'We're ready when you are.'

And with that we walk back up to the front of the room,

the registrar does what she has to do, Alison and I say, 'I will,' at the appropriate points in the ceremony, and it's over and done with. We're married.

# PART FIVE

## Then: 1998

# 1998

## Sunday, 4 January 1998

### 12.23 p.m.

It's the beginning of a new year and our family and friends have finally forgiven us for getting married in secret. Last night we went out for dinner at my friend Shezadi's house in Tufnell Park. We were too lazy to get a taxi home but, thankfully, our neighbours above us have keys and agreed to feed Disco so we ended up staying the night, sleeping on the futon in the front room. Today is a beautiful sunny day. The kind of day that puts everyone in a good mood, so I suggest to Jim that we walk down to Camden because Shezadi told me last night about a lovely little café off the high street where Jim and I could have breakfast.

Outside there are loads of people just milling about chatting and as we walk along I keep looking into the windows of amazing three-storey houses, trying to imagine the lives of the people who live there. I can't begin to imagine Jim and me in a place like that.

As we approach Chalk Farm we walk past an estate agent's window. Every picture is of a loft apartment featuring wooden floors, huge windows and tasteful furniture. I turn to Jim and say, 'If money was no object, which apartment would we buy?'

Jim laughs. 'Ladies first.'

'How about this one?' I say, pointing to a newly built duplex in Islington.

'Too small,' says Jim. 'If this is meant to be a fantasy, you need to think big.'

'All right, then,' I say, mulling over a few more. 'What about this one?'

'Not enough square footage. There's barely enough room to swing Disco in the living room.'

'It's huge.'

'Well, think huger.'

I scan the windows again and then, finally, I see it: the apartment of my dreams, in Belsize Park. It's so expensive the details don't even feature a price. 'I've found the winner,' I say, pointing, barely able to contain my glee.

Jim follows the direction of my finger. 'Nice one. Now you're talking. It's fantastic.'

'Can you imagine it? It would be amazing to live there. I wonder what it looks like in real life.'

'Pretty much what it looks like in the pictures.'

'I'd love a place of our own,' I say, sighing, then pull on Jim's hand. 'Come on, or we'll be too late for breakfast.'

Jim doesn't move. 'Well, let's do it, then.'

'What?'

'Buy a place of our own.'

'We can't afford it.'

'We can't afford this,' he says, pointing to our dream apartment, 'but surely we can afford something a little more down to earth.'

'Are you sure?' I ask.

'Definitely,' says Jim. 'I love our flat but I think we're growing out of it, don't you? Plus it seems like every other night coming home on the tube the headline on the *Evening Standard* is something along the lines of "House Prices Set to Fall", or "London Property

Bubble Will Burst in the Next Fifteen Minutes'', or ''If You Don't Buy Property Right This Very Second You'll Never Get On the Property Ladder and You'll Be Renting For Ever''.' Jim laughs. 'I must admit, in my mind renting a place was always supposed to be a short-term thing. Paying out hundreds of pounds every month for something we don't own seems ridiculous. I thought you wouldn't be into the idea, though. I thought you'd reckon it was going to tie us down.'

'Now we're married, I think we actually need to put down some roots,' I tell Jim. 'You know, establish ourselves. I think we should do it.' I look at the picture of the amazing apartment again. 'Imagine if we had loads of money and we could afford to buy this!'

'It'd be great,' he replies. He pauses for a moment and then says: 'What if . . . ?'

'What if what?'

'What if we pretended we were going to buy it?'

Before I can say anything Jim has opened the estate agent's door and is already half-way inside.

## 12.45 p.m.

Alison and I take a seat in the waiting area. Ahead of us there are three glass-topped desks with no more than a cordless phone and a laptop on them. A bespectacled, black-suited, intriguingly haircutted agent, dealing with a couple, is sitting at each. The couple to the rear of the office look like barristers; the couple in the middle look like hairdressers; and the couple nearest to us look like they work in advertising. They have one thing in common: they all look like they earn an awful lot of money.

'Let's get out of here,' whispers Alison. 'We don't fit in at all.'

'Yeah, we do,' I say confidently. 'Just leave the talking to me.'

After about five minutes the couple who look like they work in advertising stand up and say goodbye to the estate agent. The dark-haired woman who has been assisting them looks up from her paperwork and catches my eye. For a split second I think I recognise her, then she goes completely wide-eyed and I know I do.

'I don't believe it!' she says, her hand clutching at her chest. 'Jim. Jim Owen.'

I can barely believe my eyes. 'It's not you, Anne, is it?' She nods. 'Anne Clarke.'

She still looks as great as she did at university. In fact, even more so. Everything about her is really cool and sophisticated.

'How are you?' she asks, coming from behind her desk to kiss my cheek.

'Great, thanks. How about you?'

'Fine. Really good. How long has it been?'

'Six years.'

'Never.'

'Give or take a few months.'

Anne laughs.

'You look great,' I say. 'Fantastic.'

'Really? Thanks.'

'Anne,' I say, turning to Alison, 'this is my wife, Alison. Alison, this is Anne Clarke . . . We were sort of friends at university.'

Everyone smiles and there's an awkward lull in the conversation.

'So, what brings you guys in here?' asks Anne.

'We're looking for a place to buy,' I say firmly.

'No, we're not,' says Alison.

'Yes, we are,' I reply.

Anne looks at us both, confused.

'We're really interested in the apartment in your window that's in Belsize Park.'

Anne taps on her laptop briefly. 'You mean this one?' she says, turning the screen to face us. 'It's a lovely property. It's only been on our books a few weeks. It's in immaculate condition.'

'Great,' I tell her. 'Immaculate condition's what we're looking for, you see.' I pause for a microsecond, then add, 'What with me being away on tour a lot. I'm in a band, you see. We've just signed to a record label in the States.'

'How exciting,' says Anne. 'This isn't the same band you were in at university, is it?'

'No,' I reply. 'We're called . . .' I pause and attempt to come up with the most 'band-like' name I can think of, '. . .Sidewalking.'

'And you're their singer?'

I nod.

'I can't believe you're famous.'

'I wouldn't say I'm famous exactly—'

'I'm so impressed,' says Anne. 'And to think I knew you at university. You must be so excited about everything that's happened.'

'We are,' says Alison tersely. 'We're over the moon.'

'Well,' says Anne, 'I've got some good news for you. We've got the keys here in the office so if you like we can go and view it now.'

'We're not doing anything special,' says Jim. 'That'll be great.'

'Excellent. Do you have transport?'

'Not with us.'

'That's okay, we'll take my car. Well, let me take down

your details and put them into the computer. Then, if you can give me a moment or two to fetch my coat, we can get off. I'm parked round the back so I'll meet you outside in a few moments.'

Anne takes down our completely fabricated details, then disappears through an exit marked 'Office', leaving Alison to stare at me in total disbelief.

'What are you doing?' she says. 'Are you mad? You are, aren't you? What was all that stuff about being in a band?'

'Do you know who she is?'

'I'm guessing she's more than just "a friend from university".'

'She was several months of torture and heartache.'

'Even so, you're not a millionaire rock star, you're an accountant. All she has to do is look up the band on the Internet and she'll know you're lying.'

'She won't do that. Trust me. She wants to believe it.'

'Believe what?'

'That some guy from her university days who used to worship her is now in a famous band. She'll dine out on this story for years.'

And with that we get up and make a swift exit.

## Sunday, 11 January 1998

### 3.56 p.m.

Alison and I are at our kitchen table taking a long, hard look at our financial situation to work out whether we'll be able to get a mortgage. Which is why I'm currently surrounded by credit-card receipts, store-card statements, bank statements and a million other bits of paper. Things on my side are fine. Things on Alison's side, however, aren't quite so good.

Job-wise it is going well for her: she's had two pay rises since she's been at Cooper and Lawton but her money-management skills have let her down. Her financial situation is dire.

'I can't believe it,' I say, reaching for the remains of a packet of mini-doughnuts we'd bought on a supermarket expedition yesterday.

'What?' asks Alison.

'How much debt you're in,' I say, taking one of the five sugar-coated doughnuts that are left. I drop it into my mouth and in three chews it has disappeared, leaving me free to moan at Alison. 'I mean, I always knew you were awful with money but not to this extent.'

'It's not lots of debt,' says Alison defensively. 'It's just a regular amount.'

'Alison, you're thousands of pounds in debt.'

'I know.'

I eye the doughnuts again, take another one and almost inhale it. 'According to your statements, you consistently go several hundred pounds' overdrawn five days before pay day.'

'It's when my half of the rent goes out.'

'You're up to your limit on three of your four credit cards and paying a huge amount of interest every month. When was the last time you tried to pay off any of what you owe?'

There's a long silence, which I use to have another two doughnuts one after the other.

'Oh, Alison,' I say despairingly, once I've finished chewing, 'tell me the answer isn't never.'

'I thought that was why you had credit cards – to put credit on them.'

'But you're also up to your limit on two store cards.'

'They offer it to you in the shop while you're standing at the till. How unfair is that? It makes you feel like you're getting it for free.'

'But that's not the end of the story. You've still got your student loan to pay off . . . and as if that's not enough, you've got a four thousand pound bank loan.'

'But that was for a car. A car's essential.'

'Alison, you haven't even got a car!'

'I know, I had the money sitting in my account for weeks and gradually it just sort of disappeared.'

'The fact is, Alison, whichever way we look at this, you're skint.'

'It's terrible, isn't it?' she says wincing. 'I've been meaning to sort it out for ages. Has it ruined everything? Is it bad?'

'Well, it's not looking very good.'

'But we can still get a mortgage, can't we?'

'They'll take all of this debt into consideration when we ask for the money, which will mean they might offer us less.'

Alison puts her head into her hands and I take the opportunity to sneak one last doughnut. 'They'll give us next to nothing and we'll end up living in some really rough part of London where the police don't go without guns and armoured trucks, and the flat we buy will have a crack den on one side and a brothel on the other and it will all be because I bought a couple of pairs of shoes in Selfridges.' She sighs heavily. 'Don't let me near a shop again, will you? If you see me get my cheque book out for anything other than a bill, shoot me.'

I can't help feeling sorry for her. 'We'll be fine,' I tell her. 'All it means is that we're going to have to tighten our belts a little and I'm going to use my savings for the deposit.'

'But that's the money you got after your dad died—'

'No buts,' I interrupt. 'I'm doing it and that's final. One way or another we're going to get a home of our own.'

Alison smiles weakly at me and then I smile weakly at her and then we both look at the empty packet of doughnuts. I suddenly feel guilty. Alison didn't get to eat a single one of them even though it had been she who had put them in our shopping basket. By all rights she should be having a go at me for this. But she doesn't of course because you can't really have a go at someone for eating a whole pack of mini-doughnuts when they've just done what I've just done. It wouldn't seem right. But it wouldn't have been all that wrong either.

## Friday, 6 February 1998

### 8.07 p.m.

We're on the Piccadilly Line just coming back from our first viewing. It was a second-floor flat in a house conversion on Green Lanes. I fell in love with it just looking at the estate agent's details. We both agreed it had potential. But the second we stepped out of Manor House tube station I knew Jim would hate the area because he saw an old man urinating against a lamp-post.

It has been difficult getting started on the house-hunting because we've got quite a limited budget even with the benefit of Jim's savings. The other problem is deciding whereabouts in London we want to live. I don't mind but Jim won't go anywhere except North London so with that decision made we've concentrated our search. We've agreed always to look at the places together and we've also agreed that we both have the right of veto. We've even come up with a system: I go round to as many estate agents as I can, making the appointments, while Jim concentrates on the money side and approaches mortgage-brokers and banks for the best deal. It feels like we're a real team.

'I still think we're casting our net too wide,' says Jim. 'I think we need to concentrate our search on proper North London.'

'What do you mean by 'proper North London'?'

He thinks for a moment. 'Anything on or near the Northern Line and in zones one to four.'

'Are you making this up?' I say incredulously. 'I've never known you to be so picky about anything like this before.'

'I'm not picky. I'm just being careful.'

I get out the mini-map of central London from the back of my Filofax and read out places on or near the Northern Line. Jim rejects Camden as 'too touristy and overpriced', Kentish Town as 'not too touristy but definitely overpriced', Primrose Hill as 'so overpriced it makes your eyes water', Tufnell Park as 'too grim for words', Archway as 'too desperate', Highgate as 'ideal, but too expensive', Muswell Hill as 'absolutely perfect', Crouch End as 'several million light years from the nearest tube'; and finally East Finchley as 'Okay, but it's not Muswell Hill, really, is it?'

'So basically,' I say, folding away the map, 'you're saying it's Muswell Hill ideally, Highgate if we win the lottery in the next few weeks and East Finchley at a push.'

Jim laughs. 'It sounds picky but you know it makes sense.'

## Saturday, 14 February 1998

### 8.34 a.m.

I'm just thinking about getting up when I hear the post being delivered. I look across at Jim who is fast asleep, quietly slip out of bed and sneak out to the front door to get the mail. Today is Valentine's Day and although I know it's wrong I'm still curious to see whether I'll get a card from Damon this year or whether he's finally decided to move on. As soon as I get to the door I can see a medium-sized cream envelope resting on top of a pile of bills. I open it immediately. Inside is a crisp white card with the word 'Love' embossed in small gold letters. Inside it reads: 'Hope this finds you happy. Thinking of you, D.'

## Tuesday, 17 February 1998

### 4 p.m.

I'm sitting at work looking through a heap of property details that came in the post this morning from a half-dozen different estate agents. So far I've managed to persuade Jim to look at a couple of places in East Finchley because they were considerably cheaper than Muswell Hill, but he always manages to find something wrong with them, a leaky roof, mad neighbours, noisy roads – you name it, he'll find it. He persuades me to look at a flat in Highgate that's on the very edge of what we can't afford, a tiny purpose-built one-bedroom flat in a horrible sixties block, and I hate it. As a compromise, a few days later, we look at some properties in the bit of North London that pretends to be Highgate even though it's just a posher version of Archway. We see some okay flats but Jim hates them all. We look at a few places in Muswell Hill. They're still pricy but I can tell from Jim's face that this is really where he wants to be.

## Saturday, 7 March 1998

### 12.47 p.m.

We've just seen a garden flat off the Broadway. It belongs to an Australian couple. They've done it up really well but they're going back to Australia and tell us that they need a quick sale. They're leaving carpets, curtains and even the cooker, and they want to sell us other stuff really cheaply. I think it's perfect. Like the answer to a prayer. I feel, deep in the pit of my stomach, that this is the one, but I have no idea what Jim thinks because he always does his grumpy poker face to keep the estate agent on his toes.

'What did you think?' I ask, once the estate agent is out of earshot.

'What did *you* think?' Jim replies.

'You can't answer a question with another question!'

Jim laughs. 'I just did.'

I decide to conceal my enthusiasm in case it makes Jim play devil's advocate, which he loves doing and winds me up beyond belief. 'Well . . . I think it's got potential,' I begin sceptically. 'Obviously it will need decoration and I wasn't sure about the size of the second bedroom—'

'Are you joking?' says Jim. 'It's bloody perfect. I love it. Two bedrooms. Tastefully decorated. A massive kitchen. And a garden for Disco to play in. It doesn't get any better than this. You're not going to veto, are you?'

'Maybe,' I say slyly. 'And then again maybe not . . .' As I say the words my own poker face crumbles. 'I can't keep this up, babe. I love it. I love it more than any flat we've seen so far. I think we should offer the full asking price right now.'

'Right now?'

'It's Saturday. Think how many other couples are probably booked in to see it.'

'But the full asking price? We're first-time buyers, we've got nothing to sell. We can use all this as leverage to get the price down.'

'I don't care about leverage, Jim. I want us to have this flat. I can just see us in it, can't you? This could be our home. The home we have a first child in. The home that will give us the best memories of our life.'

Jim laughs. 'Well, I can't argue with destiny, can I? Let's put the full offer in now.' He gets out his mobile phone and calls the estate agent. I'm so nervous I have to walk away.

'What did they say?' I ask anxiously, when it's clear the conversation is over.

'They say they'll call us back by the end of the day.'

### 4.56 p.m.

We're standing in WHSmith on the Broadway looking for a belated birthday card for Nick three weeks after the event, when Jim's mobile rings in the pocket of his denim jacket. He takes it out and we both look at it in shock before he has the good sense to answer it. Once again I have to walk away to keep my composure so I stand by the magazine section and watch from my position of relative safety. Even though it's somewhat futile I can see that his poker face is back again. The conversation seems to last for ever with no indication of whether it's bad or good news. After a few minutes or so Jim ends the call and I walk back to him. The poker face is gone. In its place is the biggest, brightest smile I've seen in ages.

'It's good news,' he says. 'They've accepted. I'm going to contact our solicitor and get a survey under way for next week because part of the agreement is that we're supposed to exchange contracts within six weeks.'

'It's really going to happen?' I ask him incredulously.

'Looks like it,' he replies.

And right there in the middle of WHSmith, next to a whole display of *Good Housekeeping* magazines, we kiss.

## Monday, 6 April 1998

### 1.34 p.m.

I'm standing in the furniture department at the Oxford Street branch of John Lewis having just ordered a cream sofa. For the past few weeks I've spent my lunch breaks visiting what feels like every furniture store in central London in search of the perfect sofa (right colour, shade, size and material) that would look perfect in the living room of our new home. My excitement about the flat is building to such an extent that I can't concentrate on anything but homes magazines and home makeover programmes on TV. I'm obsessed, yet happily so.

## Friday, 24 April 1998

### 1.31 p.m.

Jim and I went to the solicitor's to sign the contracts yesterday evening. We're supposed to be exchanging with the couple we're buying from this afternoon. I'm heading out to a sandwich shop to get my lunch when I pass a small printer's shop. I can't help myself. Right there and then I order fifty change-of-address cards. They say I can pick them up the following afternoon. When I get back from lunch there's a message from Jim. I ring him back immediately.

'The estate agent rang,' says Jim.

His voice isn't right. I can tell something is wrong. 'What did they want?'

'They've taken it off the market.'

'Who?'

'The couple we're buying the flat from.'

'I don't understand.'

'We've lost the flat. They said they've changed their minds about going to Australia.'

I can't believe what I'm hearing. 'We should phone them,' I say tearfully. 'Explain to them that they can't do this. They can't treat people like this. Maybe they'll understand and change their minds.'

'It's their home. They can do what they want.'

'But what about all the money we've spent already?'

'We've lost it.'

'But – but I've bought change-of-address cards. They have to let us buy the flat.'

'I know, babe,' says Jim. 'But there's nothing we can do.'

### 2.02 p.m.

It's strange but I'm not prepared for how hard this news has hit me. I just burst into tears when I put down the phone after talking to Jim. I'm inconsolable. Here Jim and I are, trying to sort out our future, and the present won't even let us get off the ground. I really don't think I've ever felt so let down in my entire life. People at work keep telling me that there will be other flats and that this is all part of the game, but I don't see it like that. I don't see it like that at all. Jim's the only one who understands, I think. He's the only one who knows what this feels like.

## Saturday, 9 May 1998

### 9.07 a.m.

'I think Jim and I have become a lot closer,' I tell Jane on the phone. 'Closer than we've ever been. I feel like it's me and him against the world.'

'What are you going to do now?' she asks.

'We've decided to stop looking for a while. I don't think either of us is in the right frame of mind to carry on. We're already down quite a bit of money because of the last deal falling through. The whole thing is just so demoralising. The downside, of course, is that now it feels like we're stuck here in this flat. Things that we used to ignore before, like the leaky tap in the kitchen, or that the front door won't open without brute force, or the guys in the flat above us who leave their mountain bikes in the communal hallway, really get us both down. Even worse it turned out that the couple were lying about not going to Australia. Jim spotted the flat go back on sale with a different estate agent last week with a new sale price several thousand pounds higher than before. They'd just got greedy. When Jim told me this, I said to him, "Why are we even bothering? Everything seems to be against us."'

'What did he say?'

'He didn't say anything. He just put his arms around me and gave me a hug.'

## Friday, 22 May 1998

### 6.37 a.m.

Our depression about losing the flat has gone. We've come right through to the other side. In fact, now it almost feels like what happened has brought us closer. Jim and I are so happy together that it's almost ridiculous. We laugh and joke all the time, and even the flat's not getting us down. Things are perfect. He's got a meeting in Leeds today, which is why he's up early. I'm up early because I woke up this morning with the desire to be the perfect wife. While he got ready I made him breakfast, even though I could've quite legitimately stayed in bed for another hour at least. Love, I think, makes you do the strangest things.

'Right, then,' says Jim, putting on his suit jacket. 'I'd better be off otherwise I'll miss the train.' He walks into the hallway and I follow him in my dressing-gown, yawning. 'I have no idea how long I'm going to be in Leeds so don't worry about dinner for me. We'll probably eat up there.' He kisses me. 'See you later tonight, then.'

As he pulls away I notice a speck of shaving cream on his cheek. I lick my thumb and, in one swift movement, rub it off. 'Shaving cream,' I explain.

'Cheers, I would've been like that all day if you hadn't spotted it.'

'Well, we can't have you looking like a scruff, can we?'

'No, we can't', he says. 'See you tonight, babe.' He kisses me again, picks up his bag and walks out. And as I close the door behind him I suddenly think about all of the things that need doing that I think of as my responsibility: the washing-up in the sink, the huge pile of dirty clothes in the laundry basket, all of the ironing waiting for me in the spare room and the cat's litter tray that needs emptying and I think to myself, just for a second, When did I become this person?

## Monday, 1 June 1998

### 7.05 a.m.

I'm standing in the bathroom post-shower staring at the partially steamed-up mirror in front of me. I've been like this for ten minutes or so and, with each passing second, I have been getting more and more depressed.

'What are you doing in there?' says a muffled Alison, from the other side of the bathroom door. 'I need the loo.'

I open the door and let her in.

'Have you finished whatever it was you were doing?'

'I'm going to ask you a question,' I say, returning to the mirror, 'and I want you to be truthful. Don't sugar-coat it. And don't worry about my feelings. Just tell me how it is, okay?'

Alison studies me with a mixture of amusement and curiosity. 'Okay.'

'Are you ready for the question? Okay, here we go: am I losing my hair?'

I lower my head so Alison can get a good look at my scalp.

'It's fine,' she replies, after a few moments. 'You're worrying about nothing.'

I look in the mirror again. 'Are you sure?'

I lower my head and she looks again. 'Yeah, absolutely.'

'Are you sure you're sure or are you just saying that to make me feel better?'

'I'm sure,' says Alison firmly.

I nod, then peer into the mirror again, moving my head into the weirdest angles to get a good view of my scalp.

'I am losing my hair, aren't I?' I say.

'No. It's fine.'

'It's okay, you can tell me straight.'

'There's nothing wrong with your hair. It's great. It's fantastic.'

'But, Al, I can see my scalp from here. It's definitely thinning.'

She looks again. 'Maybe a few hairs have gone from where you're looking but that's all.' She examines the back of my head. 'You've got loads of hair here. Loads of it.'

'But it's at the back where I can't see it. The bit I'm worried about is here . . .' I point to my crown '. . . where all the light is bouncing off my head. Look, just admit it for my own peace of mind so that I can come to terms with the loss of my youth, okay? I'm losing my hair, aren't I?'

Alison nods apologetically. ''Fraid so.'

'How bad is it?'

She puts down the loo lid. 'Sit down here and I'll give you a full diagnosis.

I do as she says despondently and wait for her verdict. 'How's it looking?' I ask.

'It's pretty bad,' she replies. 'Some thinning at the front. Major thinning on the crown. Overall it's not looking too good. There's no doubt about it, you're going B-A-L-D.' She pauses, then adds: 'But bald is sexy. Think about it. Bruce Willis is bald and still a major Hollywood star, Michael Stipe from REM is definitely losing his hair and Jane really fancies him . . .' she begins laughing '. . . and Homer Simpson from

*The Simpsons* is bald and Marge adores him, just like I adore you.' She bends and kisses my crown and, though I hate to admit it because I was determined to sulk about this, in less than five minutes she's made me feel a lot better about saying goodbye to my hair.

## Sunday, 21 June 1998

### 10.30 p.m.

Jim and I are in bed and we're reading, which is nice in a cosy kind of way but extremely dull in a married-couple-not-having-sex kind of way. Jim's half-way through the latest issue of *What Car?* because he's been promised a company car and I'm reading *Cosmopolitan*.

'Jim?'

'Yeah?'

'Do you think we have enough sex now that we're married?'

'Pardon?'

'I said, do you think we have enough sex now that we're married? It's just that I'm reading this article and according to this chart,' I wave the magazine in front of his eyes for effect, 'we're below average for a married couple.'

'It's nothing to worry about.'

'Well, I know this is going to sound paranoid but that's the average, yeah?' He nods and I continue, 'So that means there are people out there like us who are having less than the national average.' He nods again. 'And there are people having more than their fair share.'

'True.'

'In which case there are married people out there who are having more sex than we are.'

'So?'

'Don't you wonder who they are? Who are these above-average married people having more sex than we are?'

'But it's not like they're having our fair share, is it? It's not like the very fact that these people are having sex means that we can't have more sex. In fact, it's the opposite. It means that we can have less sex – not that that is a desirable thing,' he adds hastily. 'But it's like this, they have more, which means there's more in the pot, so to speak, for the rest of us to share.'

'I don't want somebody else's sex,' I say, semi-outraged. 'That's horrible. A complete stranger's sex-life is making up for our own. No,' I slam down the magazine, 'if I'm going to have sex I want it at least to be our own.'

'Look, Alison, don't you think this is a little ridiculous? You're going to give yourself a heart-attack at this rate.'

'At this rate? What rate? When was the last time we did it?'

'Last weekend.'

'Nope. It was the weekend before that.'

'But I've been at work.'

'And I've been busy at work too but that's no excuse. Aren't you worried that we're not normal?'

Jim looks at me blankly. 'Fine, then,' he says. 'Let's do it.'

## Saturday, 27 June 1998

### 9.37 a.m.

I'm lying in bed watching kids' TV on my portable while trying to motivate myself to get out of bed when Alison returns to the bedroom from a trip to the loo.

'I think I might be pregnant,' she says.

At the mere mention of those words my stomach muscles tighten and I sit bolt upright in our bed. 'You think you might be what?'

'Pregnant.'

'Are you late?'

'No,' she replies. 'I'm not due for another two days.'

'Did you forget to take your pill then?'

'No,' she says, 'I never forget.'

'So why do you think you're pregnant?'

'I don't know,' she says. 'I've just got a feeling.'

'A feeling?'

'Well, I do have a feeling. I don't know where it came from but it's there and it won't budge for love or money. It's a nightmare. It's like I'm possessed.'

I glance at Alison's stomach to see if she looks any different. 'You'll have to give up smoking, won't you?'

'If I'm pregnant.'

'But you've just said you think you are.'

'I said I think I might be, which isn't the same thing.'

'But if you think you are, shouldn't you give up smoking now, just in case?'

'And what if I'm not?'

'Then you'll have given up smoking.'

Alison doesn't reply. She just sighs, gets her dressing-gown and leaves the room.

## Sunday, 28 June 1998

### 6.06 a.m.

I've just woken up and I'm busy trying to get myself back to sleep again when I realise that Jim's awake too, as is Disco, who is lying at the end of the bed.

'Has it arrived?' he asks.

'What?'

'Your . . . you know.'

'No.'

'Oh.'

## 3.30 p.m.

Jim and I have gone out for lunch with some friends of mine from work. I've just returned from a trip to the loo to check my makeup when he whispers something in my ear.

'Pardon?'

He whispers again.

'Jim, I have no idea what you've just said. Speak properly.'

He coughs and suddenly looks shifty. 'I was just asking if . . . er . . . you know . . . there's any sign yet?'

'Of my—?'

'Yes, of that.'

I roll my eyes in despair. 'No.'

'Oh.'

'Jim?'

'Yeah.'

'Are you going to ask me constantly until it arrives?'

He thinks for a moment. 'Yeah, I think so. Is that going to be a problem?'

I sigh heavily. 'As soon as I know anything you'll be the first to hear about it.'

## 6.01 p.m.

I'm off to Brighton for the company's annual conference, so Alison's decided to see me off at the station.

'Well, I'd better be off,' I tell her.

She kisses me. 'See you on Wednesday. Have a good journey.'

I pick up my bags and manage to walk about three steps before I have to turn around. 'Al?'

'Before you ask,' she says, 'the answer is no. As in no sign at all. As in nothing. As in there are no biological signs that my period is on its way.'

'Nothing at all?'

'You do know that I'm going to have to kill you if you carry on like this.'

I still can't help myself. 'But you're sure?'

## Wednesday, 1 July 1998

### 9.15 p.m.

I've dragged Nick, who moved to London a few months ago, to the pub on the pretext of drinking alcohol and talking. I haven't touched my pint all evening and have barely said a word.

'So come on,' says Nick. 'Are you going to tell me what's wrong? You've been about as much fun as a corpse all evening. Was Brighton *that* bad?'

'I'm going to tell you something,' I reply, 'but you have to remember that it's top secret.'

'Great,' he says grinning. 'I love secrets. Al's not pregnant, is she?'

'How did you—?'

Nick lets out a huge deep laugh. And continues so uncontrollably that he can barely breathe. 'I was only having a laugh,' he says, between guffaws. 'She's not really . . . you know . . . is she?' I shrug. 'What do you mean?'

'I mean, women and their hunches,' I explain. 'Just because they have a slightly more complicated biological mechanism than ours they think they're in tune with the moon and the sea and all the elements. What is it about women that makes them all think they've latent psychic powers just because they've got a uterus? It's ridiculous and all this horoscope nonsense just feeds the frenzy. Because without any proof at all Alison has managed to convince herself that she's pregnant.'

'But there's no proof?'

'I've tried to tell myself that there isn't a single shred of evidence but in the face of a wave of overwhelming hoopla from Alison I've lost my nerve. It's the way she keeps banging on that she's just got a feeling. What kind of proof is that? Science isn't based on having feelings. It's based on having completely and utterly one hundred per cent irrefutable proof.'

'Well, from what I can remember of my O level physics a lot of it is initially based on gut feeling, then they go out and prove it scientifically.'

'You're not helping, you know.'

'I know. Look, just forget it. Chances are that she isn't.'

'The thing is, Alison's good at spreading the paranoia. The more she goes on about it the more worried I become that I have super sperm that could somehow single-handedly defeat the pill—'

'Tails.'

'What?'

'Sperm don't have hands they have tails. If they were going to defeat the pill with anything they'd use their tails.'

'You're loving this, aren't you?'

'What's the worst thing that could happen? She'll be pregnant, you two guys will become parents and I'll be a godfather.'

'It's not just the baby though – although that's enough in itself – it's . . .'

'It's what?'

'I don't know,' I sigh. 'I'm not thinking straight. I haven't been sleeping well and it's got me talking rubbish . . . Let's just have another pint, eh?'

Nick shrugs. 'Why not?'

## Friday, 3 July 1998

### 8.01 a.m.

Alison's in the shower and I'm lying in bed thinking about whether or not she might be pregnant. I've barely slept all week and every conversation I've had with her has started with the words, 'Before you ask . . .' The thing is, a big part of me isn't convinced I want a baby yet. But I can't help feeling that maybe I'm being selfish; if Alison really wants a baby then why should I stop her? After all, we're happy, married . . . A baby might be the best thing that could happen to us right now . . . When I hear her coming out of the bathroom I get out of bed; despite feeling faintly sick, I'm determined to tell her of my new state of mind.

'Morning, babe,' I say, as she enters the room wearing just her towelling dressing-gown.

'You can stop panicking,' she says. 'It's here.'

'It as in "it"?'

She nods.

'You're a hundred per cent sure?' She nods. 'How do you feel?'

'Relieved . . . and maybe a little bit disappointed. Life's about building and creating things, isn't it?'

'I suppose,' I reply.

'Why don't we put it on the list?'

'What list?'

'You know,' she says, brightly, 'the big list. The life list. The long list of all the things we want to do with our lives. We're already doing well so far. We're together, our careers are going well, we're married, and if we ever get a flat we'll have another one done too.'

I frown. 'How high on your list do you want it?' I ask, noncommittally.

'How about a millennium baby?' she replies.

'Fine,' I say, even though two years seems too close. 'But for now let's just concentrate on the present.'

## Saturday, 4 July 1998

### 11.09 a.m.

Alison and I are currently standing in Flat 4A, Crescent Gardens. It's a garden flat half-way between Muswell Hill and Crouch End. Alison spotted it in the estate agent's window last Thursday and got the details even though she knew it wasn't exactly close to the tube. She persuaded me to come and see it, and now that I'm here I absolutely love it. It belongs to an elderly lady, who's going into an old people's home, and it needs pretty much everything doing to it – new wiring, new bathroom and kitchen, redecorating from top to bottom – but I can definitely see the potential. It's so much bigger than the majority of places we saw last time, and with it being a garden flat there's the possibility of extending it and maybe getting an extra room. Half-way through the viewing I can see that Alison's getting excited but I tell her we shouldn't jump the gun this time, we should make sure we're happy with everything before we make an offer. She agrees, and appears to be putting on her best poker face until we visit the kitchen for the second time.

'Look,' she whispers, so the estate agent won't overhear us.

'Where am I looking?'

She's pointing at the door that leads to the back garden. 'We have to buy it now,' she says. 'It's already got a cat-flap.'

'And?'

'Well, we wouldn't have to put one in for Disco, would we?'

'You want to buy this flat above all others just because it's got a cat-flap?'

'No, but you have to admit it's a good sign. It's cat-friendly.'

'Okay,' I reply. 'I think we should make an offer. But, cat-friendly or not, we should be prepared for it not to happen because they're asking way too much for this place.'

Alison laughs. 'Great,' she says, adopting a poor American accent. 'Let's play hardball.'

## Thursday, 9 July 1998

### 12.45 p.m.

I'm sitting at my desk, thinking about what I'm going to have for lunch, when my phone rings.

'Hello, Publicity.'

'Hi, it's me,' says Jim. 'Good news.'

'You've heard from the estate agent?'

'Yes.'

'And?'

'And . . . they've . . .'

'"They've" what?' I say exasperatedly.

Jim lets out a yell. 'They've accepted!'

## Thursday, 6 August 1998

### 5.25 p.m.

We've been asked to come into our solicitor's office to sign the contracts. Now it's all done we're standing outside the offices of de Gray and Hampton.

'How does it feel to be officially in debt for hundreds of thousands of pounds?' I ask Alison.

'Not bad, I suppose,' she says, grinning.

'No regrets?'

Alison shakes her head. 'None whatsoever.'

As we head back to the flat we pass an off-licence so I go in and buy a bottle of Moët and Chandon. When we get back to the flat we drink the lot with our first Indian takeaway in months while Disco eats a very posh brand of cat food – gourmet chicken dinner, the most expensive we can find in the supermarket.

## Saturday, 22 August 1998

### 10 a.m.

We're in our flat. Our new home. When the estate agent handed the keys over to us half an hour ago I thought Alison was going to cry. Right now, however, she seems deliriously happy. She's wandering around all the rooms in our poorly decorated flat squealing with delight. 'These are our walls!' she yells in the kitchen, so loudly that Disco runs out of the room.

'These are our light switches!' she screams in the hallway.

'See this horrible 1970s brown carpet in the living room?' she asks, pointing to it. 'It belongs to us!'

'And what about the smell of old ladies?' I ask. 'Who does that belong to?'

Alison sniffs the air. 'You're right. It doesn't so much *smell* of old ladies as *reek*.' Alison walks across to the door and sniffs the wallpaper. 'I think it's in the bricks, you know. I think the actual bricks that make up our home have been permeated with the essence of old lady. We're never going to get rid of this smell, ever. It's going to live with you, me and Disco for the rest of our lives.'

## Friday, 28 August 1998

### 9.09 a.m.

I'm at work thinking about the flat. Jim and I spent all last night talking about it. It's only now we've moved in that we can see how much work it's going to take even to get the place looking okay. It's more work than we can do by ourselves, which means we're going to have to get builders in. The only thing stopping us is money: we have none. I've just had an idea, though, that might solve all our problems.

### 10.03 a.m.

'Jim, it's me,' I say, when he picks up the phone.

'Hi, babe. What can I do for you?'

'I've been thinking about the flat and I might have got a solution.' I pause for dramatic effect. 'I've asked my dad to lend us the money.'

'You've done what?'

'He's said it's fine and we'll have a cheque by the end of the week.'

'I wish you'd asked me before you did this.'

'Why?'

'So you could've heard me say, "No." As nice as he is, I don't want to borrow money off your dad. He'll think I can't look after you properly.'

Jim's words stop me in my tracks. It has never occurred to me that he wants to look after me in the old-fashioned sense of the phrase. I think it's possibly the most adorable thing I've ever heard him say to me. I don't mention it to him, though, because I know he'll get embarrassed and say something that will spoil the moment.

'You're right,' I tell him. 'Shall I call him back and tell him not to send the cheque?'

'Do you think I'm overreacting about this?'

'No, you're right. I'm a grown-up. I shouldn't need to be borrowing money off my parents.'

Jim laughs. 'But, then, again, the carpets in the living room are very brown and very seventies . . .'

'. . . and there's the old lady smell . . .' I reply.

'. . . and if we don't get the place rewired soon we'll probably be fried to a crisp in our sleep . . .' adds Jim.

'. . . and winter's coming and the draughts coming through the windows are ridiculous . . .' I put in.

'. . . and we've got no central heating,' says Jim, laughing. 'I think I've just talked myself out of having any principles at all.'

## Saturday, 12 September 1998

### 11.01 a.m.

I'm about to put out the bins when the doorbell rings. I know who it is, though. It's the builder we're thinking of hiring. We couldn't get anyone to recommend one because everyone we knew who had had builders said they wouldn't recommend them to their worst enemies so I did some research. I got six from the *Yellow Pages* to come round and give us quotes so I could see what they were like face to face. Of the six we've waited in for, this is the only one to show up.

'Hi,' I say, answering the door to a tall ferret-like man with a beard.

'I'm Mr Norman from A1 Plus Building Construction Ltd,' he says, in a strong Essex accent, offering his hand.

I shake it and invite him in and as we walk into the living

room Disco takes one look at him and disappears behind the sofa. Alison and I show him round the flat and tell him what we want done – a new kitchen, the wall knocking down between the living room and the dining room, replastering in the two bedrooms, a new bathroom and all the floorboards sanded and varnished. He doesn't seem fazed by any of it.

'So,' I say, leading Mr Norman to the front door having agreed a rough estimate for the job, 'how long do you think it'll take you to do the work?'

He looks at his pad as if making a rough calculation. 'Six weeks,' he says eventually.

'Six weeks?' I say. 'Are you sure?'

'Absolutely. We don't hang around, Mr Owen. We should be done in four but I've said six to be on the safe side.'

'But no matter what happens, you'll be done in six weeks?'

'On my mother's life.'

'I know I've just asked you this,' I tell him, 'but you're one hundred per cent sure that the whole job will be finished from top to bottom in six weeks? It's just that we've had a lot of friends who've had builders in and, well, their six weeks quite often ends up being a lot longer.'

'They've probably used cowboys,' he says. 'There's a lot of them about. And, frankly, they're a blot on the face of the trade. But I guarantee you, Mr Owen, that when I say six weeks for a job I mean six weeks . . . or less.'

While Mr Norman puts away his notepad Alison and I exchange glances. I shrug, Alison nods and the deal is done.

I clear my throat as if making an announcement: 'I'm pleased to tell you, Mr Norman, that you've got the job.'

'Great,' he replies. 'We'll see you bright and early Monday morning.'

## Monday, 14 September 1998

### 7.33 p.m.

Jim and I have just got back from work and we are amazed. Our home now looks like a bombsite. They got off to a good start at seven this morning when ten men arrived on our doorstep in four flatbed trucks, and it seems that the work continued at top speed all day because there's now a huge skip outside our home, which is full to the brim. Jim is flabbergasted. 'I can't believe how much they've done,' he says. 'It's a good job we took Disco to the cattery. She'd hate all this.'

'You're right,' I say. 'Looking on the bright side, though, she'll be home soon. There's no way it's going to take them six weeks to finish. At this rate they'll be done before we know it.'

## Tuesday, 15 September 1998

### 12.17 p.m.

I'm just about to go to a lunch meeting with a new cookery-book author when the phone rings.

'Hello, Publicity,' I say.

'Could I speak to Mrs Owen, please?'

I can tell straight away that it's Mr Norman.

'Hello,' I say cheerily. 'It's Alison Owen here, Mr Norman. What is it you'd like to talk to me about?'

'Ah, yes, it's just to let you know that there's been a bit of an accident.'

'What kind of accident?'

'One of the lads managed to burst a pipe in the bathroom.'

'What?'

'There's nothing to worry about, Mrs Owen, just some water damage, but that's not the real problem.'

'First,' I snap, 'how much water damage is there? And second, what is the *real* problem?'

'I'll be straight with you. The water in the bathroom was an inch deep but we've mopped it up now although the people in the basement flat might want a word with you. We've managed to stop the water coming out but we need to get a plumber in before we can do any more work.'

'How long will that take?'

'Well, that's the thing. The plumber we use is booked up for the next three weeks, which, of course, will have a knock-on effect on all the rest of the work so basically we've packed up and we won't be back till then.'

'But you've only been working two days,' I say desperately. 'And you said you'd be done in six weeks.'

'That was more of a rough estimate. To be truthful, Mrs Owen, I think we're looking at quite a bit longer.'

## Monday, 2 November 1998

### 11 p.m.

The mattress that Alison and I are lying on is currently the closest thing we have to a bed as everything else is in storage. Alison is so grumpy because of the builders that I'm afraid for my life. The six-week self-imposed deadline has come and gone and they are now slowly driving us insane. They don't listen to anything we say, they've installed things upside down and the wrong way round – you name it, they've done it. Worse still, Alison and I have been living, sleeping, eating (and dying a little on the inside) in one room – the rear bedroom – for weeks. For the past week and a half we've had no bathroom so we've been showering at the gym. We haven't had a cooker for even longer so we've been eating either takeaways or microwaved food. I bought a camping-gas stove a fortnight ago but after one evening meal too many of beans on toast Alison now screams at the mere sight of the can-opener. And if that's not enough, it's now costing twice the original estimate to do all the necessary work. We had to go back to the mortgage-lenders a month ago and practically beg them for some more money. For a while, it was touch and go as to whether they'd give it to us.

'I'm going to go to sleep,' I tell Alison, and I turn off my light. She doesn't reply. Regardless, I reach across to kiss her goodnight and she pulls away.

'What's wrong with you?' I ask short-temperedly.

'Nothing,' hisses Alison.

'Fine,' I snap.

'I feel like the builders are taking over our lives,' says Alison, unprompted.

'That's because they are.'

'Well, it's all your fault that things are like this.'

'My fault?'

'You let them walk all over you. You're a man, you should be standing up to them.'

'Hang on. Whatever happened to sexual equality? Why don't you bloody well stand up to them if I'm such a lady-boy?'

'I'm just saying you should stand up to them. I'd do it myself but they never take me seriously. I don't see why I should do everything.'

'But you don't do everything.'

'This is just great,' snaps Alison. 'You'd much rather lie here arguing with me than argue with the builders.'

'I tell you what, you're wrong. At this exact moment in

time I'd rather be in bed with one of the builders than with you. They might be a bit rough around the edges but at least they'd have the decency not to be a walking gob on legs.'

### 11.11 p.m.

Once again we're lying in neither of our usual positions that involve touching or spooning but rather we're silently fuming with each other.

'Jim?' whispers Alison.

Here we go again. It's our post-row, pre-making up ritual, only this time . . .

'Hmm?' I mutter noncommittally.

'Are you talking to me?'

I say nothing because I'm not talking to her.

'So you're not talking to me?'

I allow myself to shrug because it's not really talking.

'Well, listen,' she says quietly. 'I'm sorry.'

'That's okay.' I sigh. 'I'm sorry too.'

'Friends?' she says, rubbing my calf with her foot.

I don't reply, but Alison takes my silence as an affirmative.

'I hate those sodding builders,' says Alison vengefully. 'I'm not just saying that. I do, really. I *hate* them. Any excuse and they stop work – a national shortage of trained plasterers, suppliers sending the wrong parts, adverse weather conditions, too cold, too wet, too hot, too windy, mysterious electrical faults . . . The list is endless. Do you know what? I came home tonight and it looked like the only thing they'd moved all day was the kettle so that they could make themselves a cup of tea.'

'I think that's what they do all day – drink tea and read the sodding *Daily Star*.'

'What I'd give to have five minutes with them with their

hands tied behind their backs and me armed with a blunt instrument.'

'That's a bit violent,' I say, coolly.

'That's how they make me feel. I feel like they're taking our dream and smashing it. Honestly, they're like the children in that Graham Greene short story where the kids systematically vandalise a house just for the sheer fun of it. What's it called again? It's going to bug me all night if I can't remember.'

'I have no idea what you're talking about. I've never read any Graham Greene.'

'I thought everyone did that story at school. It's like Shakespeare. Didn't you do it?'

'Afraid not. Anyway, it's late now. Let's try and get some sleep.' I kiss her. 'Goodnight, then.'

'I've got his short stories somewhere,' she says grumpily. 'I'm going to find out what it's called.'

As I watch her pull on her dressing-gown and leave the room, I begin to wonder if she's not joking about the builders driving her insane. She's gone for almost half an hour. I'm considering going to find her, even though we're suffering sub-zero temperatures in the flat, when she finally returns.

'"The Destructors",' she says, wearily flopping into bed. 'That's what it's called.'

'Oh,' I reply. 'Well, goodnight, anyway, babe.'

There's a long silence and I think she's drifted off to sleep so I turn over on to my side.

'Jim?' she says, through a stifled yawn.

'Yeah.'

'At least once this is done we'll have everything fixed before we try for a baby, won't we?' 'Hmm,' I reply, and then I fall asleep.

## Friday, 4 December 1998

### 4.02 p.m.

The decorators have gone, the last of the builders went this morning, and we've wiped the brick dust off the entire flat and it sparkles. Our home is ours once again and it looks amazing.

'We're here,' I say to Jim, J-cloth in hand, as we stand in our brand new kitchen.

'Where?' asks Jim.

'You know. That place. That place where you're supposed to be. The place where everything comes together. Where everything works. Where everything is just right and exactly the way you want it to be.'

'What about the cracks in the plaster in the bathroom?' says Jim.

'After all we've been through these past few months a few cracks in the bathroom plaster are the least of our problems. Everything is as it should be. All we need to do now is live happily ever after.'

## Thursday, 31 December 1998

### 11.59 p.m.

The four of us are standing on Prince's Street watching the fireworks, having decided to drive up in Nick's new company car and spend New Year's Eve in Edinburgh. As it gets closer to midnight a countdown begins from ten. On the stroke of midnight a million and one fireworks explode into the air, filling the sky with colour. We all wish each other a happy new year and join in with everyone around us singing 'Auld Lang Syne' even though I'm sure we don't know all the words.

'Just think,' says Jane, 'this time next year will be the year 2000. A brand new millennium.'

'Technically speaking,' says Nick, 'the millennium isn't until 2001, given there wasn't a year nought.'

Jane and I roll our eyes.

'Stop being such a boy,' says Jane. 'The fact is, everyone in the world – apart from Nick – will be celebrating the millennium this time next year.'

Nick laughs. 'I bet you there'll be a huge rise in births too. People always make big decisions around momentous occasions.'

'Jim and I have decided we're going to start trying for a baby in 2000,' I say, smiling at Jim. He doesn't return my smile, though. He just looks at the ground.

'That's brilliant,' says Jane. 'I can't wait to be a godmother.' She adds, 'I do get to be your baby's godmother, don't I?'

'Absolutely,' I say. 'Jim and I wouldn't have it any other way.'

'And I'm going to be their baby's godfather,' interjects Nick. 'Jim's already given me the okay. So you can abandon any ideas you might have of sole responsibility for imparting spiritual wisdom to their kid because I'm going to have a few things to say.'

'About what?' says Jane. 'You can't just read out the contents of a packet of fortune cookies.'

'Now, now, children,' I interrupt. 'If you both carry on like this neither of you will get the privilege, okay? Anyway, Baby Owen isn't here yet, and there's a whole year ahead of us before we even have to think about making him arrive so let's just enjoy 1999, shall we? It's going to be mine and Jim's last chance to be recklessly youthful before we have to settle down and become parents for the rest of our lives. So, let's go back to the hotel, raid the mini-bar and drink until we fall over.'

Everyone laughs, except Jim, so I walk over to him and put my arms around him.

'What's wrong, sweetheart? Got the new-year blues?'

'I don't know how to say this,' he begins.

I can see from his face that he's serious. 'Say what?'

'This. Us. This whole thing. I'm really sorry but it's not working any more. At least, not for me. I think we need to spend some time apart.'

I can't believe what I'm hearing. 'You're not making sense, Jim.'

There's a long silence.

'I just need some space to get my head together, that's all.'

'You can't do this,' I say, fighting back tears. 'We've made a home together. We're happy. Whatever's going on with you it's just a blip . . . We'll be okay.' I put my arms around him and squeeze tightly as the tears roll down my face. 'We still love each other,' I tell him. 'I still love you.'

'That's just the thing,' he says. 'I'm not sure I do love you any more.'

# PART SIX

## Then: 1999

# 1999

## Friday, 1 January 1999

### 2.10 a.m.

Nick and I are in his car going back to London. Alison and Jane are back at the hotel and I assume will get the train to King's Cross tomorrow. We haven't spoken about what's gone on and it's unlikely that we will for a few days as I'm not even sure myself. The car's heaters are on so it's warm, and pitch dark outside. Combined with the constant purring of the engine and the music coming from his CD player, I feel like I'm in the safest place in the world. As we travel into the night I think about Alison. I'm devastated that I've hurt her this way. And I'm not the kind of person who uses a word like 'devastated' lightly. I'm not devastated when the video craps up and doesn't tape *Seinfeld*. I'm not devastated when I walk out of a tube station, step on a loose paving slab and a puddle of rainwater soaks my trousers. I'm not devastated when my computer breaks down and I lose a whole day's work. I am, however, devastated to realise I'm no longer in love with the woman I wanted to grow old with.

It hit a couple of weeks ago, in the supermarket of all places. It was Saturday morning and Alison and I were at

Sainsbury's in Muswell Hill. It appeared to be populated entirely by cute, trendy, cohabiting couples several years younger than us. They were everywhere I looked, with their faded jeans, logoed T-shirts, perfectly coiffed hair and obligatory air of smugness. They paraded around with their tiny shopping baskets as I piloted a hulking pushalong trolley – which held only a copy of *The Independent* and a large bag of watercress – and I thought to myself, *Alison and I used to be like you. We used to do our shopping with tiny baskets. We used to be trendy. I used to be cool. I even used to be the lead singer of a band. Really I did.*

As I stood in the fruit-and-veg aisle I spotted an incredibly beautiful girl coming through the doors. She was stunning. Absolutely beautiful in a million different ways. A goddess. She looked about twenty and had long dark brown hair. She wasn't wearing anything special: a denim jacket, a blue V-neck jumper, jeans and workwear boots, yet somehow she transformed the whole ensemble into the most attractive clothing I've ever seen on a woman. I was convinced that she could wear a bin-bag and look cool. To top it all, she was with a tall, moody-looking guy, who looked like a part-time model.

They walked past without noticing me. I don't know why but I turned my trolley and followed them. As they walked up and down the aisles she held his hand and seemed to laugh at everything he said. It was clear to me that they'd only just got together. It was also clear to me that they were in love. And I couldn't help but feel jealous of what they'd got. This guy standing in front of me had the kind of girl that men put on a pedestal. As I followed them up the aisle lined with cereal packets I wondered if part of me missed all that. Alison wasn't on a pedestal. She wasn't even raised slightly off the floor. She was the same as me – imperfect, with feet of clay. I knew everything about her. There weren't any secrets left to uncover.

I didn't know whether this girl before me shaved her legs in the bath with her boyfriend's razor or got them waxed in a salon. I didn't know whether she sometimes went out in pants that didn't match her bra. I didn't know if she thought nothing of brushing her teeth while her boyfriend was sitting on the loo. But I did know these things about Alison. Just as she knew everything about me. We were no longer distinct from each other. Somewhere along the way we'd blended. Become less than ourselves. And all the mystery we used to hold for one another, all the questions about how our lives were going to turn out, had disappeared. Because other than the prerequisite two-point-four children Alison and I had nowhere left to go because we'd ticked nearly all the boxes in the list of things couples are supposed to do.

In a lot of ways I was proud of all the obstacles we'd overcome in the years we'd been together – the arguments, insecurities, temporary break-ups, being separated by distance, my dad's death, the whole lot – because each one had seemed to imbue our relationship with more worth. Some of the things we'd faced might've stopped other people's relationships in their tracks but not us. In fact rather than being a threat they were the reason we'd lasted so long. They helped define us. They helped us focus on our relationship. They gave us direction. But what do you do when you reach the destination you've been trying to get to for a whole lifetime and discover you don't really want to be there?

## Saturday, 13 March 1999

### 12.03 p.m.

I'm in the kitchen making a cup of tea when the doorbell rings. Taking a deep breath, I walk through the hallway and out of the front door to the communal entrance. I open the door and Jim is there. I can tell straight away that he's not in the right frame of mind for this to be anything other than the most miserable experience of my life. Just from the way that he's standing in the doorway, legs slightly apart as if bracing himself for a blow. He's wearing the dark blue Levi's I bought him for his birthday, Adidas trainers I bought him for Christmas, a T-shirt saying 'Beatnik Revolution' which I bought him from a shop in Endell Street last summer, and a heavy grey parka I bought for him from Selfridges for his last birthday. I strongly suspect that the only thing he's wearing that I didn't buy for him are his boxers as I've never really liked buying men's underwear – it's too ugly.

This is the first time he's been here in three months. After we got back from Edinburgh I think we managed a night under the same roof. Jim slept in the spare room and when I woke up I found him packing some of his clothes into a couple of bags. When I saw what he was doing I left the flat and went for a walk. I ended up in the off-licence on the Broadway and bought a packet of cigarettes. After he left I got into a bit of a state and Jane stayed here a few nights. Fortunately my boss at work was really sympathetic and I managed to scrape together enough holiday for a week away in Madrid with Jane. The weekend after my return was the most difficult. Weekends are all about couples and suddenly I wasn't in a couple and I became aware that I didn't have anything to do. When you're in a couple you don't worry about doing nothing. In fact, you look forward to it.

Jim and I met up to talk about what was going on. He said that in the time we'd been apart he'd come to the conclusion that the best thing was to split up permanently. He said he didn't know what he wanted from life any more but he was certain that what we had wasn't it. He even apologised at one point for putting me through it, which I think was him trying to be nice but that just made me cry. I told him I didn't understand what had happened to make him suddenly change his mind.

When he answered, he couldn't even look at me. He said that for a while he'd been feeling as if we were on a conveyor-belt going through life and our plans to have a baby made his fear crystallise. He said he just couldn't escape the feeling that he'd made some awful mistake. He said he didn't want to wake up one day and ask, 'Is this it? Is this how my life has turned out?' He said he thought he still loved me but he didn't think that love was enough any more. I asked him if there was anything I could say to change his mind and he said no. Everything he said, and especially the way he said it, made me angry. In the end we got into an argument and I called him a coward and told him to leave.

Part of me wonders if I'd managed to persuade Jim to carry on living here whether we could've come out the other side somehow. But with the two of us leading separate lives I think the longer we spent apart the easier it was for us to live apart. After two months, I came to realise that my world wouldn't fall apart without Jim. The turning point was losing my fear of being alone. I just woke up one morning and it was gone. I didn't cry when I saw the empty space beside me in the bed. I didn't cry at the thought that there was no one to say 'good morning' to. I didn't cry when I could tell that Disco was wandering around the flat looking for Jim. And once that happened everything stopped hurting quite so badly. And because Jim had moved out I felt bitter and because I felt bitter he was bitter too. And because we both felt bitter, whenever we spoke on the phone we argued and because we argued we spoke less, and because we spoke less, after three months we seem like total strangers. And now because we're total strangers it seems logical to dismantle our lives together. Which is why he's here now. We enter the flat in silence and he closes the door behind him.

'Do you want a cup of tea or coffee?' I ask.

'Yeah,' he says. 'Why not?'

When I return from the kitchen with the tea Jim is standing in front of the bookshelves staring intently.

'So, you want to start with the books, do you?' I ask.

'It's as good a place as any,' says Jim. 'Let's just get this over with.'

**12.17 p.m.**

Alison takes a pile of books off the shelf and begins reading their titles: '*The Importance of Being Earnest*.'

'Yours,' I reply, and she puts it on the floor at her feet and picks up another.

'*Less Than Zero*?' she asks, waving the book.

'Yours.'

She places it on her pile of one.

'*Moon Palace*.'

'Who's that by?'

'Paul Auster.'

'That'll be yours, then.'

'*Neither Here Nor There*.'

'Bill Bryson?'

'Yes.'

'That'll be mine.' I take the book from her and put it on the floor beside me.

Alison picks up another. '*Get Shorty*.' She hands it to me.

I study the cover. 'No, actually it's yours.'

'I've never read an Elmore Leonard book in my life.'

'I know.'

'So how can it be mine?'

'I bought it for your birthday because it was my favourite book.'

She opens the cover and looks inside. Inside I've written: 'Happy birthday, Alison, hugs and kisses, Jim.' She hands it back to me. 'Here, you can keep it.'

'Why would I want to?'

'You've just said it's your favourite book.'

'I've already got a copy.'

'Well, I don't want it, do I? I don't like Elmore Leonard. I'm never going to read Elmore Leonard so there's no point in my having one of his books, is there?'

'Is it absolutely necessary that you have to be so hateful all the time?'

'Yes. Absolutely.' Alison sighs and picks up another book. '*The Black Album* by Hanif Kureishi.' She looks inside. 'It's a signed copy.'

'That'll be mine, then.'

She picks up another book. *'Star Wars: A New Hope?'*

'Mine.'

'Actually, you'll find it's mine,' says Alison.

'You don't like even *Star Wars*. You said it was the most stupid film you'd ever seen. Why would you buy the book?'

'It is stupid, but this came free with a film magazine. Look.' She shows me the cover. And, yes, it had indeed come free with a magazine.

'Well, can I have it?' I ask.

'No.'

'No?'

'As in, no, you can't have it.'

'But you don't want it.'

'I know.'

'So what are you going to do with it?'

'I'm going to give it to Oxfam along with the Elmore Leonard.'

'That was below the belt. I am about to retort with something equally malicious but I stop. 'Look, I haven't come here for a row. I've come here to try and sort out our stuff. And it's taken . . . ooh, all of five minutes for us to start having a go. Can't we just be reasonable and sort this out like mature adults?'

## 1.08 p.m.

'The TV's got to be mine,' says Jim. 'I spent ages looking for that TV. I trawled up and down Tottenham Court Road for an entire day playing off electrical store against electrical store until I got the lowest price. Of course it should be mine. Plus you don't watch that much TV.'

'I don't want the TV,' I inform him. 'I think it's too big. I said so at the time and you didn't listen to me . . . as usual. And I think it's ugly but the fact remains that I paid for the majority of it.'

'That's irrelevant,' says Jim.

'I think it's very relevant,' I snap. 'I tell you what. You can have the TV but I want the video and the washing-machine.'

'You can have the washing-machine but I really want the video,' replies Jim.

'I think it's a fair swap,' I tell Jim. 'The TV cost a fortune.'

'Fine,' he says eventually. 'You have it. I'll buy myself a new one.'

## 1.23 p.m.

'I think I should get the sofa,' I tell Alison. 'It's the most expensive thing in the flat and, as I remember, I paid for it too.'

'The sofa's mine,' says Alison. 'You might have paid for it but it was me who walked round every furniture store in central London on my own looking for it. Every time I asked you to come along you'd cry off with some excuse about having to work late or something. This sofa is the culmination of all my blood, sweat and tears. I chose the perfect colour, I chose the perfect size, I selected every last thing about it down to the last detail. It should go to me.'

'Where's the negotiation in that?'

'There is none. It's mine.'

### 1.45 p.m.

'I've cut you out of all our holiday photos,' I tell Jim defiantly.

'You did what?'

'I cut you out of our holiday photos. You've been erased from Crete, summer 1996, the Lake District, summer 1998, and New York, 1997. I took all the piles of mini-yous and set fire to them. It was very therapeutic. It's a shame, actually, because I was telling a friend of mine, Lucy, in the art department at work, what I'd done and she seemed to think that she could've Photoshopped you out on her computer and put someone much nicer in your place – she suggested Keanu Reeves in a wetsuit like in *Point Break*, but I said if I was going to do it I'd sooner have a golden retriever because they're more faithful.'

'Do you know what's the worst thing about that?' says Jim angrily. 'It's not that you'd swap me for a dog – that doesn't surprise me in the least. It's the fact that they weren't your bloody photos. They were mine! Taken on my bloody camera. With my bloody film!'

'Your photos, my photos, what does it matter?'

'This is stupid. Stupid and pointless. We're getting nowhere very slowly. So far all we've managed to do is sort out a few books and a few CDs and you've ruined our holiday photos. We've got a whole flat to do.'

## 3.03 p.m.

I'm on the phone to Jane.

'How did it go?' she asks.

'Not well,' I reply. 'We didn't manage to get much sorted at all. He just wasn't in the right frame of mind and neither was I. Part of me even thinks that Jim's deliberately dragging his feet over all this separating business and making it a bigger deal than it needs to be. All he has to do is claim what's his so that I can claim what's mine, and then we can get round to deciding the fate of what's ours.'

'Did you manage to sort out who's getting Disco? I know you're worried about that.'

'He didn't mention her once, but I can tell he's been dying to. He adores her. And she thinks he's the best thing since sliced bread.'

'I thought men weren't supposed to be into cats. At a push they're allowed to like dogs or dangerous animals like snakes, venomous spiders and sharks – basically animals that will kill or maim you given the opportunity – because they're manly. Cats aren't manly. They're the girliest animal in the book.'

'I know, but Jim loves Disco. And Disco loves him right back. Given a choice of laps to sit on, she'll take his over mine any day of the week. Not that she doesn't love me too. But it's like this: their love is unspoken. While I make the biggest fuss over her at any given opportunity, Jim will try his best to ignore her and she'll do her best to ignore him, but at the end of an evening in front of the TV they always end up together. It's like a perfect match.'

## Sunday, 21 March 1999

### 7 p.m.

It's the weekend again and we've really made some progress. Jim came back to the flat at midday and, though it took a while, we've sorted nearly everything, even some of the deal-breakers.

The living room no longer looks like a living room. It looks like the place that Walkers' crisps boxes go to die. There are boxes everywhere: on the sideboard, on the coffee-table, on the two armchairs and the sofa. And they are all full of our stuff. The stuff that Jim and I have collected during our relationship. And each and every one of the items has a sticker on it that reads: 'His' or 'Hers'. Originally the stickers were going to read 'Jim's' and 'Alison's', which was my idea, but Jim said it would be easier if we just wrote 'J' on his stickers and 'A' on mine. I wasn't happy about that for no other reason than that he had come up with the idea. So in the spirit of compromise I suggested 'Mine' for me and 'His' for him because it made him suitably anonymous. His counter-offer was the 'His' and 'Hers' that we have now, and although I didn't like it I reasoned that I was too tired to argue any more over something I really didn't care about. The stickers are on our things because some of the items are too big for Jim to take back to Nick's, where he's still living, so we've agreed that most of the stuff will be left in the spare room of the flat until we've sold up.

The only 'thing' we've got to decide about is currently circling the boxes that we've spent all afternoon labelling and sniffing the corners suspiciously.

'So what are we going to do about her?' I ask, as Disco rubs her body against my ankles.

'I don't know,' replies Jim. 'I've been sort of avoiding that one. I'd like to take her with me but she's your cat. I mean . . . I did give her to you, after all.'

'But she's really our cat, isn't she? Maybe we could have joint custody like they do with kids?'

Jim laughs, for the first time in what feels like years. 'You know what cats from broken homes are like – they're sneaky,' he says. 'She'll play us off against each other.'

'But what about it?'

'Are you serious?'

'I don't see why not.'

His face falls. 'Because it'll mean that you'll still be in my life and I'll be in yours.' He stands up. 'I think it's probably best if you keep her. I'll go and say goodbye to her now.'

And as he picks her up and walks into the kitchen with her, I can't stop the tears as I think, *This is how much he doesn't love me.*

## Saturday, 3 April 1999

### 10.57 a.m.

Jim's and my official separation is beginning to gain momentum. Terry Mortimer from Merryweather estate agents is here because I've arranged to have the flat valued. As I let him into the flat it strikes me that he is approximately twelve years old. And the fact that he's wearing a pinstripe suit and is trying to grow a goatee beards makes him seem even younger. I have tidied up in preparation for his visit and now all the boxes that Jim and I have sorted out are in the spare room, the carpet is free of fluff and I have even dusted. Terry visits all the rooms in turn and writes things down on his clipboard. He tells me he likes what I've done in the kitchen, the bedrooms are a great size (although the second bedroom could do with being emptied of the boxes), the bathroom is 'pristine' and, overall, the flat is in first-class condition.

I'm pleased with his verdict, I suppose, because it's always nice when someone says something complimentary about your home even if it's a home you're selling under difficult conditions. His comments make me feel moderately well disposed towards him so I ask if he wants a cup of tea. He asks if I've got any coffee and I tell him only decaffeinated and it's been in the cupboard for ages. We both examine the jar to spot the sell-by date but it seems to have disappeared altogether. He tells me he doesn't mind if it's gone off a bit so I open the jar and scrape away at the solid contents within until I have sufficient chippings for a mug of coffee. We stand in the kitchen staring at the kettle waiting for it to boil. I've run out of conversation and for a moment, I think, so has he.

'Can I ask why you're moving?' he asks.

'I'm splitting up with my husband,' I reply.

It's strange to witness first hand but Terry's eyes light up magically, as though the first thing I'm going to do with my freedom, following the end of the longest relationship of my life, is have a torrid affair with a cocky teenage estate agent.

'You don't look old enough to have an ex-husband,' he says smoothly.

'You don't look old enough to be selling my flat for me. How old are you by the way?'

'Twenty-two,' he replies. 'I've got a baby face. How old are you?'

'Old enough to be your big sister,' I tell him.

## Tuesday, 6 April 1999

### 10.58 a.m.

I'm just about to go into a meeting when my phone rings. I think about letting the voicemail get it but then I wonder if it's the journalist from *The Times* I've been trying to get hold of for the past few days who wants to do a feature on one of the cookery books I'm working on. I pick up the phone.

'Hello, Publicity.'

'Hello, I'd like to speak to Alison Smith, please. It's Terry from Merryweather estate agents.'

'Hello,' I say brightly. 'It's Alison here.'

'How are you?'

I look at my watch. 'Fine.'

'I just thought you'd like to know that we've valued your property.'

I hold my breath and listen. He then proceeds to tell me a figure that I would never have imagined our flat to be worth. I'm too shocked to speak.

'How does that sound?'

'Are you sure?' I ask. 'That seems very high.'

'Properties in your area are selling very well indeed and, given the A1 condition of the flat, I actually think I'm being a little conservative. Would you like us to start marketing the property?'

I tell him yes, and suddenly tears are streaming down my face. I wipe them away, sniff deeply and glance around the office to see if anyone has noticed. 'I'm sorry, Terry, I have to go.'

'Oh,' he says disappointedly. 'Can I just ask one thing before you do? I know this is very unorthodox, and I would never normally do this in a million years, but I can't help but feel there's some sort of connection between us.'

Even though my cheeks are still damp with tears I find myself having to suppress a laugh. 'You do?'

'Yes. I was wondering whether you'd like to go out to dinner some time. Maybe this Friday, about seven o'clock. I know a couple of nice places we could go.'

I think for a moment about Jim.

I think for a moment about how the last six years have been wasted.

I think for a moment about the future.

And then I find myself saying yes.

'That's great,' he says, as though he can't believe his luck. 'I'll call later this week.'

I put down the phone and immediately regret giving Terry the teenager even the faintest glimmer of hope. I scribble a note on my Cooper and Lawton promotional Post-it pad: 'Leave two days, then cancel with a cold.'

## 12.09 p.m.

My meeting went badly. I was supposed to be giving a report to my boss on how the campaign for one of our lead titles has gone. I kept losing my place and stumbling over my words. I wondered whether she could tell that I was thinking about the conversation I was going to have with Jim this afternoon. I wonder if she knows that I've set in motion events that will lead to my selling my home. The home I lived in with Jim. Our home.

## 1.17 p.m.

'Jim,' I say into the phone, 'it's me.'

'Hi,' he says.

'The estate agent has valued the flat.'

'How much?'

I tell him Terry's valuation.

'Are you joking? I can't believe it's gone up that much in a year. We're rich.'

'I suppose we are,' I say quietly.

'Have you got a solicitor yet?'

'No,' I reply. 'Do I need one?'

'Of course you do. I've already got one.'

I want to laugh. 'How could we have ended up in a situation where we need solicitors to talk to each other?'

'Because we're legally tied to each other,' says Jim coolly. 'It's entirely up to you but as far as the marriage goes I think the best thing for us is to wait two years and then apply for a *decree nisi* as long as we both agree that's what we want. And then six weeks after that we'll be awarded a *decree absolute* and we'll be officially divorced.'

'You've done your research, haven't you? You've got it all worked out.'

'I'm only trying to do what's best for us both,' he says, and I have to put the phone down because I don't want him to hear me crying.

## 1.29 p.m.

'Well, you need one too,' says Jane, when I call to tell her about Jim's I've-got-a-solicitor-I-think-you-need-one-too surprise.

'Why?'

'To make sure he doesn't rip you off when the flat's sold,' she replies. 'You should have the guy my sister Kate had when she split up with her awful boyfriend, Paul. I'll just get his number.' The line goes quiet and I listen to the sound of papers rustling.

'Found it,' she says eventually. 'This guy's name is Graham Barnet and he's from a firm called Fitzsimmons and Barclay.'

I scribble down the name and number carefully.

'Jim's solicitor is a woman,' I tell Jane. 'She's called Penny Edwards from Saunders and Elcroft. Now, thanks to us, two solicitors – a man and a woman, no less – who have never met will be sending each other letters in legalese and charging us a fortune for the privilege.'

'Maybe it'll be like some kind of romantic comedy where the counsel for the warring sides end up together,' says Jane. 'After all, they say that opposites attract, don't they?'

'They certainly attract,' I say quietly, 'but I think in the end they lack a certain staying power.'

## Monday, 26 April 1999

### 1.12 p.m.

Now that the flat is going on the market, I tell myself it's time to start looking for a place of my own. It's all very well sharing with Nick but after so long living with Alison what I really want is my own space. My own four walls.

During my lunch-hour I go on the Internet and register with some estate agents in and around East Finchley because I know I won't be able to afford a flat in Muswell Hill on my own. Even in East Finchley I can't believe how much money people want just for a one-bed flat. I even think briefly about moving out of London and back to Birmingham. On the plus side, I'd be able to afford something decent. On the minus side, it's been a while since I lived there. Times have changed. Things have moved on. And it wouldn't be anything like the old days.

## Saturday, 1 May 1999

### 11.11 a.m.

I'm viewing my first place in East Finchley. It's the ground-floor flat of a converted two-storey house on a quietish road off the High Road. On the phone the estate agent told me it was only a few minutes from the tube. It takes me nearly ten minutes to get there. The only way that those ten minutes could be converted into a few would be if I were to sprint full pelt from the station, which I can't really see myself doing every day.

The estate agent's name is Sourav. He's wearing a badly fitting suit and cheap shoes, and it's his first day in the job. I know this not because he tells me but because he's clearly out of his depth answering any questions other than 'Are you the guy from the estate agent's?' I try not to give him a hard time even though it's the one thing I want to do.

Instead I decide to focus on the flat but my mind wanders. It's weird looking for a place all on my own. It's weird thinking I have no opinion to take into account other than my own. In a way it's thrilling. This is one of the first times I've enjoyed not being part of a couple – the idea that I can do what I want when I want is exhilarating because, for the past six years, I haven't made a single decision that hasn't involved Alison even in some small way – even if it was to do the opposite of what she wanted. That's a long time not to make a decision that's purely your own.

After five minutes or so I'm pretty sure I hate the flat. Not only is it too far from the tube but the guy tells me that they don't have cable in the area and a satellite dish might be a problem because it would need to be mounted up high near the roof on a section of the house that wouldn't technically be mine. Cable TV or satellite is essential to my new life-plan. Without it there's no way I can become the happy new bachelor I intend to be. However, I poke around it for ten extra minutes or so because I don't want to dismiss the flat based on criteria that aren't entirely mine. At certain points, as I roam around with Sourav shadowing me, I find myself saying, 'The hallway is too narrow,' and 'The living room's a funny shape,' and 'There's not enough natural light in the bedroom.' Now, since when did I give a toss about 'natural light'? I don't. It was only Alison who cared about that kind of stuff, not me, and I feel like she's haunting me. I begin to wonder if I'm haunting her too. How can you not be haunted when you've been with someone as long as I've been with Alison?

## Tuesday, 4 May 1999

### 2.29 p.m.

Terry the teenage estate agent calls me at work about the flat. I listen carefully to his voice to see if he's annoyed that I cancelled our date. I made up a huge lie that I had a bad cold and I even fake-sneezed several times. He didn't get the message, though, and kept pushing me for a date when I thought I might be better. In the end I had to tell him it was too soon for me to be seeing someone else because I still had a lot of hurt to heal. He said he understood and that if I ever needed anyone to talk to he was only a phone call away. Fortunately today he sounds ridiculously jolly so I feel less guilty than before. He tells me that three couples are booked in to view the flat tomorrow at six in the evening. 'Will you be in?' he asks.

'No, I'm working late.'

'Oh, that's a real shame. Maybe next time?'

'Hmm,' I murmur. 'Maybe.'

## Wednesday, 5 May 1999

### 7.38 p.m.

I've just got home and I'm checking all around the flat to see if anything has changed. It's strange knowing that strangers have wandered around my home forming opinions about both me and it. I wonder what they thought of the colour of the kitchen. I kick off my shoes in the hallway, make my way to the fridge, take out a carton of cranberry juice and pour myself a glass. As I head to the living room sipping my drink I hear the answerphone beeping from its home on the sideboard near the radiator. There's one message. It's from Terry. One of the couples, a Mr Blake, a graphic designer, and his girlfriend, a Miss Quilliam, a photographer's assistant, have already booked a second viewing. I decide to be brave and stay in this time.

## Thursday, 6 May 1999

### 7.30 p.m.

The doorbell has just rung.

As I walk along the hallway I think that perhaps I should've set about filling the air with the aroma of brewing coffee or baking bread to make the flat appear more homely. I can't help but smile as I sniff the air and realise that they're going to have to make do with the aroma of my microwaved Singapore noodles emanating from the kitchen.

When I open the door Terry is standing there looking more youthful than normal without his goatee. Next to him are the couple who have come to view the flat. They look very arty and hopelessly young. He has long hair tied back in a pony-tail and is wearing olive green designer army trousers, trainers and an artfully distressed-looking leather jacket; she is dressed exactly the same, even down to the fact that her auburn hair is in a pony-tail too. They look like bookends.

'This is David and Amanda,' says Terry. 'They really love your home.'

'We think it's amazing,' says Amanda. 'I like what you've done with the bathroom.'

'It's great,' says David. 'It's exactly what we're looking for.'

David and Amanda tell me they're prepared to borrow a lot of money from their parents and mortgage themselves to their eyeballs to afford the flat. They look so cute and so utterly happy that I say that if they make the right offer they can have the fridge and cooker for free. I don't care that Jim is probably going to argue with me over that. If he'd seen their faces light up when I said this maybe even his cold heart would've melted. When they leave I cry again because I know in my heart that this couple are going to be so much happier here than Jim and I were.

## Wednesday, 9 June 1999

### 11.35 p.m.

I'm sitting on the sofa. Disco is on my lap (because it's the only lap that's available). A plate that once had a jacket potato and baked beans on it is on the seat next to me. The TV is on, but the sound is off, and I'm reading the lonely-hearts section of last weekend's *Guardian*. I'm reading every single one written by a woman. Not the men. The women. It's the women in those pages that interest me. Behind each '30-ish leftish n/s with gsoh seeking similar' entry is an attractive, intelligent and financially solvent woman who likes theatre, music and long walks in the countryside, and they're all looking for love. And I think, How am I ever going to get one of the good ones when the cold hard reality of life is that beautiful, intelligent women are being forced to hawk themselves in newspaper ads?

I grab a pen and spend the next few minutes writing my own lonely-hearts message. This is the best I can do:

> *Happy Go Lucky? Late twentysomething looking for love. Me: romantic, loyal, easy going, ex-leftie, likes cinema, theatre and badminton. You: tall, funny and skilled in the art of conversation. Let's get together and see where we go.*

Writing the fake ad makes me think about me and Jim. I still can't believe the fact that we are really over. We'd been together for so long. I thought it would never end. And now the longest relationship of my life has fallen apart. I can't think about work. I can't think about anything. I just want to curl into a ball and cry. I've done a lot of crying over the last few months and in a way I'm a little bored with it. There are only so many tears you can shed before you use them all up. Once you get to that stage all that's left is anger and bitterness, and an incredible sense of having been wronged.

The thing is, I don't understand how we got to this point. I don't understand at all. I'd been with Jim since 1993. And I just can't get over the fact that something that was once so good has now somehow turned into something that's so not right. I've been focusing on it day in and day out. And time and time again the same questions keep coming back to me. How did this happen to us? Why did this happen to us? When did this happen to us? I ask myself, time and time again, 'What went wrong?' Of course I talk it over with friends – Jane especially. But as great as friends are, deep down I know I'm never really going to get the truth from them because they're on my side. They always come to the conclusion that it was Jim's fault. And while I agree with what they say in part, it doesn't feel like it's enough. It feels empty. I'm not hearing anything I don't already know. I want . . . I need to know, without any shadow of doubt, that I didn't drive him away.

I spot my mobile phone out of the corner of my eye.

I pick it up.

I put it down.

I pick it up again.

Then put it down.

Finally I pick it up, scroll through the phonebook, find Jim's number and press Dial. It rings out several times before his voicemail kicks in. I take a deep breath and leave a message.

### 11.56 p.m.

It's late. And London is loud. The sound of taxis, buses, mobile burger sellers and revellers leaving nearby bars and pubs fills the air. I'm still in my work clothes. My tie is stuffed into the inside pocket of my suit jacket and I smell of cigarettes, even though I don't smoke. I've been out drinking with Nick. We've talked about stuff on TV, work, why they always serve that Belgian white-beer stuff in a girly glass, music we've bought in recent weeks and a bit of politics. I've drunk way too much and now I feel sick and sorry for myself as Nick and I stand on Tottenham Court Road waiting for the bus to East Finchley.

My phone beeps. I take it out of my jacket pocket and look at it. Apparently I've missed four calls and have several messages.

Message 1: 'Jim, it's me.' Long exaggerated sigh and pause for breath. 'Look, I know that we've both said a lot of terrible things to each other since . . . well, since we split up . . . but now the flat's being sold and we're talking to solicitors and I just feel like – like we should give our relationship one last shot. I think a relationship counsellor could really work for us—'

Message 2: 'Jim, it's me, Alison, again.' Long exaggerated sigh and pause for breath. 'I think I got cut off.' Pause. 'I can't even remember where I'd got to now.' Long pause. 'Oh, right, yeah, the counsellor. The fact is, Jim, we need help. I know you've given up on us but I haven't.' Pause. 'Look, whether you come or not I'm going to see her the week after next. She's one of the authors I look after at work. She did that self-help book I brought home once, *How to Make Love Flourish*. Anyway, her name's Caroline Roberts, and she's in Crouch End just off the Broadway. I'll pay for all the sessions. Please come at least once, okay? All you need to do is turn up. How easy is that? All you've got to do is turn—'

Message 3: 'This is getting ridiculous.' Long exaggerated

sigh and pause for breath. 'Why don't they sort these things out so that they work?' Another long exaggerated sigh and pause for breath. 'I'm not on a quiz show, and on the telephone I will not be hurried by anyone.' Even longer exaggerated sigh and pause for breath. 'This – in case you were wondering – is Alison again. I really think we need to sort out things between us and I can't do that on my own. Surely we can't throw away what we had without—'

Message 4: 'This machine is pathetic! It's me. You know what I want by now. Look, please call me and let me know ASAP.'

Even drunk I know better than to call her. It's best to leave well alone. I can't understand why she's going on about relationship counsellors. It is possibly the worst thing she could've said to me. The idea of involving a third party to sort out what was wrong with us makes me shudder. I can't begin to think how excruciatingly painful it would be. I can't even read the problem page at the back of the *Mail on Sunday's You* magazine without wincing at people's distinct lack of shame.

## Wednesday, 7 July 1999

### 5.34 p.m.

I'm near Blackfriars Bridge and it's raining. I consider getting my umbrella out of my bag but there's something sweet and life-affirming about the rain so I just walk and enjoy the feeling of the droplets against my face. Within minutes I've reached my destination: Jim's work. I'm not hoping to bump into him. Instead I'm hoping that my general presence in this vicinity will be picked up by his psychic radar and will somehow shame him into action. I can't believe he hasn't phoned me after all those messages. I can't believe he doesn't want to give us another go. Or, at the very least, find a way that we might be able to sort things out between us. I reach into my bag for my phone and scroll through the numbers until I reached Jim's, then press Dial. I'm not the least bit surprised when the call goes straight to his voicemail as his phone has been off for weeks.

'It's me again,' I say wearily. 'It's been ages now and I've heard nothing from you. I know that you're about because I saw you and Nick in the Yorkshire Grey on Langham Street – and before you say it, yes, I did go there on purpose, but, no, I wasn't stalking you . . . I just wanted to have it out with you but I reasoned that having it out in the pub in front of your mates wasn't the best idea in the world. Is it really too much to ask that you do this one thing for me? For us? I've made an appointment with Mrs Roberts. Please come. I really do think this is our last chance.'

## 11.33 p.m.

It's late, I'm tired and I want to go to bed. Instead I'm sitting in the living room with Disco, listening to the saddest music I can find but, given that I've only got two CDs, *The Best of Disco Volume 2* and *The Man Who*, by Travis, there isn't much choice. The Travis album won the day. It fits my melancholy mood perfectly – and is the perfect soundtrack while I drink three-quarters of a bottle of Merlot and chain-smoke nearly a whole packet of Marlboro Lights in less than an hour. As the album comes to a close, I look at the bottle of wine in front of me, pour the last of it into my glass and pick up my cigarettes and lighter. There's only one cigarette left. I take it out and put it to my lips. I'm about to light it when I stop and look at it. *This is stupid*, I think to myself. *I'm not even thirty and I've got a failed marriage, and a cigarette addiction that will probably kill me one day*. I put the cigarette and the lighter back into the red and white Marlboro Lights packet. Then I walk to the spare bedroom, kneel down at the end of the bed, pull out a battered brown suitcase and open it. Inside are old letters from friends and family, photographs from my younger days, keepsakes and mementoes from happier times. I drop the cigarette packet inside, close the lid and put the suitcase back under the bed.

*That's that,* I think to myself. *I'm never going to smoke another cigarette again.*

## Friday, 6 August 1999

### 9.54 a.m.

Today we are selling the flat. Through our solicitors Alison and I have agreed that we should both turn up at the offices of Fitzsimmons and Barclay in Highgate to sign the agreements. We didn't have to do this face to face. In fact, my solicitor tried to talk me out of it, saying it would cause me a great deal of emotional stress. I didn't listen to her, of course. I think a degree of emotional distress is the least my relationship with Alison deserves. Otherwise it would be too clean. Too clinical. I want to say goodbye to this relationship. I want a full stop. And this is going to be it. I don't know whether Alison feels the same. I assume she does because she agreed to it.

Fitzsimmons and Barclay is everything I expect of a solicitor's office. There's a receptionist, some fake potted palms and a waiting area where my ex-wife and her solicitor are now seated. Alison's wearing a black shirt, dark blue jeans, and heeled black boots. She's had her hair cut and is wearing a new shade of lipstick. I, on the other hand, look a little scruffy. I've taken the day off work because when I woke up this morning I realised I wasn't far from losing the will to live. I'm wearing a T-shirt bearing the legend Northern Soul that I bought in a shop in Covent Garden because I'd seen a musician wearing one in a magazine, a pin-striped jacket, a pair of beige bootleg cords, a pair of red Converse All-stars. The look is deliberate. I don't want to look like a nearly thirty-year-old accountant with a failed long-term relationship. I want to look like a cool, hip and happening single man with the world at his feet.

'Hi,' says Alison, standing up to look at me directly. 'How are you?'

I give her a short smile. 'Good.'

'You didn't return my calls.'

'Things have been really hectic.'

'It doesn't matter anyhow. I cancelled the appointment. But I think I might reschedule it and go on my own.'

My gut instinct is to ask her why she wants to see a relationship counsellor on her own. But I don't ask because the answer will involve my non-compliance. Instead I introduce a new topic, one that might be less likely to result in an argument. 'How's the cat?'

'Her name's Disco.'

'Okay, how's Disco?'

'She's good.'

'Great,' I reply. 'Give her a cat treat from me.'

Alison's solicitor stands up as mine walks into the reception area. There's lots of polite smiles and shaking of hands, then we walk along a short corridor into an office. My solicitor says something in legalese, then Alison's says something else in legalese and, in the meantime, Alison and I attempt to look as if we know what they're talking about.

Eventually the time comes when we have to sign the necessary papers. Alison signs first and doesn't look at me. I don't know what I expected from her but it was certainly more than that. Now it's my turn. Three contracts and a green fountain pen with black ink. Helpfully they've put some of those sticky red tabs on the places where we're supposed to sign. The red tabs make me feel like I'm too stupid to know what's going on. I feel like a six-year-old who has been practising his handwriting. I look at Alison's signature. It seems so much neater than mine. I put the pen to the paper and my heart begins to race. As my name unfurls from the nib it gets faster and faster. I'm half expecting Alison to let out a gasp or faint or do something equally dramatic. But she doesn't do anything at all.

One down. Two to go.

I look at the complete signature. Mine and Alison's side by side. My stomach now joins the party and keeps flipping over. I can't help but think that something will happen in the next sixty seconds to stop this going through. Because I know that once I've signed my name another two times there will be one less thing tying the two of us together. It'll be the start of us becoming two separate people again. I'll go back to being Jim. She'll go back to being Alison.

I sign the second paper.

Two down. One to go.

Finally I sign the third paper.

And there's nothing left to sign.

Because it's nearly over now. Soon, Alison 'n' Jim will cease to exist.

# PART SEVEN

## Now

# 2003

## Friday, 17 January 2003

### 10.45 a.m.

I'm at home waiting for the buzzer to ring. It's strange to think that in a few minutes I'm going to see Jim for the first time in nearly four years. I've been trying to imagine what his life is like without me in it and each time fail miserably. It's almost like he ceased to exist when we went our separate ways. Like it was all a dream. I'm just about to go and get my coat when the buzzer rings. I pick up the entryphone by the door.

'Hello?'

'It's me,' says Jim.

'I'll just buzz you up.'

By the time he's made it upstairs I'm standing in the front doorway waiting for him.

'Hi,' I say. 'Do you want to come in for a moment?'

He follows me into the flat and closes the door behind him.

'Nice place you've got here,' he says, sitting on the sofa. 'It's very you. How long have you lived here?'

'About six months,' I reply.

'Alone?'

'Pardon?'

'Sorry . . . I was just asking if you bought your flat on your own?'

'No, I bought it with Marcus . . . my fiancé.' I point to a picture on the mantelpiece.

'Is that the two of you together?'

'It was taken last summer in New Zealand.'

'And you're getting married?'

'This Valentine's Day. How about you? Are you in a relationship at the moment?'

Jim nods.

'Still the great communicator. Has she got a name?'

'Her name's Helen.'

'And it's serious between the two of you?'

'We're planning to live together, if that's what you mean.'

I look at my watch and stand up. 'We'd better go,' I say. 'I'll just get my coat and do something with my hair.'

I'm ready in a few moments and we leave the flat and start walking along the road. As we walk we talk generally about our lives, rather than what we're about to do. I tell Jim about my wedding arrangements. In return he tells me the odd snippet about him and Helen. By the time we reach the vet's we're not exactly strangers any more but neither are we old friends. We're more like old acquaintances who lost touch.

## 11.07 a.m.

'I've never done anything like this before,' I say, as we stand outside the vet's. 'What are we supposed to do?'

'I don't know,' says Alison. 'When I was a kid we had a mongrel, Clara, who died, but I was only eleven at the time. I think my mum must have sorted everything out.'

'What are the options?'

'I think we can either take her with us and bury her somewhere or the vet can deal with it.'

'Do you think we should bury her?'

Alison shrugs. 'I don't know. What do you want?'

'I don't know. She wasn't much of an outdoors kind of cat, really, was she?'

Alison gives me a smile and opens the surgery door. I follow behind her as she goes up to the counter and speaks to a nurse.

'Do you want to take . . .' the nurse pauses to look at a form on the desk in front of her '. . . Disco home with you?'

Alison looks at me.

'I'm not sure I can face seeing her as she is,' I tell Alison.

'Me either.'

'I think we'll let you take care of . . .' She doesn't finish the sentence. 'I know this is going to sound stupid but do you mind bringing out the box that she's in so that we can say goodbye?'

The nurse nods and disappears behind a door. She emerges moments later carrying a Walkers' crisps box and places it on the counter. Alison begins to cry and pats the box gently and I just stare at it. That stupid crisps box. And I'm almost in tears too.

That's our goodbye.

## 12.04 p.m.

Jim and I are standing outside the vet's in silence, not quite sure what to do with ourselves.

'I'm really glad you called me,' says Jim.

'I'm glad you're here,' I reply. 'The thing is . . . I don't want this to come out the wrong way but . . . when I told Marcus what had happened he was sorry for me, and sad because he was fond of Disco too, but I couldn't get away from the idea that he wasn't feeling what I was feeling.'

'I think Helen was the same. She was understanding but it's not the same if it isn't your pet.'

'But don't you think that's strange? That out of all the people in the world – Marcus, my family, my friends – the only person who has any idea of what I'm feeling right now is you? We haven't been part of each other's lives for a long time and yet here we are, two people who used to love each other saying goodbye to their pet cat.'

There another long silence.

'I'd better go,' I tell Jim.

'Me too,' he replies.

Instinctively I put my arms around him and squeeze tightly while he does the same. We hold each other in this hug for what feels like minutes but is probably no longer than a few seconds and then it's all over.

'I really had better go,' I say finally. I smile and add, 'Have a nice life. I hope you'll be really happy.'

'You too,' says Jim. 'And all the best for your wedding day.'

I begin walking towards Crouch End Broadway when I stop in my tracks and turn to see Jim standing in the spot where I left him. He walks towards me and I walk towards him and we meet in the middle.

'I don't want to sound presumptuous,' begins Jim, 'but you're not thinking what I'm thinking, are you?'

I laugh. 'More than likely.'

'It's just that . . . well, I haven't seen you in so long. It just seems odd for us to go our separate ways like that.'

'I know what you mean. I feel the same too.'

'Why don't we go for a drink? Just the one and well . . . we'll just talk.'

'That sounds great,' I reply. 'Let's just talk.'

**12.11 p.m.**

Alison and I are now sitting in a corner booth in the Red Lion. The pub is relatively empty, although small groups of people are dotted around the bar. Pop music is playing in the background – I suspect that one of the bar staff has put on a chart compilation CD from about two years ago because all the songs are annoyingly familiar. Alison has been chatty, but not too chatty, since we left the vet's. We talk about work (it's going fine); her parents (they're fine too); work for me (it's going fine); my mother (she's fine too). I'm just thinking about getting another drink when Alison clears her throat as though she's about to speak.

**12.12 p.m.**

'I don't want this to come out the wrong way,' Alison begins, 'but I was just wondering, do you ever think about us?'

'Sometimes,' I reply. 'It was such a mess when it ended.'

'It was, wasn't it?' she agrees. 'It's just that with what's happened today it's got me thinking about the past. Disco was part of our history. Our shared past. And the thing is, when things end badly – like they did for us – you never get to really find out –'

'– what went wrong?' I interject.

'Exactly.'

'Yeah, I thought that a few times.'

'I mean, aren't you curious?' she continues. 'We were together over six years. When did it stop working? Why did it stop working? Did we bring out the worst in each other? Was it just one person's fault or both of us? Aren't these the questions everyone wants to ask when they split up with someone?'

I laugh. 'I think initially you're convinced it's the other person's fault.'

'Oh, absolutely,' says Alison. I would've blamed you for starting the Second World War when we broke up.'

'But now?'

'Well, now my judgement's a bit clearer. What about you?'

'My judgement's always been one hundred per cent sound.' She raises an eyebrow. 'I'm joking. I agree with you. I can see things differently now. There are certain things I regret.'

'Me too,' she says.

'Do you want to talk about it? Us? It's sort of a weird thing to talk about, isn't it, really? But I'd like to.'

'Why not? We're both in new relationships.'

'We're both happy with our partners.'

'Then let's do it,' says Alison. 'Let's find out where we went wrong.'

**12.27 p.m.**

'The first question I want to ask you is this,' begins Alison. 'Apart from the big things, which I'm sure we'll both be talking about sooner or later this afternoon, when we were together what sort of things did I do that annoyed you?'

'This is going to sound weird,' I say, 'but do you know the first thing that sprang to mind when you asked that?'

'No.'

'You're going to laugh.'

'That doesn't surprise me.'

'Hair conditioner.'

'*Hair conditioner?* How can any normal person be annoyed about hair conditioner?'

I can't help but laugh. 'You always had loads of it, as though you were stocking up in case there was ever a world-wide shortage of posh conditioner for dry and damaged hair,' I explain. 'Your idea of financial parsimony was to buy anything that was in a Boots three-for-two offer. Which meant you constantly had six different brands of shampoo and conditioner on the go at once. I don't know whether you've noticed but you've only got one head.' Alison laughs. 'And while we're at it, I don't even know what conditioner does. Shampoo I understand. Shampoo, good, cleans your hair. Conditioner, useless, because it does bugger-all. I know this because I tried it several times during the course of our relationship and it didn't do a bloody thing. My hair was exactly the same after as it was before. It didn't feel fuller or softer or anything, it just felt like hair. So you buying three bottles of stuff that does nothing at all to your hair for the price of two bottles of stuff that does nothing at all to your hair isn't a saving – it's just money thrown away.'

I pause for breath, and we both laugh, and then I add, 'But apart from that you were fine.'

## 12.38 p.m.

'Sometimes I used to wish that you'd be a little more vulnerable,' I tell Jim. 'I mean, I wouldn't have wanted you to be weeping every five seconds just because you watched the last five minutes of *Pet Rescue*. In fact, I liked that you were quite blokey. I liked it if only because your behaviour was so weird and different from mine. But then again – and I'm sure, Jim, you'll disagree with me here – I actually think you do have a little bit of a feminine side that most people don't know about, and I wouldn't have minded seeing more of it.'

Jim laughs in what I assume is him adopting a manly manner. 'I haven't got a feminine side. You're making that up.'

'I'm not saying it's huge – because it's not – but there were things about you that surprised me.'

'Like what?'

'Okay, this is only a very small example but the way you used to dry your legs when you stepped out of the bath fascinated me.'

'You what?'

'You used to step out of it really delicately like you were a prim and proper Victorian lady, then you'd sit on the edge and dry your feet. But you didn't bring your foot closer to your body like most blokes would, you pointed it like a ballerina, then leaned forward to dry it. It wasn't just once it was all the time. I know because I checked.'

'I can't believe you dedicated brain cells to that kind of nonsense. You know what? I can't defend myself against your accusation because I have no idea how I dry my feet when I get out of the bath.'

'You would say that because you never notice the details. But in a relationship the details are everything because they can remind you – just when you need to be reminded most – why you fell in love with someone in the first place.'

'Are you saying you fell in love with me because of the way I dry my feet?'

'I fell in love with you for a million different reasons. The way you dry your feet was only one of them.'

'I know you're trying to make a positive point but don't you see that the details were part of the problem with us? If you're always looking at the small stuff you're always going to find something most people don't notice.'

'That's exactly the point.'

'Well, that's all well and good for the positive "small stuff" – the things you think are cute and adorable. But what about the negative "small stuff", the million and one different things I did every day that you must have hated and I didn't even know I was doing?'

'Like the way you used to have to channel surf through the adverts even though you knew I liked them?'

'Who watches the adv—'

'Or the way you used to think that taking out the rubbish to the wheelie-bin at the side of the house was somehow doing me a massive favour.'

'But you never did it in all the time we were together.'

'And never put the washing-machine on. How do you think your clothes got clean? By magic? And, anyway, you're putting me off my stride now because I'm trying to remember the thing you did that used to annoy me most.' I pause and run through a mental list of grievances. 'I've got it,' I say finally. 'The most annoying small thing you used to do was eat a packet of twelve mini-doughnuts from the supermarket before I'd even had one.'

'But if I'd left them until you'd got round to them they would've been stale and they'd have gone to waste.'

I laugh and shake my head. 'You're right about one thing,' I tell him. 'The details are dangerous. They can turn a woman to love one day and to loathing the next.'

## 12.56 p.m.

Jim is looking at me curiously.

'What?' I ask.

'This is something I've always wanted to ask you.'

'Go ahead.'

'About four months after we split I sat down to watch *The Professionals*.'

'*The Professionals?*'

'Yeah, you know the one. The seventies TV show with Bodie and Doyle, a Ford Capri and lots of chasing after criminals.'

'Oh, yeah, that one.'

'Good, so you remember? They repeated the first series of *The Professionals* on cable. Do you remember?'

'I remember you boring me to tears with it.'

'I told you I was going to tape every single episode.'

'I remember that, but only because you said that you weren't going to watch them.'

'Well, I was sitting at home and I put the first videotape into the machine, pressed Play, expecting to see the first episode of the first series, and do you know what I saw?'

'No.'

'I'll tell you. It was an episode of *Ricki Lake*.'

'And you think I did that?'

'Yes, you must have done it after we'd had a row because you knew it would ruin the experience for me.'

'Couldn't you have just watched the other episodes?'

'No. I wanted to watch them all in chronological order – it was very important to me.'

'Well, you're probably right about it being me,' I say breezily. 'I can't imagine you taping *Ricki Lake* in a million years. Was it a good episode?'

'You did it on purpose, didn't you?'

'Well, it probably would've pleased me then to see you annoyed so I more than likely did do it but not on purpose. I'm not that vindictive. I suspect what happened was you left the videotape in the machine and I assumed it was a blank one.'

'You didn't check? How irresponsible is that?'

'It was very irresponsible,' I say, trying to stifle a snigger. 'You're really annoyed about it still, aren't you?'

'Just a bit,' says Jim, trying to play it down.

'Well,' I say humbly, 'I consider myself well and truly told off.'

## 1.05 p.m.

'When it looked like it was inevitable that we were going to split up did you think we'd stay in touch?' I ask Jim.

'I knew we wouldn't,' he replies.

'Me too. I couldn't see how we could possibly remain in each other's lives after all that time together.'

'We'd gone too far for that.'

'How could we have been just good friends after having once meant the world to each other? I'd rather I never saw you again than have you consider me your friend. I'd rather you vanished into thin air. Or stopped breathing.'

'What if I'd died?'

'If you'd died at the time I would've come to your funeral. And I think I probably would've been sad and openly shed tears.'

'Why?'

'Because it's hard to hold grudges against dead people.'

There's a long pause and then, for no reason at all, we both burst out laughing.

## 1.10 p.m.

'I can't believe we've been talking like this for an hour,' I say to Alison. 'I bet you've been wanting to leave for ages.'

'No, actually, I haven't. I've really enjoyed talking with you.'

'But you have to go now?'

'Don't you?'

'I'm supposed to be working from home today but I'm not too worried. What about you?'

'There's nowhere I've got to be.'

'Do you want another drink?'

'I'll have a glass of white wine, if that's all right,' says Alison. 'Dry.'

'Are you hungry? I could get us a lunch menu.'

Alison laughs. 'But then we'd be having lunch together, wouldn't we? And that would be a bit strange, don't you think?'

'I can see what you're saying. Peanuts, then? No one can misconstrue a packet of peanuts, can they?'

'Okay. Peanuts it is.'

## 1.17 p.m.

'I was just thinking at the bar,' I say, as I return to our table with peanuts, a dry white wine and a pint of Guinness, 'how in the early days of our relationship you were sceptical about everything.'

'Was I?' asks Alison.

'Yes, you were.'

'I didn't feel like I was.'

'I'd go so far as to say that in the early days of our relationship you were more like a bloke than I was. I'll admit this much – and I don't say it lightly – in the early days it was me who was insecure in our relationship. I could never get over just how hard you could be sometimes. The fact is, when we got together I was mad about you. I never thought that kind of thing would ever happen to me. So in the early days, because you showed so much restraint sometimes, I think you commanded more respect than any woman I've been involved with. I mean, I've had women who weren't interested in me – I think most men have been there. But to have a woman who's interested in you but still remains in total control of her emotions is another.'

'Are you saying that most women aren't? Because you'll be on very dodgy ground there.'

'I'm not saying that. I'm just saying that you were . . . balanced. That's the way I'd describe you. Balanced. But the further we got into the relationship the more your defences came down. And that was good at first because it meant we weren't playing games any more. We were equals with equal commitment to the relationship. The thing is, if at that point you were to have plotted a graph – with commitment on the vertical axis and time on the horizontal and my line in blue and yours pink—'

'Pink!' laughs Alison. 'You're making my line pink? I don't even like pink. When have you seen me with pink anything? I can believe what a Neanderthal you're being.'

'What colour do you want?'

'Green.'

'Fine. You be green, then. The point is that at the beginning my line would've been high and yours would've been low, but as the relationship continued our two lines – blue and green – would've come together. They would've been on top of one another. In fact, they would've stayed that way for quite a while, but then suddenly while mine would have stayed the same, yours would have started going up sharply, like it was a rocket heading towards the moon or something. It was freaky. It was disconcerting.'

'Not that I'm agreeing with a single word you've said, but why did that worry you?'

'Because I felt like my line was in exactly the same place. It wasn't going up and it wasn't going down. It was the same.'

'But by your admission in the beginning yours was high and mine was low, and you didn't think that was such a bad thing, did you? In fact, you said that you "respected" me. So why, all of a sudden, did the rules change?'

'I don't know. It's just . . . it's just that . . . well . . . women don't know anything about balance, do they? They're so binary, it's scary. They're all so all-or-nothing, in or out, off or on, not at all interested in you or "I'm going to dedicate my life to you," and while both are useful on occasions, too much of one or the other can drive a man insane.'

'Face it, Jim, you're like a living, breathing, eating, sleeping version of the biggest male cliché in the book. You want it when you can't have it and when you've got it you don't want it.'

'No, you're wrong. Yes, I wanted it when I couldn't have it, but when I'd got it I just wanted you to pretend – not all the time, just every now and again – like sometimes you didn't want it either.'

'Why?'

'To remind me.'

'To remind you of what?'

'To remind me . . . why I fell in love with you.'

## 1.41 p.m.

**'Is it a crime to fall out of love?' asks Jim. 'When we said we loved each other I'm pretty sure we meant it. But weren't we talking about how we felt right at that moment? Is it the kind of thing you can predict? Isn't it a little bit random? Chemistry mixed up with the unknown? How could we know that we'd always feel the same way about each other? Doesn't having to love take away the incentive to love voluntarily? Is it better that we put up with each other because we promised to do so rather than cut ourselves free so we can love people we want to love rather than love out of a sense of obligation?' Jim pauses and laughs. 'Am I asking a lot of questions? Or is this just me?'**

**'I don't know the answer to any of them,' I tell him. 'I don't think anyone does. I think that's why love is what it is: the most complicated, intense and indefinable emotion. And yet without it . . . well, life wouldn't really be worth living, would it?'**

**1.45 p.m.**

'I think a lot of our problems began when we moved in together,' says Alison.

'Yeah,' I say, nodding. 'It was weird how we fell into traditional male-female roles. I mean – put it this way – we're both adults and we'd both lived on our own for quite a while. I can cook. I can clean a house without being told to. So can you, and you can even put together flat-pack furniture.'

'Yeah, but I'm not sure how seeing as I never understand the instructions.'

'Neither do I. But that's not the point. The point is gradually I forgot these skills and somehow turned into my dad.' I pause to sip my pint. 'I never asked you to do this once but somewhere during the second year we lived together you started doing all the washing and ironing. And then I started doing all the things my dad used to do at home. Anything mechanical became my realm. Anything financial became my realm. Anything practical became my realm.'

'Why does that disturb you so much?'

'Because . . . I don't know. Because I'd expected things to be different between us. I'd grown up in a world where women could do and be anything. The longest-serving prime minister in my lifetime was Margaret Thatcher. We were taught about sexual equality. We learned domestic science at school and the girls were allowed to do woodwork and metalwork. That was the world I was brought up in. And it was a little undermining to realise that . . . oh, I don't know.'

'I'd never have taken you for a feminist,' says Alison, laughing. 'I only did your washing and ironing because I loved you and wanted to do everything for you.'

'I suppose I looked after all the blokey stuff for the same reason. But didn't you find it a bit disappointing?'

'Not in the beginning,' she muses. 'Well, okay, not all the time. I used to vacillate between doing it because I loved you, and feeling stupid and taken for granted. But back then I wanted to do everything for you. I wanted you to need me. There's nothing in the world quite like that feeling of being needed by another human being.'

'But that's it. That's what you did. You made yourself indispensable. You filled in all the gaps. For instance, I'm crap at remembering people's birthdays and always forget the card. You have a sixth sense for remembering them so gradually you started buying them for me, then buying and writing them for me and getting me to sign them, then buying, writing and forging my signature. Gradually I – the unreliable variant in this – was completely erased from the process.'

'I just got too annoyed by your uselessness sometimes. I know this sounds awful but I did it because it reflected badly on me. The worst thing is it got to the stage where I resented doing it so much and resented you so much that I used to go out deliberately and buy really ugly birthday cards just because I was annoyed. You didn't even notice when I sent your mum an awful padded card with glitter on it.'

'But if you resented it so much why did you do it?'

'Because it wasn't a choice between doing it and not doing it. It was a choice between me doing it and you doing it badly.'

'But it was impossible to keep up with you. You used to buy Christmas cards in the middle of October. How was I supposed to compete with that? Christmas never used to get a look-in in my head until a few days before Christmas Eve.'

**3.09 p.m.**

'It sounds stupid saying it aloud but women really are so different,' I explain to Alison. 'Do you know, I'd always thought that men and women were pretty much the same under the skin – the thought processes and all that. And it's not until you live with a woman that you realise just how – how not like men they are.'

'Tell me about it. What was the biggest surprise to you about living together?' asks Alison.

'For me it was your lack of priority.'

'What lack of priority?'

'Well, for instance, the fact that we didn't have a proper TV for ages when we first moved in.'

'You call that a lack of priority? We had a TV. In fact we had two.'

'Yeah but mine was tiny and yours was black-and-white and you could only ever get three channels on it.'

'So you're having a go at me because we had two crap TVs.'

'No, I'm having a go at you because you'd have put up with it for ages. When I first met you you had a video-player that was the size of a tank, you didn't even get a CD player until you moved to London. All you had was millions of tapes that friends had given you. I'm not saying that any of this makes you a bad person. I'm just saying I didn't understand how you could live like that.'

'And you only noticed this when we moved in together? What about every other weekend that you came to stay?'

'It was quaint then.'

'Quaint?'

'Relatively speaking.'

She pauses and then says, 'I knew it. I always felt like you wanted to change me.'

'Well, that's interesting, because I always felt like you wanted to change me too.'

'You weren't overt about it or horrible, it was just small things that you picked up on, I suppose. I definitely think you thought I couldn't survive without you. By that I mean you thought that my life before you moved in was the equivalent of some kind of third-world country and us living together was you bringing me into the modern era. I suppose if you want a metaphor I think you thought I was India under British occupation. You know how historians always go on about how Britain gave India the railways, as though the poor Indians should have been grateful that the country was being illegally occupied just because they could now get the nine fifteen to Calcutta? It was like that. I always felt like you thought you were making improvements in my life when what you were doing was putting in a railway I hadn't asked for.'

'Give me a bloody example of one of my so-called railways,' I say laughing.

'Okay, how about the way that you were always giving me books to read, CDs to listen to and films to watch as though you felt obliged to educate me. For instance, you bought me the *The Wild Bunch* on video one Christmas. I hate violent films *and* Westerns.'

'I thought you'd like it.'

'I think you thought I ought to like it. Just as I think you thought I ought to like Elmore Leonard novels, *The Simpsons*, *The Fast Show*, Stereolab, Northern Soul and whatever other bands, books, TV programmes, musical genres you thought I needed educating in.' She laughs. 'Still, if I'm being honest I have to admit I did try to change you too. For instance, do you remember those horrible cut-off jeans you wore on our first holiday together? Do you remember why you didn't wear them on our holiday to New York?'

'I could never find them. They got lost in the move to yours.'

'Nope.'

'You threw them away?' I say, outraged.

She nods. 'I threw a lot of your stuff away when we moved in together, and you never noticed. Your collection of 1970s TV annuals that you never looked at? Oxfam. All the shoes you hadn't worn for years but wouldn't throw away? Cancer Research. The acoustic guitar that had no strings on it? Jane's thirteen-year-old niece. If I hadn't got rid of half the rubbish you brought with you from Birmingham we'd have needed a mansion to house it all.'

'I can't believe how devious you were.'

'Yes, I was devious but at least I was subtle. And it was always for your own good.'

## 3.32 p.m.

'So where do *you* think it all went wrong?' I ask.

'When we got married,' Jim replies, without hesitation.

'You seem very sure of that.'

'It's not that I think it was the only reason things didn't work out,' he tells me. 'It's just that we did it too early. I think I knew then that we were making a mistake.'

'So why didn't you say anything?' I frown.

'I could ask you the same question.'

'I thought it might keep us together. The truth was that we'd got together too early. There were still too many things you wanted to do with your life and, in retrospect, there were probably things I needed to work out in my head before I was ready for something as serious as marriage. I think we were very good at papering over the cracks – I can see that now.'

**4 p.m.**

'Do you want another drink?' I ask Alison.

'No, I'm fine,' she says. 'Do you want me to get you another?'

'No. I'm fine with this one.'

'You're sure?'

'Yes, I'm sure.'

'What about peanuts?' I ask. 'Your packet's empty.'

'No, I'm fine. I don't like to eat too many of those things.'

'I know, but I like the way that whenever you get to the end of a packet you lick your finger and put it in the dust at the bottom. There's something childlike about it. I always imagined that if we'd had a kid it would do that too.' Alison laughs and looks at her watch. 'I'd better be going.'

'Yeah,' I reply. 'Me too, I suppose.'

She smiles at me. 'It was nice, though, eh?'

'What?'

'This afternoon?'

'Yeah, it was.'

She stands up and puts on her coat while I drain the contents of my glass. And then we head for the exit. Once there, we realise it is raining.

'One last question,' I ask as we shelter in the doorway getting bearings. 'Do you ever hear from Damon these days?'

Alison laughs. 'Before I answer that question I have a confession. For a couple of years after he and I split up he used to send me Valentine cards swearing undying love.'

'And you never told me?'

'It was stupid, really. I didn't want to upset you.'

'But you kept them anyway.'

'How do you know I kept them?'

'You had them in an old shoebox marked "Household Bills". I came across them in the flat one day while I was looking for – would you believe it? – household bills.'

'Why didn't you say anything?'

'What's to say?'

'Weren't you jealous?'

'Not in the slightest. I got the girl, didn't I? I lost her, mind you. But I did have her for a while.'

Alison smiles awkwardly. 'He used to swear undying love in those cards. But I think his love must have popped its clogs somewhere along the way because they petered out about 1998. I didn't hear anything from him until last April when an invitation arrived at my parents' house inviting me and a guest to celebrate the wedding of Damon Guest and Camilla Forsythe. I wondered why he'd invited me, especially as I hadn't seen him since we split up, but curiosity got the better of me and Marcus and I went.'

'How was it? Had he changed?'

'It was the weirdest wedding I've ever been to. He was exactly the same. Absolutely lovely and adorable. He never made it in the music business, like he wanted to. He works for a French bank. But you'll never believe this Camilla – the woman he was marrying looked just like me.'

'You're joking.'

'Okay, we might not have passed for twins but we definitely could've been sisters. We had the same hair, colouring. We were even about the same height. If I'd been wearing a white dress that day Damon would've been hard pressed to tell us apart. I didn't know where to put myself. I really didn't. The worst thing was that we'd been invited to the sit-down dinner thing and as we were all queuing to going in I suddenly realised we were also queuing up to greet the bride, groom and all the in-laws. As I shook their hands their jaws dropped in amazement. They all asked me the same question, "So how do you know Damon and Camilla?" to which I replied with a tactful, "I went to university with Damon."'

'So do you think he never got over you?'

'He didn't have to get over me, did he? He just found himself a better version of me.'

'Why better?'

'Because this version didn't fall in love with someone else.'

## 4.10 p.m.

'I think I'll probably take a cab home,' I tell her. 'I can get it to drop you off, if you want.'

She smiles. 'I'll walk. I am waterproof, after all.'

There's an awkward few moments and then Alison says, 'I'll say goodbye then,' and gives me a hug. 'Thanks for this afternoon.'

'Maybe if we'd done more talking when we were together it might have worked out,' I say.

'Maybe,' she replies. 'The thing is, what was nice about this afternoon was remembering the old days, all of those small moments that made them. We never treasured them when we had them because there were so many of them. But they *were* special. And you only know they're not going to go on for ever when it's all over. The thing is, no matter how much either of us explains to someone, they'll never quite understand why our stupid in-jokes were so funny to us, they'll never understand why, because of you, I never went on a Monday-night date with Marcus, they'll never understand why losing Disco today felt like the worst thing in the world. They can't understand these or a million and one things that happened to us because they weren't there. Those moments are unique to us. And sometimes all it takes to feel like things are okay in the world is to know that someone else was there with you at the time.'

'Like now,' I say, and, without thinking, I kiss her and she kisses me back. Once the kiss stops, however, we look at each other. I want to say something but I don't know what. But before I can speak she puts her index finger to my lips, shakes her head sadly and walks away.

# PART EIGHT

## Sixteen hours before Alison's wedding

# 2003

## Thursday, 13 February 2003

### 4.00 p.m. (US time)
### 10.00 p.m. (UK time)

'We're going to miss the flight.'

I look at the stationary traffic surrounding our yellow cab, then at the cab driver, who almost seems to have given up on life altogether, and then at my watch before sighing heavily. Helen's right. We are going to miss the flight. Getting on another will be the biggest pain in the arse. Airport people – especially American airport people – hate it when you miss flights. They look at you as if you're an idiot and ask a million and one questions about why you were late as though you're a six-year-old. 'I think you're right,' I tell Helen.

'What are we going to do?'

'What can we do?'

Helen looks at me, exasperated. 'What's wrong with you today?'

'What do you mean?' I ask.

'I mean, what's up with you?'

I wonder for a moment about whether to tell Helen the truth. After all, she may understand. But, then, again, for her to understand I'd have to tell her everything. Absolutely everything with no editing. And would she want to hear everything with no editing? Probably not. If the tables were turned, would I want to know everything about Helen without editing? Not really. I've always thought that there's a lot to be said for the expression 'Ignorance is bliss'. There have been many situations when people have told me things I wished they'd kept to themselves. The truth is I need to talk about what's on my mind because the constant churning of my mental processes isn't producing any results. Neither had my other strategy of surprise-your-girlfriend-with-a-trip-to-Chicago, spend-a-lot-of-money-that-you-can't-afford-on-things-you-don't-want-in-the-hope-that-you-will-forget-about-it.

Much as I hate to admit it, talking is the only way to get it out of my system. But talk to who? Not Helen, that's for sure.

'You're not having regrets, are you?' asks Helen.

'About what?'

'About us moving in together?'

I laugh. 'Do you think it's part of some sort of evil plan that I ask my girlfriend to move in with me just so I can hate every second of it?'

Helen nods thoughtfully. 'You've been so quiet, I thought it must be a problem with me.'

I give Helen a reassuring kiss. 'I love you, you know.'

A big grin spreads across her face. 'Six.'

'What?'

'That's only the sixth time you've told me that you love me.'

'It is? Are you sure?'

'Absolutely. The first time was three months after we'd got together. We were standing on the Northern Line platform at

Tottenham Court Road station after a night out with Nick and his girlfriend. You put your arms around me and said it then. The second time was a few weeks later when we were watching TV at my flat. The third time was during the summer, when we went for a walk on Clapham Common. The fourth time was when we stayed at your mum's and I'd fallen asleep on the sofa. The fifth time was on Monday in our hotel room after we . . . And the sixth time is now.'

'How many times have you said it?'

'Millions. But I'm like that.'

'I'd say it more, only I don't like to wear it out.'

'It's not a criticism. It's just an observation.'

'Do you want me to say it more often, then?'

'Like a performing seal?' Helen shakes her head. 'No. I quite like you being sparing with it. It makes the times when you do say it that bit more special. It's just funny that this is the first time I've had it twice in the space of a week. I just wondered if it has some sort of special meaning.'

'Other than I love you?'

Helen smiles. 'I'm over-analysing again aren't I?'

'Just a smidgen.'

Helen laughs.

'What's so funny?'

'The way you said "smidgen". I love it. Promise me that from now on you'll say the word "smidgen" to me every single day.'

'I'll try my best.'

We sit in silence for some moments and then Helen asks the driver a question. 'How long until we get to O'Hare?'

'Not long,' he replies. 'A few minutes, maybe.'

Helen turns to me and asks, 'How long have we got before they close the check-in?'

'Plenty of time,' I say, closing my eyes. 'Just give me a nudge when we get there.'

### 4.10 p.m. (US time)
### 10.10 p.m. (UK time)

Helen and I arrive at the airport with about five minutes to spare and race to the check-in desk. There are four sets of people ahead of us carrying what I estimate to be about a million pieces of luggage and only three check-in personnel. I'm coming to terms with the idea that we might not get on the flight when all of the people in front of me suddenly realise they're in the wrong queue. With a minute and a half to go we're waved towards the desk. The attendant gives us the 'Did you pack your own bags? And has anyone given you anything to carry in your luggage' speech. Everything seems to be going smoothly until she hands back the tickets and passports and wishes us a nice flight. 'Er . . . excuse me,' I say, examining the two boarding passes. 'You seem to have made a mistake. According to these,' I hold up the passes, 'my girlfriend and I aren't sitting next to each other.'

'That's correct, sir.'

'But we prebooked seats before we left England. We specified that we should be sitting next to each other, preferably in the bulkhead area or by the emergency doors, and that one of us should have an aisle seat.'

'That's correct, sir.'

'So why weren't we allocated the seats?'

'You were, sir – two hours ago. I'm afraid it's company policy that we reallocate prebooked seats if passengers haven't arrived half an hour before the check-in for the flight closes.'

I can't believe what I'm hearing. 'You've given my prebooked seats to someone else?'

'That's correct, sir.'

Helen can tell that I'm about to get very annoyed indeed because she's tugging my sleeve. 'Look, Jim, let's go. It's not worth it.'

'But we prebooked!'

'Let's just leave it.'

'Fine,' I say, scowling at the check-in attendant.

She smiles back and, without the faintest hint of malice, says again, 'Have a nice flight.'

'I'm really sorry about this,' I tell Helen, as we walk towards the departure lounge.

'It's not your fault.'

'I can't believe it,' I say examining the boarding passes again. 'One of us is in 3B and the other in 36B. What do the seats go up to? We couldn't be any further apart, could we?'

'Jim, this isn't like you at all,' says Helen. 'You're getting worked up over nothing.'

'Maybe we can get the people we're sitting next to to swap?' I say, ignoring her question.

We've got the seats in the middle, sweetheart,' says Helen, laughing. 'No one wants a seat in the middle.' She pauses and sighs. 'I don't think I'd be much of a buffer anyway. It'll be eleven o'clock in the evening on Thursday in the UK right now and around seven fifteen in the morning when we arrive home. We'll have missed a whole night's sleep unless we do some serious napping on the flight. So I suggest we just get on the plane and try to sleep.'

'I suppose,' I say reluctantly. 'But I bet I get the nutter.'

## 11.00 p.m. (UK time)
## 5.00 p.m. (US time)

I'm lying in bed in my room at the Great Eagle Hotel in Warwickshire staring at my wedding dress with the phone in my hand. In less than twenty-four hours I'm going to be married for the second time. Of all the people in the world right now, I think, my fiancé, Marcus, is the one I most want to talk to. Which would be fine in any other circumstances.

In spite of this I dial his number and wait. 'Marcus,' I whisper into the phone, when he picks up, 'it's me.'

'Is that you, Claire? I'm really glad you called.'

'Who's Cla—' I stop as it dawns on me that I'm being had. Marcus lets out a burst of deep, resonant laughter. 'You'd better be joking about this Claire woman.'

'We're getting married in the morning,' he says. 'Of course I only have eyes for you, Alison. Anyway, never mind all that. What's wrong? I thought you were going to get an early night? Can't sleep?'

'No.'

'Too excited about the big day?'

I think for a moment, and even though I know it isn't the answer I still find myself saying, 'Yes, I think so.'

'Have you tried counting sheep?'

'I've tried sheep, elephants, zebras, pigs, gerbils and – I don't know where this came from – koala bears. Before that I tried drinking. First the bottled water in the hotel room mini-bar. Then some low alcohol lager that tasted awful. After that I made myself a double gin and tonic to take away the taste of the lager and followed it with a double vodka and orange juice, then a small Bailey's washed down with a diet Coke, and another double gin and tonic.'

'That'll be your problem then.'

'Drinking?'

'Alcohol's a stimulant – you'll be awake all night on that lot.'

'But I always fall asleep when I drink. It's like my party piece – Alison has a few drinks and falls asleep in the pub. Can you think of a single time that I've had lots to drink and not fallen asleep?'

'Now you put it that way, no.'

'So why aren't I asleep?' I felt myself becoming a bit tearful. 'Will you come over?'

Marcus laughs. 'Is that the drink talking?'

'No, it's not,' I snap. 'I'm sorry. Look what I'm doing. I'm sniping at you when you're only trying to be nice. Why would you want to marry someone like me?'

'Because I love you. I love everything about you. I especially love the fact that you call me and wake me up to tell me you can't sleep. That's what I've always looked for in a woman.'

'Why are you so reasonable?'

'I don't know. It just comes naturally to me I suppose.'

'But you're always reasonable, aren't you? You're never in a bad mood or miserable for no reason. You never yell or moan or do any of the things normal people do. You're just nice. Nice all the time and I don't deserve someone like you.'

'Come on now, Ally, you know I can be quite stroppy when I want to be.'

'No, never. You're never stroppy. You are always lovely. You know in the Walt Disney version of *Snow White*, when all the animals help her do the washing-up? Snow White is so radiantly wonderful that she almost seems to glow and all the animals are practically falling over themselves to help her out. Well, that's you, that is. Me? I'm the evil queen lurking about in the background with a poisoned apple.'

'The good news for you is that I find evil queens very, very sexy.'

'So you're not going to come over?' I say, trying make my voice stay on just the right side of pathetic.

'Isn't it meant to be bad luck to see the bride the night before the wedding?'

'Do you think we'll have bad luck, then?'

'No, I didn't say that,' he says quickly. 'I said it's supposed to be bad luck if we see each other the night before the wedding. But you know that's just an old wives' tale.'

'I'll be an old wife one day.'

'And I'll still love you because I'll be your old husband.'

'You will, won't you?'

'Absolutely.'

'And you do love me, don't you?'

'One hundred and ten per cent and then some.'

'And I love you too. I love you so much that I don't know what to do with myself.'

'If you want me to come over I will. It won't take me twenty minutes to get there.'

'No,' I say resignedly. 'You're right. I'll be fine. I'm just a bit tipsy and feeling sorry for myself and nervous about the morning . . . I just wanted to talk to someone, really.'

'You can talk to me all night if you need to but I get the feeling this might be one for a lady in your life. Why don't you try your mum? She's in the room next door, isn't she?'

I try to imagine myself talking to my mum about what's on my mind. I can't picture it at all. My mum would never get it in a million years.

'Mum's asleep,' I say, after a moment, 'and I'd only wake Dad.'

'What about your sisters?'

I try to imagine waking Emma for a late-night chat. I can't see that either. When we were kids Emma was never much of a night person and now that she's got kids of her own keeping her up at night she craves sleep more than anything. As for my baby sister, I can't imagine she'd be much help. What I need is a good listener and Caroline has always been better at talking than listening.

'I don't think any of my family are the right people for the job.'

'What about Jane?'

'She's still in London and won't be here until the morning.'

'Well, if they're no good,' says Marcus, 'I'll come round right now and you can talk to me.'

'You're such a sweetheart,' I reply, 'but I promise I'll be okay. I just need to get to sleep . . . I'll see you in the morning. Don't be late, will you?'

'I'll be there on time. You just worry about yourself. The last thing I need is for people to think I've been stood up by my bride.'

I let out a small laugh as tears roll down my cheeks. 'I love you,' I say, trying to mean it with my whole heart. 'I love you more than anything. Sleep tight.'

I put down the phone, lean across to the bedside table, grab a few tissues, wipe my eyes and give my nose a good blow. With the tissue now balled tightly in my fist, I try to work out what I'm going to do. I'm supposed to be having breakfast with all my family at nine o'clock. The hairdresser's booked for eleven. Jane's friend Jo, who's a bit of an amateur whiz with makeup, is coming at midday and the wedding itself is booked for two o'clock. Time. I haven't got enough of it. I need more. I want more. Because in just a few hours time I'm going to be a married woman.

## 7.22 p.m. (US time)
## 1.22 a.m. (Friday, 14 February, UK time)

It's a couple of hours into the flight. The peanuts have been distributed and the miniature cans of soft drinks and alcohol have been passed around. The resultant rubbish has been collected and the lull that normally falls over a fully booked flight travelling from one time zone to another has filled the cabin. The majority of passengers are, like me, sitting in darkness with blankets across their knees and plasticky headphones on their ears, watching the in-flight entertainment, which consists of a CNN news round-up bulletin. War. Death. Presidential walkabouts. And the odd celebrity gala.

I haven't even closed my eyes, let alone fallen asleep. I know there's no point in trying when there's so much on my mind. In a way I'm glad Helen's sitting so far from me. If she was next to me right now there would be no hiding anything from her.

I'm sitting between two people. On my left, in the window-seat, there is a young Englishman in his twenties, wearing a baseball cap and a thick padded shirt. The moment he sat down he'd plugged himself into his portable CD player, delved into his rucksack and produced a handheld computer game. On the other side of me, in the aisle seat I craved for its extra leg room, is a friendly looking middle-aged woman with light brown hair. She's wearing jeans, a mohair jumper and Scholl sandals. When she sat down she'd smiled at me warmly and said hello. I thought for a moment I might have a talker sitting next to me, but then she took out a thick paperback from a carrier-bag under the seat in front of her, switched on the light above her head and began to read. From that moment on she was silent.

Until now.

*'Pauly the Talking Parrot.'*

I hear the words quite clearly through my headphones. I take them off and turn to her. 'What?'

'I'm sorry . . . I didn't mean for that to come out like that. I was just taking a break from reading and I was looking at everyone watching the screen over there.' She points to the in-flight entertainment. 'And I was trying to remember the name of the last film that I watched all of the way through on a plane.'

'And it was *Pauly the Talking Parrot*?'

'I know it's ridiculous, really, but once I started watching it I couldn't stop.'

I smile politely and put my headphones back on, only to see out of the corner of my eye that the woman is still looking at me. I take them off again.

'Business or pleasure?' she asks.

'The trip? Pleasure.'

'Me too. My oldest friend moved to Chicago in 1974 and we take it in turns to see each other.'

I knew it. A talker. I consider putting my headphones on again but there's no way I can do it without being rude. Out of politeness I ask her why her friend moved to Chicago, which leads to a long monologue on the pros and cons of moving around the world for the sake of work. This leads to a conversation about the news in the UK, which leads to an even longer one about the book she's reading, then to why discipline in schools isn't as good as it used to be.

During all of these conversations, however, I find myself warming to her. I'd known women like her at school. They were the cool mums who were invariably the mums of the cool kids. They were the mums so unlike your own as to be almost completely unmum-like – Kate Raddick's mum in junior school, for instance, who, when I'd gone to her house for dinner one evening, allowed us to eat our dessert before the main course, which would never have happened in the Owen household. Or Nigel Ross's mum, in secondary school, who managed to combine being just that little bit too good-looking to be a proper mum with the fact that she let Nigel take girls up to his bedroom and close the door. Those were things you can only truly appreciate if you had a mum like mine.

## 1.55 a.m. (UK time)
## 7.55 p.m. (US time)

I've decided to turn on the main bedroom light now as if to usher away any pretence that I might miraculously fall asleep. I pick up the book on my bedside table, *Harry Potter and the Chamber of Secrets*, open it where it has been bookmarked and begin reading. Within minutes my mind is wandering. I'm not getting into this one as quickly as I did the others. This thought leads me to work. I wonder who'll be looking after my authors when I'm on my honeymoon, which reminds me that I'm getting married in the morning, which reminds me again of the reason I can't sleep.

I look around my room for a diversion. It's an ordinary hotel room that has probably been slept in by thousands of businessmen and -women. On the wall near the door is the infamous Corby trouser press. I wonder if anyone has ever pressed their trousers in it. To the right is a small dressing-table and mirror, then a red armchair, and a table with a little kettle and some cups and saucers. That's it. I'll make myself a nice cup of tea and everything will feel better.

I swivel out of bed and, on my way to the table, put on my dressing-gown. I grab the kettle, head to the bathroom to fill it, then return to the room. I set the kettle on its stand, press the button and listen as it begins to hiss and bubble. I set out a cup and saucer and grab a packet of sugar. There's a problem, though. I check through all the sachets on the tray. There's coffee, hot chocolate, brown sugar, white sugar and even artificial sweeteners but no teabags. Under normal circumstances I would've taken this omission in my stride. It's only some missing teabags, I tell myself, not the end of the world. But for some reason this is the last straw. I'm never going to get to sleep now. Never. And it's not my fault. It's the hotel's fault. Specifically that of the person who has neglected to replenish the stock of teabags in my room.

I dial room service but no one answers. Now I really am annoyed. Is it too much to expect to be able to make a cup of tea in the middle of the night? I ask myself, as I climb out of my pyjamas and begin pulling on my clothes. Who did the Great Eagle Hotel think they were, charging a fortune for a room with no tea in it? And then having no one answering the room-service calls. If they can't get the teabags right what will they do to my wedding reception? Will the starters be missing? Will guests who ordered the fish get vegetarian moussaka? Will meat-eaters get the steamed turbot? Will the vegetarians be served a whole leg of lamb? It doesn't bear thinking about.

Fully dressed in jeans, trainers (without socks), a T-shirt I'd borrowed from Marcus and a thick brown jumper, I pause to tie my hair away from my face with a scrunchie and storm out of the room in search of someone to shout at.

**8.01 p.m. (US time)**
**2.01 a.m. (UK time)**

'My name's Jim,' I say to the woman sitting next to me. 'Jim Owen.'

'Pleased to meet you. I'm Marian. Marian McCarthy.' She picks up the book from her lap, closes it and puts it back into the plastic carrier-bag, as if signalling that she's going to give me her full attention. 'Was it your first time in Chicago?'

'Yes, it was a surprise for my girlfriend.'

'Really? That's nice. Why did you choose Chicago?'

'My girlfriend spent a year at the University when she was twenty and had a great time but hadn't been back since she left. She was always telling me how she'd love to go back some day so I thought I'd make it happen. We've spent the week sightseeing and meeting up with her old friends.'

'That's lovely,' says Marian. 'Where's your girlfriend right now?'

I point to the front of the plane. 'Up there. We couldn't get seats together.'

'Oh, that's such a shame. I'm quite prepared to swap, if you'd like.'

'It's a middle seat,' I explain. 'You wouldn't want a middle seat . . . Anyway, she said she was going to try to sleep, which is more than I'll achieve on this flight.'

'Oh?'

'I haven't been sleeping very well.'

'Jet-lag?'

'I think it started before we arrived in the States.'

'Hmm,' says Marian. 'Can I ask what you do for a living?'

'I'm an accountant.'

'Is it a very stressful job?'

'Aren't they all?'

She smiles. 'What else is going on in your life at the moment?' I look at her, puzzled. 'I'm not being nosy – I read in a magazine once that stress is the main cause of sleeplessness.'

'It's probably work,' I reply.

'You don't seem so sure. Could it be anything else?'

I laugh nervously. 'This is very strange, if you don't mind me saying so.'

'Yes, it is,' she acknowledges. 'But strange is good, isn't it? Who wants life to be safe and straightforward all the time? Do you? I doubt it. Now, this not sleeping business . . . what's on your mind?'

## 2.05 a.m. (UK time)
## 8.05 p.m. (US time)

'I'd like to speak to the manager,' I say firmly.

'I'm afraid I can't help you there,' says the man standing behind the hotel reception desk. 'I'm the night porter. The manager doesn't arrive here until seven a.m. She's very nice, though, and she'll be quite happy to talk to you.'

'Well, that's not good enough,' I reply, without thinking. I'm annoyed now, and when I get this way I don't think straight at all. A normal me under normal conditions is far more civilised. 'It's absolutely outrageous the way this hotel is being run,' I continue. 'Absolutely outrageous. I demand to talk to someone in authority now.'

'I see,' says the night porter. 'You seem very . . . upset, if you don't mind me saying so.'

'Yes, I am,' I snap, and then, as if suddenly awakening from a dream, I feel awful about shouting at this middle-aged man with the friendly face and freckles and once red hair that's now fading to white. Did I detect an accent too? Polish, possibly. Or Russian? Slovakian? Something like that, perhaps. This makes me feel even worse. Here he is, away from his homeland, and I'm behaving little better than a British lager lout or soccer hooligan. There's no reason at all to shout at this poor man, who, chances are, had little to do with putting teabags in rooms.

'Can I ask what the problem is? I might be able to help.'

'Look, I'm really, really sorry.'

The night porter looks puzzled. 'Why are you sorry?'

'For being rude to you. I shouldn't have spoken to you like that. It was awful of me.'

'But you seem upset.'

'A little bit.'

'What is the problem?'

'My . . . er . . . my room has no teabags.'

He nods understandingly. 'I have noticed that tea is very important to the British . . . So, you are unhappy because there are no teabags?'

'Well . . . not really.'

'So, you're not upset because you have no teabags?'

'I wanted the teabags to make a cup of tea because I couldn't sleep.'

'Tea will keep you awake, though – the caffeine.'

'Is there much in it?'

'I read it in a magazine once.'

I laugh. 'You sound like my fiancé. He's just been telling me that anything I drink to get me off to sleep will keep me awake.'

The night porter smiles. 'You're getting married?'

'Tomorrow.'

'And you're getting married here?'

'In the Hampton Suite.'

'Congratulations,' he replies, and offers me his hand. Although I feel odd doing it, I shake it. His hands are huge, freckled, slightly clammy, yet reassuringly strong. 'You will be very happy,' he says warmly.

'How do you know?'

'I just know these things. Don't you think you will be?'

It's a simple question. Certainly not worthy of tears. And yet here they are again for the second time in less than an hour. One after another, they roll from the corners of my eyes, down my cheeks into the crevice by my nose and along the edge of my mouth so that when I lick my lips I can taste salt. 'I'm sorry,' I say, turning away from him.

'Have I upset you?'

'No, it's just me. I'm being silly.'

'I didn't mean to upset you. I was just making pleasant talk about your wedding.' At the very mention of the word 'wedding' the tears increase tenfold. 'I make things worse.'

'No, you haven't,' I say, trying to sniff away the tears. 'It's just me. Please ignore me. If you could just find me a couple of teabags I'll be out of your way.'

'No, no, no. I can't give you teabags when you are this upset. I must make you the tea.'

'No, really. Honestly I'll be fine. I don't want to bother you.'

'Please, it's no bother at all.'

For a moment I stare at the night porter looking at me so kindly that I just want to cry even more. 'I'd love to have a cup of tea with you,' I tell him, between sobs.

'You wait here,' he says, 'and I'll be back in several moments.'

**8.10 p.m. (US time)**
**2.10 a.m. (UK time)**

I check my watch and calculate the time in England. I'm not feeling the slightest bit tired and, despite the distraction of Marian, my mind is still churning away at the problem in hand. 'It's a woman,' I say to her. 'It's a woman on my mind.'

'But not your girlfriend?'

I lower my voice. 'No, not my girlfriend.'

'Is this a woman you're currently seeing?'

Instinctively I look up the plane towards Helen's seat. 'No . . . but it's complicated. I used to be married to her. It was the longest relationship I've ever had. But it didn't work out.'

'So why is she on your mind now?'

'If I told you she was getting married again tomorrow you'd think that that was the reason, wouldn't you? But you'd be wrong, because a couple of months ago if I'd found out she was getting married it wouldn't have bothered me in the slightest. Not for a second.'

'So what's changed?'

'I saw her about a month ago.'

'By accident?'

'She called me . . . and . . . well, I can't really explain it but something happened that . . . well, all I can say is it put a seed of doubt in my mind. I'm not sure I didn't make a huge mistake in letting her go. And, well, when she gets married in the morning that'll be it. I'll never know.'

'What changed your mind?' asks Marian, looking intrigued.

'I could tell you but it wouldn't make much sense.'

'Why?'

'Because you have to know the full story. You had to be there.'

'So why don't you tell me the full story? We're not landing for quite a few hours yet. You can't sleep and I love listening.'

'Look, this isn't very me. I don't do this sort of thing.'

'It's just talking. A problem shared is a problem halved and all that. But who knows? In telling me about this woman—'

'Alison.'

'In telling me about Alison you might clear things up for yourself.'

I have my reservations even though what she's saying makes total sense. But, given that I don't have a better solution and she seems a nice person, I decide to give it a go. 'Are you sure you won't get bored?' I ask.

'Absolutely not,' she replies. 'I love hearing people's stories.'

I clear my throat. 'Okay, I'll tell you all about me and Alison.'

## 2.15 a.m. (UK time)
## 8.15 p.m. (US time)

As cups of tea go, the one in my hand has probably been one of the best of my life. While I'm drinking it I'm learning several things about the night porter. His name is Anatoly, he's fifty-five and has been living in Warwick for the past five years since he moved here from London. He's originally from Siberia, has two grown-up daughters (one my age who lives in Moscow and a younger one in Ottawa) and an ex-wife still in Siberia. I love listening to him talk about his life: his whole manner is comforting. I can't help but feel there is something not only wise about this man but trustworthy too.

'Now do you feel better?'

'Yes, much better, thank you.'

'But not tired?'

I laugh. 'It must be the tea.'

Anatoly laughs with me, then looks serious for a moment. 'Do you want to tell me why you cry? Is it because of the wedding?'

I nod.

'Is he not a nice man?'

'He's lovely.'

'You don't love this man, then?'

'I love him to bits.'

'But?'

I smile. He's right. There is a 'but'. 'It's complicated.'

'Love is always complicated,' says Anatoly. 'That's why it's love.'

'The reason I can't sleep is that I've got something on my mind . . . or maybe it would be more accurate to say that I've got someone on my mind.'

'Not the man you marry tomorrow?'

'A man from my past.'

'I see.'

'Do you?' I ask. 'Do you really? Because I don't. I don't see at all.'

'This other man – do you love him too?'

'I don't know.'

'Does he love you?'

I let out a small laugh. 'I don't know that either. He more than likely doesn't. All I do know is that a month ago I saw him for the first time in nearly four years and something happened and it's made me . . . well, it's made me unsure. How can I not be sure if I love someone else when I'm going to get married in a few hours? It isn't fair on Marcus. It would always feel like he was getting second best.'

'Why don't you contact this other man?'

'Tonight? I couldn't. It wouldn't be right, would it? The morning of my wedding.'

'But surely you have something to say to him?'

'No, he's been on my mind a lot, that's all. We were together a long time, you see. We even got married. It was the longest relationship of my life.'

'And this thing that happened, what was it?'

'It's hard to explain without telling you everything.'

Anatoly smiles. 'Then tell me everything.'

'Everything?'

'Well, you can't sleep. And I am sitting here all night. And you say you want someone to talk to. Why not?'

'Because . . . well, because you don't want to hear about me and my ex-husband.'

'But I tell you I do.' Anatoly raises his eyebrows.

'Really?'

'Yes, really. I'll make us another cup of tea and then you tell me everything about this other man. What's his name?'

'Jim,' I reply. 'His name's Jim.'

**9.15 p.m. (US time)**
**3.15 a.m. (UK time)**

'Would you like a mid-flight snack?' interrupts the stewardess.

'What is there?' I ask, even though I'd heard her, less than twenty seconds ago, give Marian the options.

'A cheese roll, a tuna roll or a ham roll.'

'What kind of cheese is it?'

'Cheddar.'

'I'll have the ham,' I reply.

The stewardess hands me a tray, then has to go through the whole thing again for the benefit of the man next to me because he was listening to his headphones.

'How's your food?' I ask Marian, who ordered the tuna.

'Good,' she replies. 'I love airline food. How does yours look?'

I take the cellophane off my roll. It looks about as unhappy as me. 'Unappetising.'

Marian laughs. 'Right then, well, if the food's that bad there's no excuse for not getting back to your story.'

**3.17 a.m. (UK time)**
**9.17 p.m. (US time)**

'Taxi in the name of Perkins,' says a large bespectacled man in a thick grey jumper, interrupting my conversation with Anatoly.

'Which room?' asks Anatoly.

The taxi driver shrugs so Anatoly has to look up the name on the hotel computer.

'Room twelve,' he says eventually. 'I'll ring them.' He picks up the phone and dials their number. 'There's a taxi here for you,' he says, when they pick up. There's a long silence while Anatoly listens to the reply. 'They say they didn't order a taxi,' he tells the driver.

'I'll check with base,' says the taxi driver gruffly.

Anatoly smiles in my direction, as if to apologise for the interruption. A few moments later the taxi driver returns.

'It wasn't Perkins,' he says. 'It was Hodgkins.'

Anatoly sighs wearily, then goes through the same process all over again. This time it's the right person. 'They'll be down in a moment.'

'I'll wait in the cab,' says the driver.

Anatoly turns to me. 'I'm sorry about that.'

I laugh. 'There's nothing to be sorry for. You have a job to do.'

'But, still, it's not nice, these interruptions. They break up your story.'

'Right,' I say, smiling. 'Now, where were we?'

## 10.01 p.m. (US time)
## 4.01 a.m. (UK time)

'Excuse me,' says the bloke sitting next to me, stopping my narrative.

I notice it's that curious time on flights when people start getting up *en masse* to use the loo as if they've all got synchronised bladders. I unbuckle my seat-belt, Marian undoes hers and we shuffle into the aisle to let him go through.

'It feels good to stand up,' says Marian.

'Hmm,' I say absentmindedly. I'm looking towards the front of the plane trying to spot Helen.

'Looking for your girlfriend?'

I nod. 'I'm suddenly feeling a bit guilty telling you all this stuff. I mean, right now you know stuff about me that Helen has no idea about.'

'The way you've got to look at it is this: whatever happens, us talking is going to benefit her. If you decide to stay with her at least you know that you've thought it all through. If you decide that Alison's for you, you'll be doing Helen a big favour because it's better that you let her down now rather than later.'

I think for a moment. 'Do you think it's inevitable I'll let her down?'

'Only if you're in love with someone else.'

Suddenly I feel uncomfortable. 'I do love, Helen, you know . . . I'd better go and see her.'

I walk up the aisle towards her seat, looking for the top of her head as I get closer. I can't see it and only realise why when I'm standing parallel to her row: she's fast asleep. Her head's resting on her shoulder and a blanket is covering her legs. She looks absolutely peaceful. The woman next to her eyes me suspiciously. I give her an awkward half-smile and head back to my seat.

**4.07 a.m. (UK time)**
**10.07 p.m. (US time)**

'Would you like more tea?' asks Anatoly, as I pause in my narrative to get my bearings.

'I'm fine,' I reply.

'Do you mind if I have one?' he asks.

'No, by all means, carry on,' I tell him, and he disappears.

Bored, I begin leafing through the in-tray for anything interesting. I'm just about to check the out-tray when I hear someone behind me.

'Hello,' says a girl in her early twenties. 'I wonder if we could have the key to room eighteen.'

'No problem,' I reply, and stand up to get it off the board. This is the moment, however, when I realise the girl in front of me is not alone.

'Alison, is that you?' It's my cousin Martin. He's about the same age as me and works as a solicitor in Barking.

'Hi,' I say sheepishly. 'I bet you're wondering what I'm doing behind the reception desk of the hotel at this late hour.' I look at the girl. 'Hi, I'm Martin's cousin. I suspect you might be staying here because you're coming to my wedding in the morning.'

'Er . . . hi,' says the girl. 'I'm Jessica, Martin's girlfriend.'

'Hi, I'm really pleased to meet you.' I turn to Martin, who is wearing a very puzzled frown. 'It's good to see you, Martin. You look great.'

'Thanks,' he replies, clearly bemused. 'And you're doing what in Reception?'

'I didn't have any tea in my room,' I explain, 'so the nice night porter, who was sitting here less than a minute ago, made some and we've been talking ever since.'

Martin laughs. I step out from the counter and kiss him. 'It's good to see you,' he says. 'You just took me a bit by surprise, that's all. We've been to dinner with some friends I hadn't seen for years, which is why we're so late. Anyway, we'll be off to bed now. I'll see you in the morning.'

'I'm back,' says Anatoly, returning from the office at the rear with two mugs of tea. 'I made you one anyway . . .' His voice trails off when he realises we're not alone.

'Anatoly, this is my cousin Martin and his girlfriend Jessica.' I gesture to Anatoly. 'Martin and Jessica, Anatoly the night porter.'

'Nice to meet you,' they chime, and Martin fakes a yawn. 'Anyway, we'd better get off.'

'They seem like nice people,' says Anatoly.

'They are, but I think I'm going to be the gossip of the day among my dad's side of the family after this . . . Anyway, where were we?'

## 10.53 p.m. (US time)
## 4.53 a.m. (UK time)

I'm just about to tell Marian the next instalment of the saga when I look up and spot Helen heading down the plane towards us.

'It's Helen,' I say, panicking, 'my girlfriend! She's coming down the plane.'

'What are you worrying about?' asks Marian. 'It's not like she's got supersonic hearing, is it?'

'Good point,' I say, trying to calm down, even though I can see her getting closer by the second. 'What's going to be our cover story? I'll tell you what. You were just sitting next to me and you asked me what the time was and I told you and that was that.' Marian laughs. 'You can't laugh,' I tell her. 'Helen will know I've made you laugh and then—' It's too late, she's here.

'Hey, babe,' she says, standing in the aisle. 'The turbulence woke me up so I thought I'd come and stretch my legs and see you.'

'I came up earlier to see you but you were fast asleep.'

I can feel Marian looking at me expectantly, waiting for an introduction.

'This is Marian,' I say hesitantly.

'Your boyfriend has been keeping me company,' she explains. 'I know his entire life story.'

Helen laughs, then gives me a secret look as if to say, 'Oh, no, you've got the nutter, after all.' Then she turns to Marian and says, 'I bet you know more than me—'

Fortunately she's cut short by the pilot requesting passengers to return to their seats as there's more turbulence coming up.

'I'd better go,' says Helen. She blows me a kiss, then

mouths the word 'Sorry', and says aloud, 'I'll see you a bit later.'

I breathe a deep sigh of relief.

## 4.55 a.m. (UK time)
## 10.55 p.m. (US time)

Once again the story of Jim and me grinds to a halt. An attractive young woman in a cream overcoat is at the reception desk. She's standing next to a much older man wearing a navy blue jacket and grey trousers. They're both looking curiously at me, probably because I'm sitting on a chair in the small office at the rear of the desk looking decidedly scruffy. I smile back as if to say, 'Mind your own business,' even though I'm curious as to where they've been until this late hour.

'Could I have the keys to room eight, please?' asks the young woman.

'Of course, madam,' says Anatoly. He hands them to her. 'Goodnight.'

The couple take a last look at me and frown, as if there's something improper going on but they're not sure what it is.

'I'm sorry about that,' says Anatoly, sitting down. 'Where were we?'

'Never mind that,' I say. 'What was their story? That man was old enough to be my grandad. What was he still doing up? It's practically morning.'

'A good night porter knows when not to ask questions,' says Anatoly, smiling knowingly. 'Now . . .'

## 11.13 p.m. (US time)
## 5.13 a.m. (UK time)

'Hot towelettes?' asks the stewardess, interrupting my flow once again. Fortunately I'd all but finished telling Marian the story of me and Alison. All that remained was what happened after we sold the flat and our meeting a month ago.

'No, thanks,' I reply, but Marian takes one so, for no reason at all, I change my mind. 'I'll have one, actually,' I say, as the stewardess passes one with plastic tongs to the bloke next to me. She hands me a towelette so scaldingly hot I'm sure I can smell my flesh singeing.

'Am I fully up to date with your story now?' asks Marian.

'Not quite,' I reply. 'There's just one thing left, really. It's the reason why I'm not sleeping and why I can't think straight. It's the reason why I'm telling you my story.'

'What happened?'

'Of course I'll go into more detail if you want me to, but in a nutshell it was this. The cat I bought Alison ten years ago died and she called to let me know. I went to the vet's with her, to keep her company, and we went for a drink afterwards. And during an afternoon of talking, it felt like we were the only two people in North London, I felt like we reconnected to such an extent that the last four years hadn't happened. And as we said goodbye, we kissed, and for her I think it was just a momentary slip but for me it was everything. That's why I'm not sleeping. I'm still in love with my ex-wife.'

## 5.15 a.m. (UK time)
## 11.15 p.m. (US time)

Anatoly and I are now in the hotel kitchen. As well as manning Reception during the night, one of the other roles of the night porter is to look after preparation of food ordered from the limited room-service menu. While he makes a club sandwich for room nine I make ham rolls for us to eat in Reception. I walk up to the room with him to keep him company as he delivers the sandwich, then together we return to Reception. I can heard the birds singing outside even though it's still quite dark. And I'm beginning to feel tired. I'm starting to worry about how I'm going to get through the day ahead. I know, however, that even if I do go to bed now I won't sleep. At least, not until I've told Anatoly the reason why I'm having so much trouble sleeping in the first place.

'So where are we in your story?' asks Anatoly, as we sit down.

'I think we're nearly done, apart from the main event. A meeting with Jim after a four-year break, which ended with a kiss that has turned my whole world upside down.'

## 11.26 p.m. (US time)
## 5.26 a.m. (UK time)

'So what are you going to do?' asks Marian, now that my narrative has drawn to a conclusion. 'You've admitted you still love her. And if she's getting married today this is going to be your last chance.'

'To do what?' I reply, as the man next to me opens the blind on the cabin window. 'To tell her not to marry the man she's been happily living with?' I pause and look out of the window. 'Let's look at what really happened, Marian. Alison and I spent an afternoon together and we got a bit sentimental because our cat died.'

'But you kissed her.'

'But that's it – it was just a kiss. I can't change my entire life for a kiss. Helen's supposed to be moving in with me today. I really can't imagine that when I get off this plane I'm going to split up with Helen and travel all the way to Warwickshire, or wherever it is she's getting married, to beg her to reconsider just because I've had some sort of epiphany. I don't live in Hollywood, Marian. I live in East Finchley. Things like that don't happen in East Finchley.'

'Well, maybe they ought to,' says Marian, with a smile. 'Today is Valentine's Day after all. If things like that can happen in the real world then a day designed for lovers must be the best day for it.'

I'm about to reply when I'm interrupted by the pilot over the intercom. He informs us that we'll be landing at Heathrow in twenty minutes.

'Regret is a terrible thing,' continues Marian. 'I can't think of anything much worse than knowing you had the power to change a sad event into a happy one and choosing not to do so.'

There's a long silence, and as I look out of the cabin window again I catch my first glimpse of the sun.

'You're right,' I reply sadly. 'Absolutely right. But this isn't about me, is it? It's about Alison and her wedding day. The last time she got married there were only three people there to witness it and it didn't work out. Today she's getting married again and she's going to do it right this time. I know she will. And this guy she's marrying, I'm one hundred per cent sure he loves her. And that he'll care for her. And that he'll never leave her – which is the most important thing of all.'

## 5.37 a.m. (UK time)
## 11.37 p.m. (US time)

'Morning, Anatoly,' says one of the cleaners, walking through Reception.

'Morning, Anna,' he replies.

'How long until you knock off?'

He looks at the clock behind him. 'A while yet.' He laughs. 'But I set the clock a few minutes forward every now and again.'

'Don't let them catch you out, will you?' she says, laughing, then disappears through the double doors into the bar.

Anatoly turns to me expectantly.

'Now I've told you everything,' I say, 'you're going to ask me what I've decided to do, aren't you?'

'I think you know what you should do,' he says. 'I think you're just waiting for the courage to do it.'

'But I love Marcus,' I reply.

Anatoly laughs. 'See? I didn't say what you should do, and you assumed I was in favour of Jim. That's why I think you know what you should do. Your heart is speaking to you. All you need to do is listen.'

'But why would I want to run off with my ex-husband just because of one stupid kiss? We only got our decree absolute a couple of years ago. It doesn't make sense. I think it's a case of pre-wedding jitters. The brain does funny things under stress. Makes you think and feel things differently from how you would under normal conditions.' I stand up and kiss Anatoly's cheek. 'Thank you for listening to me. I really can't thank you enough.'

'It was no problem,' he says. 'In fact, it was my pleasure.'

'Well, you were kind to a woman in need. I know this might seem odd, and obviously you may prefer to get some sleep, but I don't suppose you fancy coming along to the wedding, do you? I'd love to have you there and you'd be more than welcome.'

Anatoly shakes his head. 'Thank you. That would be nice but I can't. I need to go home.'

'Of course.'

'I hope your life is a happy one, whatever choice you make.'

I smile at him but don't reply, then head up the stairs to my room.

# PART NINE

## One month later

# 2003

## Saturday, 15 March 2003

### 8.32 a.m.

I'm sitting in the back of a black cab on my way to Alison's house. It has been a month since the wedding, and although I haven't seen or heard from her since the day Disco died, I'm assuming they'll be back from wherever they've been on honeymoon. I'm hoping that Alison still likes a lie-in on a Saturday morning. I'm going to drop off a wedding present – my small way of saying congratulations to them and wishing them well. I've already decided that even if they do ask me to come in out of politeness I'm going to decline. I don't want to make a big deal of it. I just want to hand it over and leave, especially as any conversation they might have with me is bound to include some variation on the question: 'How is life treating you?' To which, if I'm going to be truthful, I'll have to answer that I've been a lot better but thanks for asking.

Helen and I split up. It happened the day we came back from Chicago. It wasn't nice. It didn't make me feel great. But it was definitely the right thing to do. I told her she deserved someone better than me. And she said she didn't want someone better than me. So then I explained that even if she didn't want to be with someone better than me at the very least she must want someone who isn't still in love with his ex-wife. Because she'd already handed in her notice on her flat, I let her stay at mine until she found somewhere else to go. Fortunately she did so a week later. I haven't seen her since, and I don't think I'm likely to hear from her again as I strongly suspect that I'll always be – at least in her mind – the man who dumped his girlfriend on Valentine's Day. When I told Nick what had happened he looked at me as if I was stupid and said, 'Why didn't you wait until the day after?'

'Because,' I replied, 'the best time to do the right thing is always right now.' I could tell he didn't understand and I wasn't all that sure I did either. All I knew was that Marian had been right. Even if Hollywood endings don't happen in East Finchley, the world would indeed be a richer place if they did. And although at Heathrow I hadn't jumped into a cab and asked the driver to take me to Warwickshire because I had a wedding to stop, I knew I had to take action of sorts. And I'm pretty sure that if none of the events of the past few months (Disco dying, my meeting up with Alison and, most importantly, our talk in the pub) had happened I would still be quite happily with Helen. I'm sure we would've been great together. Maybe we would've got married and even had kids. But those things *had* happened. And they had changed me for ever. Because from the moment Alison and I had kissed on the day Disco died, I had known the biggest mistake I'd ever made in my life was leaving her. Alison was the best I was ever going to get. And being with anyone else didn't compare.

**9.05 a.m.**

'It's this block here on the left,' I say, indicating to the cab driver to pull over. I get out of the car, making sure to take my wedding present with me. 'Can you just hang on a few moments?' I ask, checking his clock, then handing him a twenty-pound note. 'I'm only going to be a few minutes.' He nods, turns off his engine and gets out his copy of the *Daily Mirror*.

Turning my attention to the job in hand, I take a deep breath, walk to Alison's apartment block and ring the buzzer. My heart begins to race as I imagine meeting Marcus for the first time. I wonder what he'll think when he sees his wife's ex-husband standing on the doorstep holding a wedding present a month after the event. I decide it doesn't bear thinking about. Whatever happens will happen.

'Hello?' comes a familiar-sounding female voice from the intercom.

'Hi,' I reply. 'Is that Alison?'

'No, it's Jane. I'm a friend of Alison's. She's just gone to the shops. Who is it? Your voice sounds familiar.'

'No one important,' I reply hastily, as I look forlornly at the wedding present in my hands. 'I'll come back another time.'

'No, you won't,' says a voice behind me. I turn round and Alison is standing a few yards away from me. She's wearing a red Puffa jacket, faded blue jogging bottoms, trainers and a green woolly hat that has clearly seen better days.

'How are you?' she asks.

'I'm okay,' I reply. 'How about you?'

'Not too bad,' she says, smiling at me. She looks down at her jogging bottoms. 'Sorry, I must look like a right scruff. Jane insisted she wanted an omelette for breakfast. I only nipped out to the shops to get some eggs.' She waves the box in her hand. 'I wasn't expecting guests.'

'I'm not really a guest.' I look over at the taxi. 'I'm not staying. The reason I'm here is to wish you and Marcus all the best and give you a present.'

Alison smiles. 'Jim, you really didn't need to do this.'

'I know,' I reply. 'I just wanted to.'

'Is it what I think it is?'

'I don't know,' I reply. 'Depends on what you think it might be.'

Alison looks at the box with a huge grin on her face. 'Well, shall we look at the clues? One, the box you've got in your hands used to contain crisps, which is a bit of a give-away unless you've actually bought me some crisps. Two, whatever is inside that box appears to be moving pretty rapidly of its own free will. And three . . .' Alison falters and starts to laugh, then to cry, and then to laugh and cry at the same time, which is something I'd never seen before. 'I'm sorry,' she says. 'It's just that I still miss Disco so much.'

Slowly Alison walks towards me, almost not daring to look at what's inside the box. When she reaches me and we're standing right in front of each other I take the eggs from her and hand the box to her. She sets it on the ground, opens the flaps and looks inside.

'He's eight weeks old,' I tell her, as she pulls out a jet black kitten and cradles him to her. He has huge green eyes and when he yawns as he looks at Alison they seem to get even larger. I can tell immediately that for both of them it's love at first sight.

'He's gorgeous,' says Alison, trying to hold the wriggling bundle of fur while simultaneously wiping away the tears.

'Absolutely gorgeous. You really didn't need to do this, Jim. You didn't.'

'I know,' I say softly. 'I did it because I wanted to, that's all. I know how much you loved Disco. And I know that Lucy can never be a replacement for her but . . . you know, she can be something different, can't she? She can be a new beginning.'

Alison smiles, even though the tears are still falling. 'Who's Lucy?'

'The kitten.'

'But you referred to it earlier as he.'

'Yeah, I know.'

'But if he's a he, why is he called Lucy?'

'You know me,' I reply. 'I've always been terrible at cats' names. I'm sure you and Marcus can come up with something better.'

Alison smiles sadly, and there's a silence.

'If I was going to keep him,' she says eventually, with her eyes fixed on the kitten, 'I'd never call him Lucy in a million years. He looks like a Harry. And I think you should call him that.' She looks up at me briefly and our eyes meet.

Even after all this time apart I can tell when something's wrong with her just by a look, or one of the dozens of invisible signals you learn to read when you know someone as well as you know yourself. 'What's wrong?' I ask. 'Why can't you keep Harry? You haven't already got a kitten, have you?'

She shakes her head.

'So what is it?'

'I just can't accept him, that's all,' she says, as she places Harry back in the box, closes the flaps to stop him escaping, then puts it at my feet. 'I'm sorry,' she says. 'I'm really sorry.' And she walks away from me towards her front door.

'I don't understand,' I say. 'I didn't come here to upset you, Al, honestly. I came here to try to do something nice because . . . I don't know . . . you make me want to do nice things. Is it so wrong to want to give your ex-wife a wedding present?'

Alison turns to me with tears in her eyes. 'It is, if she didn't get married.'

'What?' I say, stunned. 'But it was all going to happen on Valentine's Day, wasn't it?' She nods. 'And it didn't happen?' She shakes her head. I pause before asking one final question. 'But you're still together?'

'It's a long story.'

'Yeah?' I reply. 'Well, I've got a long story of my own. Helen and I have split up.'

'But I thought you said she was the One.'

'We all make mistakes, I suppose,' I reply, looking down at the crisps box wobbling at my feet as Harry bounds around it, clearly frustrated at being parted from his new mistress. 'Some of us more than others. But that's life, isn't it? None of us is perfect. And sometimes it takes a while to get things right but we get there in the end.' I kneel down, open the flaps, reach inside the box and take out Harry. 'But wedding or no wedding,' I say, walking over to Alison, 'long story or short, I want you to have Harry. He's yours. I can tell just by looking at the two of you that this is going to be the love story of the decade.'

Alison takes him from my hands and pulls him tightly to her as she looks across at the cab. 'Don't go,' she says quietly.

'I really should clear off,' I reply. 'I told myself on the way over here that I was just going to give you the present and go.' I step forward and kiss Alison's cheek. 'Take care,' I tell her, 'and have a good life,' and then I whisper in Harry's ear, 'Look after her for me. And try to keep her off the fags because those things will kill her one day.'

'You can't go, Jim,' says Alison, as I'm half-way to the taxi.

'Come on, Al, I have to,' I reply.

'You can't,' says Alison, laughing. 'How am I going to make Jane's omelette without you?'

I look down at my hands and see she's right. 'I'm sorry,' I reply, walking back to her. 'I didn't realise.'

'A likely story,' says Alison, as I offer them to her.

She sighs theatrically. 'Can't you see I've got my hands full?' she says, indicating with her eyes to Harry, who is trying to crawl up her Puffa jacket. 'You're such a typical bloke sometimes.'

'What do you want me to do?'

'Bring them inside for me, stay for breakfast with me and Jane, and then this afternoon you and I can go to the pub and trade those long stories we both mentioned.'

'I would,' I say uncomfortably, 'but you know what happened last time we went to the pub to talk.'

'I do,' she says, and smiles mischievously. With that she places Harry back in his box, fishes out her house keys from her coat pocket and opens the front door.

I remain rooted to the spot.

'Are you coming or what?' she asks.

I look at Alison, then at the cab, and then at her again. And as I wave off the taxi and walk towards her, I'm certain that these next few steps will take my life in a completely different direction.

The right direction.

This time.